W9-BFA-203

COLD COUNTRY, HOT SUN

Christopher Nicole

Severn House Large Print
London & New York

This first large print edition published in Great Britain 2007 by
SEVERN HOUSE LARGE PRINT BOOKS LTD of
9-15 High Street, Sutton, Surrey, SM1 1DF.
First world regular print edition published 2005 by
Severn House Publishers, London and New York.
This first large print edition published in the USA 2007 by
SEVERN HOUSE PUBLISHERS INC., of
595 Madison Avenue, New York, NY 10022.

British Library Cataloguing in Publication Data

Nicole, Christopher
    Cold country, hot sun. - Large print ed.
    1. Retirees - Spain - Fiction 2. Suspense fiction 3. Large
    type books
    I. Title
    823.9'14[F]

    ISBN-13: 978-0-7278-7644-7

Printed and bound in Great]
MPG Books Ltd, Bodmin, Co

Spain is a very cold country
with a very hot sun.

Old Spanish saying

One

'Tell me what happened,' said the sleepy voice. It spoke Spanish with a heavy American accent.

'Someone got there first, Big Sam,' replied the anxious voice at the other end of the telephone

'Who?'

'It was a Belgian-registered car.'

'You saw the car?'

'Only as it was leaving.'

'You let it leave?'

'I fired at it, several times. I think I hit it. But it did not stop.'

'So they got away. What have you done?'

'I sent Salvador after them.'

'Salvador? He is a nutcase.'

'He is the best we have with a car, and with a gun or a knife. He is a born killer. And they were driving south. I think they are coming to Spain. Salvador has relatives up and down the costa. He will find them.'

'I must have that card, Pedro. No matter what it takes.'

'You will have it, Big Sam. But who would have done this thing?'

Sam considered for a few moments. 'Barton! Donald Barton.'

7

'Is not Barton retired?'

'So, ain't I retired? The boss paid us both off when he called it a day. But both Barton and I knew what he had hidden away. We were the only ones. And, like me, Barton settled in Spain; it's a difficult place to be extradited from. He has a place on that hill outside Jàvea, Montgo. If those guys are coming to Spain, it has to be Barton.'

'You will have the card, Señor Sam,' Pedro promised. 'No matter what we have to do.'

'The car!' Melissa cried. 'Those men are stealing our car!' She splashed out of the gentle surf on to the sand, waving her arms. 'David!' she shouted. 'Fred!' Fred joined her first, in a shower of water, pausing to shed the messy contents of his coat over the only other couple on the beach, who were sitting peacefully on their towels. He began to bark, but as he had been taught not to chase cars, he quickly decided the rule should apply to his own, even when it was being driven away by strangers.

'The bastards!' David caught up with his wife. 'Oh, the bastards!' The estate car was disappearing up the track to the road.

'A lonely beach,' Melissa said bitterly. 'Just the job, you said. You said, why not let's skinny dip. My God! If we *had*! If those two hadn't been here...'

'Those two' sounded German, judging by their unintelligible complaints as they tried to brush off the sticky wet sand Fred had deposited. David scratched his head, looking at his wife's slender figure, her superb, slightly aquiline features framed in her long, straight and presently wet yellow hair, and her very long legs; there was not a lot of difference between Melissa in the nude and Melissa in a white one-piece swimsuit. He supposed the same thing went for him. His black body hair had tended to spread from his chest over his shoulders and down his not so attractive legs, as middle-age crept on, and his stomach, as befitted a man who had made a fortune out of food, overhung the briefs.

'All our things!' Melissa moaned, sinking to her knees. 'Fred, stop that!' For Fred had returned to stand beside his mistress, and decided to shake again. He was a golden retriever, like his master a trifle overweight; he touched six and a half stones. His name wasn't really Fred, of course; he was entered in the Kennel Club as Speign Lord Tara of Borden, but that was a bit much for usage on walkies, quite apart from an absurdity in a dog who had actually emigrated to Spain.

'If only we had left Fred in the car,' David grumbled. 'People never steal cars with dogs in them.'

'They might have! Poor Fred.' Melissa threw both arms round Fred's neck for a hug, and received a lick for her reward. 'Oh, Dave! What are we going to do?'

David looked up and down the beach. It

was quite a long beach, stretching from a low cliff at its northern end to an outcrop of rock perhaps half a mile away at the southern. It was fringed by trees on its landward side, which all but hid the road, while to the east the Mediterranean Sea stretched into the horizon. And apart from the German couple it was deserted. Or was it? He had supposed there was no one else about when he had parked the car, but obviously the two men had been lurking in the bushes. They would have seen Melissa change; he felt quite outraged about that. Now he no longer possessed wallet or cards or laptop, or transport – or mobile. Only a pair of briefs and his watch. And his St Christopher medallion. The patron saint of travellers, he thought. 'I'll go see if those two can help,' he said, retracing Fred's trail through the soft sand, while Melissa went up to the deserted track. He rejoined her very quickly.

'What did they say?' she asked, beginning to shiver.

'I can't say for certain, but I think it was the German equivalent of sod off. Fred's fault, for shaking on them. Anyway, they don't seem to have a car.'

'Then how did they get here?'

'Probably hiked. They both have knapsacks.'

Melissa sat on the dry grass beside the track. 'Only an idiot would have left the keys in the ignition,' she remarked.

They had not seen the sun since leaving London. There had been fog on the drive down to Dover, and rain on the drive across France. The border crossing into Spain at La Jonquera had been shrouded in low cloud, and this had persisted for a good way south. But once they had passed the sign leading off to Girona Sud, ahead of them was a great glow. 'Oh, to be in Spain, now that April's here,' David had said. 'Listen, Liss ... let's go down to the coast. Find a beach and have a swim. I know Fred would like it. Wouldn't you, Fred?' Fred, wedged in the back of the estate car with sundry suitcases and cardboard boxes, had panted obligingly. So David had swung off the motorway when they were well south of Girona, descended rapidly from the National Route to a B-road, and then a dirt track, and they had seen the sea, sparkling in the sunshine. The reason for the very big decision they had made when he had received the offer for the restaurant. Sunny Spain, and not a care in the world for the rest of their lives.

'What are we going to do?' Melissa asked again. If the sun was hot, the breeze off the sea was cool, and she was shivering again; they had even left their towels hanging out of the car windows.

'Well ... we have to get to a police station, as quickly as possible. We'll have to walk back to the National Route and thumb a lift. It's not all that far.'

Melissa did a three-hundred-and-sixty-degree turn, surveying the empty expanse of sand, track and stunted dry scrub, as if wondering which spiky hassock might conceal a policeman. 'Like this? Barefoot?'

'Darling, we have no choice.'

'Spain!' Melissa remarked through gritted teeth.

'Our new home,' David reminded her, and set off before she could reply.

'God, my feet,' Melissa grumbled. 'They weren't meant for walking on hot tar. Oh, shit!' Coming down the road towards them were several men, following what looked like a very old motorbike attached to a form of cart, which was filled with some indeterminate kind of vegetable. The men stared at them, not unreasonably; they were now a mile from the sea. Melissa was instinctively trying to cover things with her hands. 'Can't we talk to them?' she asked. The phrasebook was also in the car. 'They might give us a lift in that contraption,' she suggested.

'Save that they're going the wrong way,' David pointed out. 'Do you speak English?' he asked politely.

The first Spaniard was a large man with a drooping moustache; he might have walked straight out of an early Clint Eastwood movie, but not as the hero. He looked David up and down. *'Non.'*

'Policia? Policia estacione?'

'Oh, very good,' Melissa said.

'La playa...' The man pointed back the way they had come.

'Yes, we know that,' David said. 'Our car ... ah ... *coche*. Stolen.'

'Coche?' The man looked left and right.

'National Route,' Melissa tried. 'Road. *Carretera. Carretera grande.* No, no, *carretera major.* How about that?' she asked proudly.

The man looked her up and down as well, obviously enjoying the view. Fred took offence at this, and gurgled. The man looked at Fred instead, and went on his way, followed by his friends. The last, a little fellow with several teeth missing, paused. *'Allí,'* he suggested, pointing over his shoulder.

'Oh, *gracias*,' David said.

'Phew,' Melissa said. 'I feel virtually naked.'

'You are virtually naked. Let's go.' She limped beside him, Fred obedient at her side. Thank God for Fred.

By the time they reached the crossroads, Melissa was exhausted, and when they stopped, she collapsed on to the grass. 'It's a carrying job,' she said. Fred licked her face. She peered at her feet. 'Am I going to have blisters? I simply couldn't walk another step.'

'Listen!' David said, and a moment later a car came in sight round the bend in the road.

13

Melissa scrambled to her feet while David waved his arms. The car was already stopping, probably at the sight of the scantily clad woman by the roadside. It was an extremely shabby blue Seat, and, judging by the dents and half missing bumper, there was no doubt it had been around a long time. *'Buenos dias, señor,'* David said, remembering all he could. *'Habla Ingles, por favor?'*

The driver looked at him, and then at Melissa. He was a small man, quite young, with clipped features and lank black hair. *'Bon dia. Si, si.* A leetle,' he replied. 'You 'ave *una problema.'* It was not a question.

'Oh, indeed, we have a problem,' David agreed. 'Our car – *coche* – was stolen – er, *vamoose* ... while we were swimming. Can you take us to the nearest police station?'

'Policia? Porque?'

'Well, to report the crime, and possibly get our car back.'

The driver scratched his head, then shrugged. 'Who stole the *coche?*'

'There were two men,' Melissa said.

Suddenly he was interested. 'You saw these *hombres?* You would know these *hombres* again?'

'Perhaps.'

'Thees *coche,* how is it?'

David understood what he was driving sat. 'It is a Peugeot 506 Estate.'

'An eet 'as Eengleesh plates.'

'Of course.'

14

'*Bueno.*' The Spaniard opened the nearside door, and patted the place beside him on the bench seat. '*Su esposa* seet 'ere, eh?'

'Ah...' Melissa considered. 'I think you should sit in the front, Dave.'

'Good thinking.' David got into the car.

'Up you get, Fred,' Melissa said, heaving on Fred's ample haunches to get him into the back.

'*Perro, non,*' the man said.

'Where we go, he goes,' David said. 'He's one of the family.'

The driver regarded Fred with a hostile expression. '*Demasiado grande.* Too beeg.'

'There's lots of room.' Melissa got into the back seat as well.

The driver watched in scandalized silence. 'Why you 'ave zees beeg *perro?*' he asked. 'And 'e ees all wet.'

David decided to ignore the question. 'Where is the nearest police station?' The man made a weird noise in his throat.

'Eh?'

When the noise had been repeated, twice, slowly, David said, 'Ah. Girona.' And to Melissa, 'Their G's are a sort of aitch with a sore larynx.'

'Girona's behind us,' Melissa pointed out as the car moved off.

'*Si, señora.*'

'Then, shouldn't we turn round?'

'I go to Barthelona,' the man said, firmly. '*Vacaciones?*'

15

'No, no, we have a house here,' David shouted, to help their saviour to understand.

'Een Hirona?'

'No, in a place called Jàvea. Down the coast from Valencia.'

'*Xabia*,' the man said. The word was vaguely similar.

'Well, yes, I believe some people do call it that.'

'*Xabia* ees *Valenthiano*,' the man explained. 'Zee true language. The rest ... pouf.'

'I see, yes. My name is David. And my wife is Melissa.'

'*Mi nombre* ees Salvador.'

'I can't tell you how glad we are to have met up with you, Mr Salvador,' Melissa said.

'You weesh dreenk?'

'I'd love some water,' Melissa said. '*Agua?*'

'*Agua? Non.* We dreenk Magno.' He reached beneath his seat and produced a bottle containing a suspicious-looking brown liquid. 'Very good.'

David uncorked it and sniffed. 'That's alcohol,' Melissa announced.

'Brandy. Very good.'

'David!' Melissa protested, but he was already drinking.

'Wow! Try some.'

'I don't think...'

'When in Rome...'

Cautiously she swallowed some of the liquor, and felt her head spin. David took the bottle back, corked it, and handed it to the driver. To their consternation, he removed the cork and took a long drink himself. 'You're not going to drive while drinking brandy!' Melissa protested.

'Ees good, eh?' He took another swig and handed the bottle back to David.

If you can't beat them, Melissa thought. And at least she'd die happy. And after her third swig she began to feel light-headed; the catastrophe of the stolen car seemed a very long time ago. 'Just think,' she giggled as she sat with her arms wrapped round Fred. 'Spain is full of car drivers filled with brandy. What're their road-death statistics?'

'About twice as high as ours,' David said.

'Zee trouble ees zee toureestas,' Salvador said. 'Zey cause zee acceedent. Zey do not understand.'

'Understand what?'

'*Botheena?*'Ow you say? 'Orn.' He blared the car horn several times.

'It's difficult to understand anything when you're full of brandy,' Melissa said, and fell asleep, her head resting against Fred's.

Apparently Salvador managed to stay awake, because when Melissa opened her eyes they were in the middle of a very large city, with traffic lights winking at them and *bocinas* blaring. She looked at her watch: it was a quarter to one. She was both hungry and thirsty. 'I wonder where the car is now?' she muttered.

'They've had two and a half hours to play with,' David replied. 'They could be back in France, for all we know.'

'You no want *hostal*?' Salvador asked.

'I have no money. I cannot even pay you for this ride.'

'You weel owe me. You say me *su nombre, y direcciones de su casa. Si?*'

'Right. My name is David Lytton, and my address is Villa Sagittarius, Montgo, Jàvea, Alicante.'

'Veella Sagittarius?'

'We're both Sagittarians,' Melissa confessed. 'Can't you tell, from the mess we're in?'

'What ees zees Sagittareean?'

'I'll tell you when you come to the villa for the money,' David promised. 'Do you know Montgo?'

'*Mia casa* – *el* 'ouse – ees *próxima de Montgo*. Eet ees een zee *montagnas, mas sud*.' Salvador drew to a halt before an imposing building, from one of the upper floors of which the Spanish flag was drooping.

'Oh, lord!' Melissa muttered. They were stopped on a very busy street; the pavements were crowded with people.

'I come een and explain. I know a *polithia* sergeant, *aqui*,' Salvador assured them importantly, and climbed down.

Melissa took a long breath. 'Here goes.' She stepped on to the pavement. Immediately a crowd gathered. David grabbed her arm and

18

they followed Salvador up the steps, Fred padding at their heels. They were greeted by several policemen, wearing blue uniforms and with revolver holsters on their right hips, and truncheons and handcuffs on their left; they were of both sexes, but looked equally tough, if at the moment amused at the sight of their visitors. Salvador spoke rapidly in Spanish, and after some argument, David and Melissa and Fred were allowed through. Inside, they arrived before a desk, where Salvador did some more rapid talking. A policeman then gestured them further along the corridor. '*Ahora*, I go,' Salvador said.

'You mean you can't stay to interpret?' David was aghast.

'No, I go. Zey weell take care of you.'

'Well...' David held out his hand. 'Don't forget to come to Jàvea.'

'*Xabia. Si, si.* I weell come. *El coche* was a Peugeot estate. I weel remember. *'Dios.'*

'*Gracias. Adios.*' They watched him hurrying through the now thronging policemen. 'That was a really nice chap,' David commented.

'He seems very interested in our car.'

'Well, it's a nice car.'

'But he hasn't seen it.'

Before he could think of a reply, they were shown into an interview room, windowless, and well away from the street. The door was left open, and some half-a-dozen of the male constables remained crowding it, gazing at

19

Melissa. A sergeant bustled in. He wore horn-rimmed spectacles and was bald, save for a fringe of black hair over his ears. In rapid-fire Spanish he dismissed the gawking constables, and sat himself in the chair on the far side of the table, opposite Melissa, who had taken the other chair. David remained standing behind her, Fred sitting and leaning against her legs, panting. The sergeant opened a pad of notepaper, and placed a ballpoint pen beside it. 'Your car has been stolen.' His English was very good. 'Description?'

'Peugeot 506 Estate, colour dark-blue, with blue interior,' David replied. Now they were getting somewhere.

The sergeant wrote busily. 'From where was it taken?'

'A beach. About ten miles south of Girona.'

The sergeant frowned as he raised his head. 'That is in Girona Province. This is Barcelona Province.'

'I understand that. But Salvador was coming here.'

Another frown. 'You know this man, Salvador?'

'Well, no. But he was very helpful.'

The sergeant gave a heavy sigh. 'Your name?'

'David Lytton.'

'Your passports, please.'

'I'm sorry. Our passports were in the car.'

The sergeant peered at David over the rims

of his glasses. 'You leave your *bolsa*, your handbag, in the car?'

'My handbag?'

'Every man has a handbag, *señor*. In a handbag he carries his passport, and his money, and his credit cards ... you do not have a handbag?'

'I'm afraid not. It isn't usual, in England.'

'You are in Spain, *señor*. A sensible man,' the sergeant said, 'carries his handbag with him at all times. Even when he goes swimming, he leaves his handbag where he can see it, at all times.'

'I see,' David said humbly. 'I will do so in the future.'

'When you have something to put in it, eh?' the sergeant said, jovially. 'Well, if you have no passport, what is your age?'

'Forty-two.'

The sergeant wrote. 'And the lady is your wife?'

'Yes,' Melissa said. 'I am Melissa Lytton, née Clarke, and I am thirty-four years old.' The sergeant wrote. 'Our dog's name is Speign Lord Tara of Borden,' Melissa continued. 'And he is five years old.' The sergeant raised his head, and David raised his eyes to the ceiling; Melissa could not resist poking fun at pomposity. 'Well,' she said, 'I thought it might help. We call him Fred.'

The sergeant looked at Fred, and decided not to take offence. 'Now, I wish a descrip-

21

tion of the men who did the stealing.'

'One had yellow hair,' Melissa said.

'Yellow hair.' The sergeant was writing again. 'That means he was not Spanish.' He appeared relieved.

'But the other one had dark hair,' Melissa pointed out. 'He was very swarthy.'

'Swarthy?'

'Well...' She looked hopefully at David, aware that she might be getting into deep water: the sergeant could be described as swarthy.

'Dutch,' the sergeant suggested. 'Or English. They are responsible for most of the crimes on the costas.'

'You mean the Spanish don't commit crimes?'

'This is not what I am saying, *señor*. It is matter of what crime. The Dutch and the English, they are interested only in drugs. They stole your car to make a drug delivery, or to pay for a drug delivery. We understand these things.'

'When will we get it back?' Melissa asked. 'Our car.'

'I do not know, *señora*. Perhaps never.'

'Never?' Melissa's voice rose an octave.

'In any event, what is in the car will have been taken.'

'May I use your telephone?' David asked.

'You have a friend in Barcelona?'

'No. I have a brother-in-law in Surbiton, London. England.'

22

'You wish to call this brother-in-law?'

'I must stop payment on all our credit cards, and arrange for money, and...'

'What is your occupation?' the sergeant asked.

'I'm retired.'

The sergeant raised his head. 'You are forty-two, *señor*. What was your occupation before you retired?'

'I was a restaurateur. And then someone decided to buy the restaurant, and, well...'

'You have retired, on the sale of one restaurant?'

'It was a jolly successful restaurant,' Melissa snapped. 'Have you never heard of Lytton's Pantry?' David winced. But Melissa was in full defensive flow. 'We were in *Egon Ronay*, the *Best Food Guide*, the *Best Restaurants in London Guide*, the *American Express Hundred Best Restaurants in England*...'

The sergeant waited patiently. 'And you have retired to Spain. You wish to buy a house?'

'We have a house,' Melissa explained. 'On Montgo. That's by Jàvea. We bought it last year, and have been getting it fixed up. We were driving down, and now our car has been stolen...' She looked about to burst into tears. She wasn't, of course, as David well knew. But she believed in using every weapon she possessed.

'Of course, *señora*. This is very sad. You have the licence number of your car?' David gave it to him. 'Now, *señor*, you realize that it is an offence to appear on the street in Barcelona in a bathing costume?'

'We're not dressed like this from choice. If you'd just let me telephone my brother-in-law, we'll be able to arrange for some money to be transferred to buy clothes.'

'Do you think I could have a glass of water?' Melissa asked. 'And a bowl for the dog?'

The sergeant regarded Fred, who gurgled helpfully. 'That dog has no collar.'

'We took it off to go swimming, and left it in the car.'

'It is illegal for a dog to be on the street without a collar.'

'We'll get him a new one as soon as I've telephoned my brother-in-law,' David promised.

'Has the dog been inoculated against rabies?'

'Yes. We had him inoculated because we were bringing him to the Continent. There is no rabies in England.'

'There is no rabies in Spain, either, but that is because every dog has to be inoculated against it. Then you have a certificate, and a little tag to put on your dog's collar to show everyone that he has been inoculated. This tag must be renewed every year with the appropriate date. It is like a licence, eh? Your dog has no tag. Show me the certificate.'

Melissa kept her temper. 'We have the

certificate. We couldn't cross France without it. But it is in the car.'

'You must obtain a new certificate, and a tag.'

'We will get a tag, I promise, the moment we can.'

'It is not possible now, until tomorrow.'

'Well, can't you give us a dispensation, until tomorrow?'

'What will you do, until tomorrow?'

'If you'd let me telephone my brother-in-law...'

'It is very expensive to telephone England. You must reverse the charges.'

'Of course I will reverse the charges. May I?'

The sergeant gestured at the telephone.

'And please could we have some water?' Melissa begged.

The sergeant bellowed instructions in Spanish, and a bottle of water was brought, together with a glass and a bowl. Fred drank heartily, taking his time. As was the Spanish telephone system. 'Hello. Hello,' David repeated over and over again. And at last there was a response. 'Hello? Is that you, Gerry?'

'Now look here, Dave, what's all this about reversing the charges? Where are you calling from?'

'Barcelona.'

'Good God! Haven't you any money?' Gerald always spoke as if he were addressing a roomful of delinquent schoolboys. No doubt, in his capacity as a very successful chartered accountant, he addressed board meetings in the same vein.

'At this moment in time, no,' David told him. 'We've been robbed of our car. With everything in it.'

'Good Lord! Well, that's what comes of going to Spain. Still, I suppose the removal people will be down in a week or so with the rest of your stuff.'

'Gerry, old man,' David said patiently, 'when I said everything, I meant everything. Everything!'

'I say, they didn't take Liss as well, did they?'

Melissa was Gerald's youngest sister, and David had often had the feeling that Gerry considered she had married beneath her. 'No,' he said, looking at his wife. 'But they took everything else. Our current possessions consist of one swimsuit each, one watch each, one St Christopher medallion, and one dog. We have no money, no shoes, clothes or credit cards. No laptop. And no car.'

'Give me that,' Melissa said. 'Hello, Gerry. Remember you're paying for this call, and that I am sitting here in a bathing suit, being ogled by half Barcelona. Have you a pencil and paper handy?'

'Just a moment. Right. Shoot.'

Melissa handed the phone back to David. 'One: I want you to telephone the Excelsior

26

Hotel here in Barcelona and book us in. Explain the situation, and that we need a double room with bath, and that we have a dog, who will be sharing the room with us. Two: I wish you to inform them that the bill will go on whatever card number you give them, and that we are to be allowed to buy whatever we wish from their boutiques. Got that?'

'Ye-es,' Gerald said, doubtfully.

'I'll pay you back, twit,' David said. 'Three, when you've made that call, I wish you to get on to my bank and have five hundred pounds transferred to their Barcelona correspondents, to be collected tomorrow morning. Four: I want you to telephone the card companies and cancel my cards, and those belonging to Melissa, and ask for new ones to be issued and sent to our bank in Jàvea.'

'I'll need the numbers.'

'I don't have the numbers. Do you carry your credit card numbers in your head? They'll have them on file.'

'Well,' Gerald said. 'I'll see what I can do.'

'We also need new passports. Will you get on to the Consul in Valencia or Alicante or wherever and arrange that?'

'He'll need birth certificates and things.'

'They're in my safety deposit box.'

'Then I'll need authority to get them.'

'When you call about the money, tell Morton I'll call him this afternoon to confirm – that is, the moment we get to the

27

hotel. There's no time to write. Oh, and new driving licences.'

'That's quite a list. I'm bound to say, old man, that you need a minder.'

'Gerry, I am not in the mood for lectures. You do all of those things, and do them right, and I shall refrain from punching you on the nose next time we meet. Call me back at this number –' he gave it – 'as soon as we can move into the Excelsior.'

The sergeant had listened to the conversation with great interest. 'It is all being taken care of?' he asked.

'I hope so. May we stay here until my brother-in-law calls back?' The sergeant shrugged.

Gerald, once convinced there was an emergency, was a most forceful and efficient fellow, and it was only an hour and a half later that David and Melissa, and Fred, were being driven in a police car to the Excelsior. They were taken to a side entrance, and hurried upstairs to their room, where an undermanager awaited them with the registry forms. 'Mr and Mrs Lytton,' he said. 'I am most terribly sorry about your misfortune. But now everything is taken care of.'

'Clothes,' David said. 'We need clothes.'

'And toiletries,' Melissa added. 'And a hairdryer.'

'I will have some sent up immediately.'

'Food first,' Melissa said; it was three

o'clock. 'I am starving. So is Fred.'

The undermanager indicated the room-service menu. 'Whatever you wish.'

'Do you have something for the dog?'

'I will see that something is obtained, Mrs Lytton.'

'Thank you so much. Now, let me see ... oh, *gambas a la plancha*, definitely, to start with, and ... *cordero al horno*.' She looked at David. 'How does that grab you?'

'Sounds great. We'll need some wine.'

'Well, *señor*, with the shrimps, may I suggest a Marquis de Càceres *blanco*, and with the lamb, a Marquis de Riscal *tinto*. A half bottle of each?'

'No,' Melissa corrected. 'A whole bottle of each. And now,' she said, when the under-manager had left, 'I am for a hot tub. Boy, is that going to feel good.'

David had unlocked the minibar. 'I am for champagne to be going on with. It's Spanish, but it's cold, and it has bubbles. How does *that* take you?'

'That is just what the doctor ordered.' Having washed her hair, she leaned back in the tub, sipping her Freixenet and trying not to think about her feet as the hot water got to them. 'Did it really happen, Dave?'

'Terrible luck. That we should choose the very beach where these drug addicts or what-ever were just waiting to pounce.'

'If they *were* drug addicts. Listen! That sounds like food.'

It was not only food, but a selection of garments for them to try on, as well as toothbrushes and paste, an electric razor, and some perfume which made Melissa wrinkle her nose in distaste. They opted for wrapping themselves in towels and eating before making any decisions about clothes; Fred was already tucking into a large dish of meat scraps.

'So where do we go from here?' Melissa asked, daintily popping a roasted shrimp into her mouth and washing it down with the Càceres.

'As soon as the money arrives, we'll hire a car, and go on down to Jàvea.'

'David, it's Thursday afternoon. Even if the money arrives first thing tomorrow, we cannot possibly arrive before tomorrow night. You'll have to telephone Martinez and tell him we'll be a couple of days late. He will also have to organize the hire car, as we don't have driving licences.'

'Good thinking,' David was savouring his roast lamb. 'I'll do that right after lunch.'

'I'm for bed. We can have the fashion show later.' She rested her chin on her hand. 'Dave ... everything is going to be all right, isn't it? I'm thinking about the whole thing. Moving to Spain, I mean.'

'Cars get stolen in England as well, you know. Are you still mad at me for leaving the keys in the ignition?'

She blew him a kiss. 'But it was a bloody

stupid thing to have done.' They finished the red wine.

Melissa opted for a pale-green pants suit with a white shirt, a pink cotton dress with a blue and white design, and a few changes of underwear. The problems began when she started on the shoes. 'My feet are swollen!'

David took a closer look. 'You do have some dandy blisters coming up.'

'Oh, damn! What am I going to do?'

'Go to bed, and stay there. They'll be down by tomorrow. Anyway, everyone in Spain wears sandals or thongs.'

'Who's going to take Fred for walkies, meanwhile?'

They both looked at Fred, who looked back at them. 'There's no collar and no lead,' David pointed out.

'Fred has got to go out. Soon, I would say.'

David sighed.

Spending eighteen hours in bed was just what Melissa needed. Apart from her feet, she was far more upset about the car being stolen than she had let on. No doubt David was too, but they both kept their true feelings to themselves, trying to raise each other's spirits. They didn't actually know each other that intimately. Melissa supposed it was a strange sort of marriage. For David, it was second time around. She had never met

Jennifer, and therefore had to accept everything that David had told her. Jennifer had apparently been either a magnificent companion, in bed, on a small boat – David loved sailing – or on a long walk ... or she had been an utter bitch.

When she had been an utter bitch once too often, David had opted out. It had been a very messy business, because he had already built up the Pantry into one of the most successful restaurants in London, and had had to fight for the right to keep it when Jennifer had demanded half of everything. He had won that fight, an understanding judge conceding that Jennifer had had nothing at all to do with the success of the restaurant, but only at the expense of selling his house to pay her off.

He had been living in a small flat and feeling thoroughly miserable when he had come to grips with Melissa, a high-powered PR girl who organized functions for large firms. They had been acquainted for some time, as several of her functions had taken place at the Pantry, but had been nothing more than business friends until the night they had celebrated a particularly successful evening together, and wound up back at her flat, which was of a considerably better standard than his; in fact, Melissa owned the building – and had paid half the mortgage – so that she could keep the garden flat for herself and Fred.

That evening had been fun, because she had been between blokes at the time, had almost been regarding herself as a permanent single, not altogether with regret ... but she had been utterly taken aback when, three months and only half-a-dozen shared nights later, he had proposed marriage. 'So I'm forty,' he had said. 'And you...'

'So what's eight years? I was thinking more, well ... marriage? I mean, if you'd like to move in here and see how it goes...'

'I'm old-fashioned,' he had told her.

Well, anyone could see that. 'What about Fred?'

Who was leering at them over the end of the bed.

'I love Fred,' David had declared. 'And I think he quite likes me. He hasn't bitten me yet, for all that I have been making free with his mistress's body.'

'Fred likes everybody. That's why I can afford to keep him in a town flat. One of the ladies upstairs comes in and sits with him, and lets him into the garden, when I'm at work. But what about the restaurant ... a twenty-four hour a day job, isn't it?'

'Eighteen.'

'Doesn't leave much time for kids.'

'Do you want kids?'

'I thought it might be rather nice. Not right away, of course,' she had added hastily. 'But one has to try, from time to time. And six hours in every twenty-four...'

'I don't open on Mondays,' he reminded her.

It had crept up on her without her really being aware of it. Anyway, a wedding is always fun, and more so when it happens to be your own. And in fact, life had not changed in any great detail. David had moved into her flat, but she had gone on calling herself Melissa Clarke, and continued in her job, only arranging to have every Monday afternoon off. She had enjoyed having one man, exclusively, knowing that he'd be turning up some time every night after the Pantry had closed. Even cooking for him, of which she had been very nervous, did not become a problem. David genuinely liked preparing food, and when he was home, did most of the cooking himself. She found herself learning a great deal, and the future had seemed a long way away.

Until the night he had come home later than usual, shaken her awake, and said, 'I've had an offer. For the Pantry.'

Melissa had sat up. 'What kind of offer?'

'Well ... how's your heart?'

'Thumping.'

'Two million.'

'What?' she had shouted.

'Seems there's this chain ... we've actually been negotiating for some time, but I didn't want to tell you, in case it fell through. They offered one point five in the beginning, but I turned them down. I didn't think they'd come back ... but they did. Raised it to one point seven-five. Forget it, I said. I wouldn't sell the Pantry for under two. All right, they said. This evening.'

'But ... is it worth two million?'

'Not in terms of turnover. But it's the freehold as well, you see. That's worth close to two million on its own.'

'Oh, Dave!' She hugged him and kissed him, and then started thinking. 'What are you going to do?'

'Ah. I've been thinking about that.' He had disentangled himself, got up, and began to pace the room. She knew him well enough by then to see that he was nervous about what he was going to say. 'I was thinking that perhaps we could take a look at Spain.'

'We went there last year.'

'Quite. And thoroughly enjoyed ourselves. Remember those houses we saw on that mountain behind Jàvea? Montgo? I thought we might buy one of them.'

'Sounds great. But you haven't answered my question. What will you do?'

'Well...' He sat beside her again. 'Retire.'

'At forty-one?'

'Only in a manner of speaking,' he said hastily. 'I've always wanted to write. If we settle in Spain, I'd write.'

'You mean ... leave England? For good?'

'We'd come back, of course. Several times a year.'

'But ... all my friends are here. My family. My job!' Her voice was slowly gaining octaves. 'Fred!'

'Well, Fred would come with us, of course. As for the rest ... Spain isn't the end of the earth, you know. It's a simple telephone call away from England. And a simple plane ride, too. And think of all that warm sunshine, the relaxed way of life...'

'My job?'

'Wouldn't you like to retire too? Sunny Spain,' he had said seductively. 'Fred will love it. It's an adventure, Liss. And what a perfect place to settle down to that family you're always talking about. Think about it.'

It was amazing, and intriguing, how an idea, once planted, could grow. That had been September, and they had put Fred in kennels and flown down the following weekend. Melissa had convinced herself that she was in no way committed, but a week later they had bought a house. Her enthusiasm had been every bit as great as David's, by then. It was a beautiful house, not very large, but situated high up on the mountainside, possessing marvellous views across the valley of the Jalón River which twisted its way down from the mountains only twenty-odd kilometres to the west, and above all, totally private.

Of course it had needed several things doing to it, but the agent had been happy to take their instructions and had promised to put the work in hand immediately. 'We'd like to move in next April,' David had said.

'Oh, no problem, *señor*, no problem,' Alfredo Martinez had promised. Gerald and Audrey had been horrified. So had Mum. But Gerald and Audrey were horrified by anything out of the ordinary – they had certainly been horrified when she had married David – and their idea of a foreign holiday was Guernsey. While Mum had no doubt at all that to set foot in Calais, much less Valencia, was to risk cholera, or instant rape.

Well, Melissa thought, nestling into her pillows and trying to forget her aching feet, cars *were* stolen in England as well.

Two

'*Good morning, Big Sam,*' *said the voice on the phone.*

'*Salvador! What have you got for me?*'

'*I have found the men.*'

'*Well done. You overtook their car?*'

'*Their car was kaput. Pedro's bullets must have nicked the petrol tank. So they ran out of gas, after crossing the border. I found the car by the roadside.*'

'*And the men?*'

'They were not there. I thought I had lost them. But I kept driving south hoping perhaps to see them.' Sam snorted in derision. 'Then I picked up this couple. English, I think. Their car had been stolen while they bathed in the sea. They were wearing only swimming costumes. The woman was ... mmmm.'

'Get on with it.'

'Well, I realized immediately what had happened. I got them to describe their car, then I dropped them off in Barcelona, and went on. And I found the car.'

'On the motorway?'

'No, no, señor. But my cousin works on the peaje outside Tarragona. I telephoned him and told him to watch for this car. And he called me back an hour later, and told me that he had seen the car, but that it had turned off before the peaje, taking the slip road into the mountains. So I followed. I left the motorway by the same slip road, and went to a village where my uncle lives. I asked him if he had seen a large Peugeot, and he said yes. The car had driven through the village only an hour before. So I followed, and found it parked by the roadside. Another of Pedro's bullets had hit one of the men, and he was very bad. They asked for my help.'

'And?'

'I shot them both. Then I searched them. But Sam, they had nothing on them.'

'They must have.'

'I found nothing. And there was some traffic. I could not wait, as I knew the English people would have given the police a description of the car.'

'You should have killed them also.'

'Ah, señor, you have not seen the woman. Those legs...'

'So what did you do?'

'I put the men in my boot, and I drove away. I dumped them when it was safe, and came home.'

'Without the card!' Sam's voice suddenly ceased being sleepy. 'It was hidden somewhere in the car, you cretin. And you did not even look for it.'

'There was no time, señor. A car passed me while I was searching the bodies. It slowed and then drove on again, but I think they would have gone to the police...'

'Salvador, you get back to that car and take it to pieces if you have to. But get that card. Or I will send someone to see you.' The phone went dead.

'I am sorry, señor,' the bank clerk said, picking up his cigarette and blowing smoke at the ceiling. 'But there is nothing here for Lytton. Perhaps later on...'

'Oh, for God's sake!' David snapped. And then grinned apologetically. 'I'm sorry, señor, but we have had a rough day yesterday. Our car has been stolen, and...'

The clerk wanted to hear all about it, and was most concerned. 'I am sure the money will be in soon,' he said. 'You are staying at the Excelsior? Why do you not go back there and I will telephone you as soon as it arrives.'

'Your bloody brother!' David grumbled as they emerged on to the pavement. 'Does he think we're going to spend the rest of our lives in Barcelona?'

Melissa dragged Fred from the adjacent lamppost; the hotel manager had found a leather strap for them which doubled as collar and lead. 'Let's go back to the hotel and telephone the police station; they may have found the car.'

'After we've telephoned Gerald,' David said.

Gerald promised to chase up the transfer. David had already phoned his London bank as well, and with some difficulty managed to persuade them to accept his delegated authority to open his safe deposit box without his being there, and give the necessary documentation for new passports and driving licences to Gerald. Then he called the police, and after spending nearly an hour on the line, being passed from one department to another, was finally informed that there was no trace of the car as yet. Indeed, they almost inferred he was being unreasonable asking for news so soon.

'It doesn't sound as if they're bloody well looking,' he complained. As the angry flush rose up his neck and face, Melissa began to have serious fears for his blood pressure, but just before noon the sympathetic bank clerk telephoned to say the money had been traced. The clerk was all smiles when they arrived. 'I told you it would only be a few hours delayed, *Señor* Lytton,' he said. 'Five hundred pounds, for the credit of Mr David Lytton. Will you open an account?'

'I'll take the cash. In euros?'

The clerk raised his eyebrows. 'You mean to walk around Barcelona with several hundred euros in your pocket?'

'If anyone tries to mug me I'll set the dog on him,' David promised. The clerk looked over the desk at Fred, who was sitting with his head on Melissa's lap while she scratched his ears. Fred smiled, ingratiatingly. 'Anyway, we're not staying in Barcelona,' David went on. 'We're heading south to our house in Jàvea. So we need to hire a car.'

'It is as you wish, *señor*,' the clerk said. 'I will give you the cash. But first, you must let me see your passport...'

'I thought you were going to slug that poor fellow,' Melissa commented, as she pushed Fred into the back seat of the hired Seat. Alfredo Martinez had at least done his stuff and telephoned the garage.

'It crossed my mind,' David said, fiddling with the unaccustomed gears.

'I'm glad you didn't.' She clambered into the passenger seat, squealed, and leapt out again. 'Damn! That burned my bottom.' The car had been sitting in the sun for some time.

41

She grabbed the new towel she'd bought for Fred, arranging it carefully over the seat before sitting again, while David hissed impatiently. 'He was only doing his job. And there was no problem after his manager had telephoned London and got a description of us. Fred was important there. Weren't you, Fred?'

Fred licked the back of her neck. 'And it is now half past two,' David said. 'You realize that, by the time we've sorted out the hotel, it's going to be dark before we reach Jàvea?'

'Does that matter, in Spain? I thought the shops and offices stayed open until eight?'

'It's still going to be a rush. Don't they do anything in this country without looking at your passport first? Talk about the European Community...'

'We're on our way, lover.' She kissed him on the cheek. 'Do drive carefully.'

The sense of lurking hysteria was back. But now they were on their way to their new home, racing along the *autopista* south past Tarragona, over the Ebro, then past Castellón, and on to the bypass around Valencia. The April evening was drawing in when eventually they came to the familiar signs announcing exits to Denia and Ondara, and that Alicante was the next big city, albeit more than a hundred kilometres distant. And then, just as it was getting dark, they saw their mountain, Montgo, rising to their left.

However dramatic a physical feature, Montgo was not a unique aspect of the Spanish landscape. Along the Mediterranean coast there were several of these rocky giants thrown up by some prehistoric cataclysm which had separated them from the solidly packed mountains to the west. But Montgo was the biggest, vying with the Peñón d'Ifach at Calpe as the most famous on the Costa Blanca, rising seven hundred and fifty metres out of the coastal plain, its slopes gentle on the landward side, sheer and hard where they faced the sea.

Legend had it that the earliest human inhabitants of Spain were cave dwellers on Montgo, at the end of the ice age. Since then the lower slopes had become shrouded in pine forests, thinned on the southern side by the wine-growers of Alicante Province, terracing upwards for some eight hundred feet to plant their vines; in many places the ruins of windmills which had lifted the necessary water from the valley remained stark on the skyline. Only comparatively recently had the landowners of Montgo realized that they could make far more money, fast, by selling their property to the northern Europeans, the Germans and the Dutch, the Belgians and the French, and the British, who came flooding across the Pyrénées in search of cheap living and perpetual sun.

The cheap living had largely been absorbed in the general prosperity which had overtaken Spain since the death of General Franco, and subsequent entry into the European Community, but prices were still lower in many areas than elsewhere in Western Europe – especially regarding alcohol – and the sun remained, seeming to grow hotter year by year. Mediterranean Spain had become one of the most cosmopolitan places on earth. Melissa supposed it was inevitable that there would be a few crooks around.

They turned off at Ondara and took the National Route in the direction of Jàvea. Only a generation before, Jàvea itself had been a tiny fishing port in the bay protected by Cap San Antonio and Cap Negro, with a small *pueblo*, or village, situated about two kilometres inland. Now it had expanded, with a third municipality, known as Arenal, having grown up at the south end of the bay, where there was a splendid beach. High-rises had thankfully been avoided to a great extent, although there were sufficient four-storey apartment blocks, especially in Arenal, to be depressing.

Montgo rose inland and north of Jàvea, towering above the village and port like a lion couchant, and separating it from another small and still unspoiled village, called Jesus Pobre – meaning Poor Jesus – although development had reared its ugly head here as well. The side road from the National Route skirted Jesus Pobre before becoming the Jesus Pobre Road, which bounced uneasily along the southern foot of the mountain and into Jàvea itself. Now, as Melissa and David looked up to their left, they saw the myriad twinkling lights of the many houses which nowadays crowded the lower slopes. 'I can't wait to get installed,' Melissa purred.

'Won't be long now,' David promised.

She turned round to ruffle Fred's fur. 'What a long drive,' she told him. 'And now you're home. Home, Fred, home.'

'Woof,' Fred commented. He believed everything Melissa told him.

David had to drive into the *pueblo* first, to collect the keys. They left the car in the huge central macadamized park, Fred being glad of the opportunity to lift his leg against a neighbouring hubcap, then they crossed the Ronda Norde into the maze of narrow streets which filled the area around Calle Major, and where Martinez Realtors was situated. Jàvea was a bustle of bright lights and chattering people; the period between seven and eight each evening was the most popular for both shopping and business. Through lighted windows and open doors, particularly of private homes, the heart of Spanish life was revealed. Front doors stood wide to display mosaic floors leading through stone archways, heavy curtains drawn back to allow

45

access to central courtyards filled with carefully tended ornamental palms and flowers. To either side, small rooms, colourfully tiled halfway up the walls, were filled with heavily carved furniture in rich fabrics. Stout ladies, smartly coiffed, sat together with their lace work, gossiping, awaiting the return of their menfolk from shops and offices and smoke-filled bars. It was a magic new world to visiting Northern Europeans.

The offices of Martinez Realtors had been recently refurbished with tosca stone arches and marble floors. *'Buenos tardes, señor, señora,'* said the attractive dark-haired girl at the reception desk.

'Mr and Mrs Lytton,' David reminded her.

'Ah, *si, si.*' She looked anxiously at the dog.

'Fred,' Melissa explained.

'I 'ave *las claves* for you,' the girl said, taking the keys from a drawer.

'Great. We had a bit of trouble up north,' David said. 'I mentioned it on the telephone to *Señor* Martinez.'

'Si, si, problemas, I know,' she said sympathetically. 'He tell to me, *malo. Muy malo.* You car *aqui?*'

'No.' David shook his head. 'Is *Señor* Martinez here?'

'I am sorry, 'e go out. You want I do something for you?'

'I just wanted to check that all the work has been done up at the house.'

She shrugged. *'Señor* Martinez, 'e know.

46

But I do not. I know 'e go to *la casa*, many time. *Pera finita ... possible.*'

David frowned. '*Señor* Martinez assured me that it would all be finished by the time we arrived. And when I spoke to him earlier this month...'

'April is not good month,' the girl remarked. '*Pascua* ... Easter, *comprende?*'

'Easter was a fortnight ago.'

'*Si, si. Sino la fiesta, es dos semanas.* Two weeks. Next week is two days more.' She smiled. 'Is good you come today, *si?*'

'Yes,' David said grimly. 'Tell *Señor* Martinez I'll call him tomorrow morning.'

'Call, *señor?*'

'Telephone,' David explained, making the appropriate gestures with his hands.

'Ah. *Si.* Telephone. No tomorrow, *señor.*'

'Why not?'

'Tomorrow is Saturday, *señor.*'

'Oh. Yes, of course. Monday morning, then.'

Melissa had been thinking. 'Didn't you take photostats of our passports when we were here last autumn?' she asked.

The girl frowned, trying to understand. '*Foto* ... ah, *fotocopias! De sus passeportes! Si, si.*'

'Well, could we have copies of these photocopies, *por favor?*'

'They not very good, *señora.*'

'They'll be better than nothing.'

'*Momentito.*' The girl disappeared through

47

one of the arches.

'Good thinking,' David said. 'Who's my little genius, then?'

It was eight fifteen and very dark when, having done some brief shopping, they drove up the winding road and arrived in front of the rather imposing wrought-iron gates installed by the previous owners. David got out and unlocked them by the glow of the headlamps, and then negotiated the steep slope to the yard behind the house. Built into the side of the hill, the living and main bedroom areas were all on one level with the car park, but the swimming pool and pro-jected guest apartment were on a lower floor, in front. Beyond that, the land fell away a hundred yards to the next property, where a house showed lights from several windows; they had not yet met any of their neighbours.

Further up the mountain the darkness was intense, the only sound the whisper of the wind in the pines, punctuated by the occa-sional calls of night birds. 'You stay put while I open up,' David advised, fumbling with the keys and pulling back the protective *reja*, or grille. When the door swung in, he flicked the switch, to no avail. 'Oh, hell!'

'It's probably off at the mains,' Melissa suggested. 'The box was at the end of the hallway, wasn't it?'

There was no torch in the hired car. David disappeared into the gloom, and Melissa got out and allowed Fred to descend. He headed for the nearest bush. 'Got it!' David shouted. There was a click, and the hall light came on. 'What the...?' Melissa hurried inside, leaving the door open for Fred, gazed at the totally empty living and dining area. 'Didn't we buy a vast quantity of furniture and instruct them to deliver it?' David demanded.

'Yes, we did.' She went down the passageway, threw open the door of the master bedroom. 'David!' She couldn't stop her voice giving a little quiver. 'There are no beds!'

'Oh, Jesus Christ!' He stood at her shoulder, gazed at another large area of empty tiled floor. 'Well, that's it. I'm getting that bastard Martinez up here now to sort things out.'

'He'll have gone home. It's long past eight.'

'He'll be in the phone book.'

'I should think there are an awful lot of Spaniards named Martinez in the phone book.'

'Then I'll call them all, one after the other,' David announced. 'Now, where the devil is it?'

He wandered through the house, switching on light after light and swearing, watched by an anxious Fred, who had come in and was sitting in the middle of the empty lounge, looking forlorn. Melissa followed him, attempting to suppress a rising tide of panic. 'I think,' she said, 'the reason you can't find

49

a phone book is that there's no phone.'

'Oh, shit! We put our names down for that in October, and he said it'd be in by Christmas.'

'Maybe he meant Easter. What are we going to do?'

'There's a *parador* down at Arenal. We'll have to check in there for tonight.'

'Oh, thank God for that! I thought we might have to sleep on the floor. Well...' She headed for the back door, and recoiled. 'David!' she screamed. 'There's a man!' Fred barked, but showed no immediate signs of advancing. David hurried to stand by his wife, and stare at the man who was filling the open back doorway. 'David!' Melissa grasped his arm. 'He's got a gun.'

'Now look here,' David said, stepping in front of her, and checking, because the intruder was clearly not a day under seventy-five, tall and distinguished looking, with handsome features and a full head of iron-grey hair. He was also very well dressed, in corduroy pants and a cashmere sweater over his sports shirt. But he was definitely carrying an automatic pistol.

'Forgive the intrusion,' he now said, his English only slightly affected by a foreign accent. 'I saw the lights come on and thought I should investigate. This house has been empty for some time.'

'We're the new owners,' David explained. 'David Lytton. This is my wife, Melissa.'

'Ah, yes, I heard the property had been sold, to a famous restaurateur.'

'Well, I wouldn't say that, exactly,' David said, modestly.

'But I have eaten at your Pantry, in London, Lytton.' The man tucked his pistol into his pocket and held out his hand. 'Hans von Grippenheimer.'

'Von ... ah...' David shook hands.

'And Mrs Lytton.' Grippenheimer turned to a still speechless Melissa.

But she was getting her nerves under control. 'Do you always walk around with a gun, Mr Grippenheimer?'

'When investigating odd goings-on at night, yes indeed, dear lady. One cannot be too careful.'

'Oh. Yes.' She looked at David.

Who was essaying a smile. 'Well, if we had been burglars, we wouldn't have found much to steal, would we?'

'Apparently not. Ow!' Grippenheimer grimaced as he discovered that Fred, who had finally decided to be friendly, had seized hold of his left hand with a set of perfect, large white teeth.

'Fred! Stop that!' Melissa commanded. 'He only does it when he likes you,' she explained.

'I see.' Grippenheimer gave an abortive tug. 'Ouch! What does he do when he doesn't like you?'

'Fred! Let go!'

51

Fred reluctantly obeyed, and Grippenheimer massaged his hand. 'If you own a dog
like that, you do not need a gun,' he remarked.

Melissa and David exchanged glances;
Fred liked everybody unless they actually
attempted to kick him, or, far more serious,
take away his bone. 'Oh, he's broken the
skin,' Melissa said. 'Let me put something on
it. Oh, Fred, you are a naughty fellow.'

'What are you going to put on it?' Grippenheimer was peering at the traces of
blood. 'I assume you have a certificate of
vaccination against rabies?'

'Yes, we do,' David said aggressively, in an
attempt to prevent their caller from actually
asking to see it.

'The dog has no collar.'

'Oh, dear,' Melissa said, having been
reminded of their predicament. 'I don't
suppose we *have* any medication. I am most
terribly sorry, Mr ... ah...'

'Think nothing of it, dear lady.' Reassured
that Fred was not diseased, Grippenheimer
gave the little puncture a suck. 'Welcome to
Jàvea. I hope you will be very happy here.'

'Thank you,' David said. 'And we appreci-
ate your concern about our property.'

'What are neighbours for?'

'Absolutely,' Melissa agreed, happy to have
changed the subject. 'We'd be much happier
right now if our furniture had arrived.'

'Yes, the van was up here yesterday. But the

52

place was locked up. They were quite put out.'

'But didn't they get the keys from the agent? *Señor* Martinez?'

'Ah,' Grippenheimer remarked. 'You bought the house from Martinez.'

'Shouldn't we have?' Melissa demanded.

'Who am I to say, dear lady? But apparently he had told the furniture people that the house would be open for them, and it wasn't. As I say, they were quite put out.'

'I don't blame them,' David said. 'We're quite put out as well. No furniture, and no prospect of getting any until Monday.'

'My dear fellow, now that you are here, I am sure you will get it up tomorrow.'

'Tomorrow is Saturday.'

'But the furniture stores in Gata open on Saturdays. According to the sign on the van, you bought your furniture in Gata.'

'We did!' Melissa cried. 'Well, that *is* a relief. We can spend the night in the *parador*, and get things done tomorrow.'

'The *parador*?' Grippenheimer looked astonished. 'You don't want to go down there, dear lady. Why not spend the night with us?'

Melissa looked at David. 'We couldn't possibly intrude,' David protested.

'My dear fellow, it will be a pleasure. My wife is just preparing supper.'

'But ... there's the dog,' Melissa said.

'Oh, bring him along. Antoinette adores

53

dogs. We'll expect you down in ten minutes.'

When the door had closed, Melissa looked at David again. 'What do you think? I mean, we don't know this chap...'

'He's somewhat larger than life. Hans von Grippenheimer. With a wife called Antoinette. But these things happen in Spain. I'll just get the gear out of the car, and stick what's necessary in the fridge.'

The *casa* at least came complete with fridge, freezer, stove, dishwasher and washing machine, even if the fridge was a long way from being as cold yet as the rest of the house. Melissa hugged herself in the lightweight jumper she'd bought in Barcelona. 'This place is like an icebox without any furniture in. It's these tiled floors, I suppose. I think we'll have to invest in some carpets.'

David was sweating slightly from his exertions. 'You're just tired and hungry.'

That might be why I'm not keen on Hans, she thought, trying to rub some life into a sandalled foot, as she followed David down the hill, with Fred and the washbag given them by the hotel, and a tin of dog food and some biscuits. 'Mrs Lytton! Mr Lytton! Do come in.' Melissa and David both goggled. The woman was younger than Melissa, certainly not yet thirty, just under six feet tall, with a handsome face and voluptuous figure – the latter amply displayed by her tight pants and very loose blouse – and with a mane of yellow hair tumbling down her back. 'I'm Carrie,' she announced, in a thick, unidentifiable accent.

Grippenheimer hadn't mentioned a Carrie. Must be his daughter. 'We're awfully sorry to intrude like this,' Melissa said. 'But your father...'

Carrie gave a shriek of laughter. 'You mean the admiral? Oh, he will be much amused by that. Come in. Come in.'

Melissa was totally confused. Admiral? Cautiously they stepped into an elegantly furnished lounge, the best aspect of which was the roaring log fire: the night had become distinctly chilly. 'And this is Fred!' Carrie dropped to her knees to give Fred an affectionate hug, which clearly pleased him very much. 'Oh, you are gorgeous.'

'I hope you don't mind, but I brought down his food,' Melissa said.

'Of course. And he must be starving. Bring him into the kitchen.' Melissa followed her through the lounge and equally elegant dining alcove beyond, peering around for a glimpse of Antoinette; the kitchen opened off both, and in the lounge doorway they encountered Grippenheimer with a tray of fluted glasses.

'Dear lady,' he said. 'Welcome to the Eyrie. You'll take a champagne cocktail?'

'Oh ... thank you.'

'We called it the Eyrie,' Carrie explained, 'or rather, Hans did when he built it, because

55

it was the highest house on Montgo. But since then there have been several others even higher. Including yours.'

'Oh! What a shame!' Melissa answered vaguely, still trying to work out the relationship between their hosts.

'The fortunes of war,' Carrie said. 'Now let's see...' She opened a cupboard and took out a large Pyrex bowl. 'Fred can eat from this. I'm afraid Antoinette's bowls just wouldn't be big enough.'

'Antoinette's...?'

'My Siamese.'

'Ah. Your cat!' The fuzz in her brain was beginning to clear. 'And the admiral is your...'

'Husband,' Carrie explained. 'I'm his fourth wife.'

'Ah. He said your cat liked dogs.'

'Oh, she does. I'm sure of it.' Carrie opened the tin expertly. 'You'd better add the biscuit.' Melissa did so, set the bowl down, and Fred fell to without a moment's hesitation. 'He was hungry,' Carrie observed.

'It's been a long day.' Melissa stood by as Carrie whisked saucepans and dishes about in well-practised fashion. She always felt helpless in another woman's kitchen. For the sake of polite conversation she remarked, 'So your husband is an admiral?'

'He's actually retired.'

'Oh, quite. In what navy?'

'The German.'

'Of course. Are you German?'

'I am Danish,' Carrie said.

'Oh. Do forgive me asking all these questions...'

'Why should you not? We are strangers. Whereas you are the famous restaurateurs.'

'Well, my husband was...' Melissa followed Carrie into the lounge, where Admiral Grippenheimer was talking, and David was listening, a rather desperate expression on his face.

'Dear lady,' Grippenheimer said. 'Is that man-eating beast of yours being fed?'

'I'm awfully sorry about your hand,' Melissa said. 'Is it sore?'

'Just a scratch, actually,' Carrie said. 'I tell Hans not to pull his hand away when a dog takes it.'

'Does it happen often?' David inquired.

'Hans attracts fierce dogs.'

'Fred is not a fierce dog,' Melissa insisted.

'Of course he isn't,' Grippenheimer said, and decided it was time to change the subject. 'My dear, Mr Lytton has been telling me about their ghastly experience in Barcelona.'

'It was Girona, actually,' David said. 'And do please call me David.'

'Tell me about it, David,' Carrie begged, leaning forward, all huge blue eyes and revealing décolletage.

Melissa let David get on with both talking and admiring the view; she leaned back, sipping her champagne cocktail, into which a liberal helping of brandy had been stirred. It had been a long day for her too, and it was nearly nine o'clock, and all she wanted to do was eat and go to bed. But these people were being so nice ... she found herself staring at a large, framed photograph on the mantelpiece above the fire. It illustrated a tall, very young man in a naval uniform – unmistakeably Grippenheimer some sixty-odd years ago – having his hand shaken by a slight man in military uniform, with a little black moustache, his dark hair flopping over one eye ... without meaning to she sat up straight, causing the settee to jerk and David to spill some of his drink. 'Liss?' he asked anxiously.

'I'm sorry,' she said. 'I'm afraid I nodded off.'

'I'm not surprised,' Carrie said. 'You poor darling. You must be exhausted. I'll serve dinner, and then you must go to bed.'

'You must let me help you,' Melissa said, and scrambled to her feet.

'You're very kind.' Carrie led the way back into the kitchen, where Fred was lying down, clearly in deep thought. He opened his eyes and gave a perfunctory wag of his tail at the intrusion. 'Now, let me see,' Carrie said. 'I'm afraid it's just hot soup and a cold platter. I hope that's all right.'

'That will be perfect,' Melissa assured her.

'There's this cold meat –' a large oval plate

with a beautifully arranged assortment decorated with parsley – 'and the bread, and some salad. Would you take the potatoes from the oven and cut them? Here is some garlic butter.'

The kitchen door was shut, so Melissa ventured to ask, 'Has your husband been in the navy all his life? I mean, before he retired?'

Carrie gave a little tinkle of laughter. 'He left the navy in 1946. He was eighteen. Actually, the navy left him.'

'Oh,' Melissa said. 'Yes. You mean he was ... well...'

'A Nazi? Wasn't everyone? I mean in Germany.'

'Ah,' Melissa said, a knifeload of butter poised over a hot potato. 'And you mean he was an admiral, at eighteen?'

'No, no, he was just promoted sub-lieutenant when the war ended.'

'I am completely fogged,' Melissa confessed.

Another tinkle of laughter. 'Hans has awarded himself an extra rank, every few years or so, according to where he thinks he would have been, had he stayed in the navy. And had there still been a navy.'

'How ... positive,' Melissa commented.

Carrie opened the door. 'Wine, Hans,' she commanded.

He bustled into the kitchen, and Melissa bustled out with bowls of hot soup. They sat down, and Hans poured the wine. 'You really should listen to Hans,' David told Melissa. 'He has had such an interesting life.'

'Not as interesting as operating a famous London restaurant, surely,' Hans protested.

'Why—' David was interrupted by a loud noise from the kitchen, a dreadful wailing accompanied by a frenzied barking, and a great deal of scrabbling, and the sound of breaking crockery.

'Oh, my God!' Melissa cried, springing to her feet; her nerves were still on edge.

'Antoinette must have come in,' Carrie said, getting up and going to the kitchen door. The others followed her.

She opened the door, to reveal several glasses and plates scattered in broken profusion across the floor, a large dark-grey cat standing against the outside door and its cat flap, and, on the kitchen table itself, Fred, clearly at bay, paws over the edge and teeth bared, tail pointing straight behind him like a spear. 'Fred!' Melissa screamed.

'I never knew Fred could climb on to tables. He's very heavy,' David confided to Hans.

'I think he jumped,' Hans pointed out.

'Fred!' Melissa put her arms round Fred's neck and hugged him. 'I can't take you anywhere.'

'Of course you can,' Carrie said, in turn scooping her cat from the floor and hugging *her*. 'Antoinette was probably very rude to him. You are a naughty puss,' she bawled into Antoinette's ear. 'A naughty pussy!'

Antoinette continued to regard Fred with a baleful expression, and Fred was showing no inclination to get down from the table. 'I thought you said she liked dogs,' David observed.

'Oh, she does,' Hans asserted. 'I think your dog was terrified at the sight of her, and that caused the trouble.'

'Why do you not take Fred into the lounge,' Carrie suggested. 'And I will clean up the mess.'

'You take him,' Melissa told David. David wrapped his arms round Fred and heaved him down, then dragged him out of the kitchen, backwards; Fred had no intention of taking his eyes off the cat. 'I feel so terribly embarrassed,' Melissa said. 'This mess, and you have been so kind...'

'Think nothing of it,' Carrie insisted. 'It was all Antoinette's fault.' She gave Melissa's hand a squeeze. 'We are going to be such friends. I know it.'

'Did you see the photograph?' Melissa asked in a whisper, when she and David were undressing in the bedroom they had been given for the night.

'What photograph?' David queried loudly. He had had far too much to drink, on top of the exhaustion of the drive.

'Sssh! The one on the mantelpiece. Of

61

Hans shaking hands with Hitler.'

'No! Really? I didn't notice that.'

'You wouldn't notice the Queen if she walked into the room,' Melissa grumbled. 'Hans was a Nazi, David.'

'A long time ago.' He pushed Fred away from his side of the bed and crawled under the sheet. 'He seems to have done all right since.' He fell asleep.

Melissa awoke at a sound she couldn't immediately place. On her right, David was snoring, and on her left Fred was snoring even more loudly, lying on his back against the wall with all four legs in the air. Fred was having the adventure of his life, apparently having forgotten his encounter with Antoinette. But in a few minutes he would be waking up and demanding to go walkies ... and she didn't know where Antoinette was.

She got out of bed, cleaned her teeth and brushed her hair, and went to the window. It was a marvellous morning, crisp and clear and cool. She looked up the mountain first, at their house and the pine trees, and thought how wonderful it was going to be, actually living there. Then she looked down at the pool, and realized what had awakened her: the sound of someone entering the water. Below her, Carrie von Grippenheimer was breaststroking slowly up and down, her golden hair spreading behind her like a mat of seaweed, her legs moving rhythmically, her white buttocks breaking the surface in time to the sweep of her arms.

'Oh, my God!' Melissa whispered. She counted herself as sophisticated as the next person, but nudity outside of the bedroom or bathroom, or strictly in the presence of the current boyfriend, which now meant only David, had never been her scene.

'What's the problem?' David was sitting up.

'Nothing,' she said, and left the window.

'Oh, yes?' He got out of bed and took her place.

'That's voyeurism,' she complained.

'No it isn't. The Germans and the Scandinavians never wear swimwear. Shit, is she built! I'm going down for a swim.'

'You mean you're going in with her?'

'You bet I am.'

Melissa pulled on her borrowed dressing gown. 'Come along, Fred. We'll keep our eye open for that beastly cat.'

She used the back door, and Fred advanced into the yard with the utmost caution, but the cat was not to be seen, much to Melissa's relief. When Fred had attended to all the shrubs and bushes he could find, she took him back into the house, drew a deep breath, and emerged on to the *naya*. David was already in the pool, swimming up and down beside Carrie, who had now turned on to her back. As David had said, she was *built*. Melissa began to feel like a scarecrow. It wasn't until she ventured on to the poolside patio that she realized the admiral was also up and about ... and also nude, sitting in a chair and drinking coffee. 'Come on in,' Carrie invited. 'It is cool, but very refreshing.'

Melissa looked at Hans, and he smiled at her. She dropped the dressing gown on a chair and walked down the steps, slowly, feeling more wanton than ever before in her life.

And suddenly, totally relaxed, as they sat round the pool, drinking coffee and eating croissants which Carrie prepared at the poolside bar, all without even bothering to wrap a towel round her waist, 'I suppose you are in a hurry to go into Gata,' Hans said.

If David had managed to get himself under control, no doubt assisted by the rather cold water, Hans had not even twitched at the sight of her. Melissa felt thoroughly squelched. 'There's so much to be done, one hardly knows where to start,' David said. 'But I think top of the list must be the telephone. Martinez promised me it would be in by the time we arrived...'

Carrie gave one of her shrieks of laughter.

'What's so funny?' Melissa asked.

'When did you apply?' Hans inquired.

'Well, when we were here last autumn,' David said.

'We applied five years ago,' Carrie said.

'Five years...' David looked up, for the first time realizing there were no poles or wires anywhere to be seen. 'But that's outrageous.'

'It is also Spain,' Hans pointed out.

'Can't something be done about it?'

'Well, you can go down to Alicante, to the Telefonica office there, and talk to them. Don't attempt to make a fuss. Nothing gets a Spaniard's back up so quickly as someone making a fuss. You must always be quiet and reasonable...'

'It helps if your wife bursts into tears from time to time,' Carrie put in. Melissa glared at her, sure her leg was being pulled.

'But really, you will achieve very little,' Hans went on. 'Spanish bureaucracy moves at its own speed, sometimes very fast, but more often any movement is hardly perceptible.'

'Well, we'll certainly go and see them. I think we'd better make a move, Liss.'

Melissa got up, feeling self-conscious all over again, collected her robe and hurried for the house, Fred padding faithfully at her heels. 'We have to get a bed in today,' David said as he joined her.

'Turned you on, did she?'

'Wowee!' She felt she should be annoyed, but somehow it seemed more funny than disastrous, in the context of the ongoing disasters around them.

They dressed, and found Hans and Carrie

65

still sunning themselves around the pool. 'Where are you lunching?' Carrie asked.

David looked hopefully at Melissa. 'We thought of lunching in town, or the port,' Melissa said.

'We're lunching in Arenal,' Hans said. 'Why not join us?'

'Dutch, of course,' David said.

'No, it is a Spanish restaurant. Right on the beach. And the food is good.'

'I meant, we'll split the bill.'

'Oh, of course. Shall we say, on the front, about twelve thirty?'

'We can't thank you too much for last night,' Melissa said. 'You really have been so kind.'

'It was our pleasure,' Carrie said, pink nipples glowing.

'Well,' Melissa said as they walked up the hill. 'That was an experience.' She opened the grill gate leading from the drive to their pool area. This had been in darkness last night; now it was filled with morning sunlight, and—'Oh, my God!' she shouted. Fred came bounding in to protect her, and David hurried behind him. 'It's green!' she shouted. 'And look, there are wriggly things swimming in it. It's like a cesspool.'

'I suppose it's because the pump hasn't been on for some time.'

'Didn't you arrange with Martinez to have it serviced?'

'Yes, I did. Boy, am I going to have a few words with him on Monday. Just forget about it for today. You've had your swim.'

'It looks so revolting,' she moaned.

The morning improved. They drove into Gata, were remembered by their original *meubles* dealer, and shown their furniture, neatly stacked and awaiting delivery; as they were shipping down quite a lot of their own stuff they had only bought the essentials – a king-size bed, some *naya* cane furniture, some kitchen furniture, including a table, and some rugs. 'Can you deliver it today?' Melissa asked.

'Today? Ah, *señora*, today is a bad day.'

'But we must have it today. We have nowhere to sleep.'

'I will see what can be done ... This afternoon, perhaps.'

'We'll be there, waiting.'

'Do you think he will deliver?' Melissa asked, as they got back into the car, where Fred had been waiting patiently. 'What about this *mañana* business?'

'He'll deliver,' David promised, with more confidence than he felt.

'It's eleven fifteen. We've an hour before we meet the Grippenheimers.'

'Well ... we could go back to the villa.'

'With no furniture? And that pool ... Oh, well, I suppose we can sit in the car and look at the view.'

'And open a bottle of wine.' She grunted, and he drove up the hill. The road twisted quite a lot, and that, as well as the steep incline, caused them to drive dead slow. Thus they arrived at the corner beneath the Grippenheimers' house at the same time as a couple who were walking their dog.

'Good morning to you,' said the man in perfect English. 'You must be the Lyttons. Donald Barton. And this is my wife, Lucy. We live just down the hill from you.'

Donald Barton was of medium height, had greying hair, and wore a little moustache. Melissa put him down as about fifty, but very well preserved and fit, with almost handsome features. His wife was about the same age, she estimated; Lucy Barton's hair was also streaked with grey, and she was wearing skirt and blouse and thick shoes. She was quite good-looking, without suggesting beauty. Their dog was a golden Labrador bitch, who had already aroused Fred's interest. 'Hear you've been having a rough time of it,' Lucy Barton remarked.

'We spoke with the admiral, this morning,' her husband explained.

'Well, yes, we've been having some problems,' David agreed.

'If there is anything we can do to help,' Barton said, 'don't hesitate to say.'

David looked at Melissa. 'You wouldn't know anything about pools, would you?'

'If you intend to live in Spain, you have to learn about pools very quickly. What is the matter with yours?'

'It's green,' Melissa said. 'And has things in it.'

'Well, presumably no one has been looking after it,' Barton suggested.

'Someone was supposed to, but he obviously didn't. The point is, what are we going to do about it?'

'Oh, that's not a problem,' Barton said. 'We'll just go home and get some chlorine, and I'll be up in a moment.'

'What absolutely charming people,' Melissa said. 'I like them so much more than the Grippenheimers. If he can really fix the pool...'

'I take that with a pinch of salt,' David said. 'If he thinks a couple of chlorine tablets are going to fix that lot he's an idiot.'

But Barton did not turn up with a couple of chlorine tablets; he arrived in a small van with a five-gallon drum of the high-smelling yellow liquid. 'Now start your circulating pump,' he said. 'But clean the filter first. It's probably gunged up.' Then he saw that David didn't have a clue what he was talking about. 'I'll take a look, shall I?' The two men disappeared in the direction of the pump house.

'You have a delightful *parcela* here,' Lucy Barton remarked. 'We're further down the mountain. Not such a good view.'

'Would you care to look inside the house? I'm afraid there's no furniture yet. It's arriving this afternoon.'

'Do you think I could let Corky out? She's looking a little trapped.'

'Corky? Oh, you mean the dog. Yes, of course.'

'Your dog is all right, is he?'

'He loves everybody, especially if they have four legs and aren't cats.' A moment later Corky was flirting unashamedly with Fred, while Melissa showed Lucy the house, and Lucy made all the correctly appreciative noises. By the time they regained the *naya*, the pool was circulating, and Barton was emptying his five-gallon drum of chlorine into the murk.

'You want to be careful not to let any of this splash on your clothes,' he explained. 'It burns holes in them. There we are.'

'And you reckon that'll clear it?' David was still doubtful.

'It'll cause all the algae and other matter which has turned the water green to sink to the bottom,' Barton explained. 'It'll still have to be vacuumed up, of course. What I suggest you do is buy one of these automatic pool vacuums, which run all the time the pool is circulating. They cost about four hundred pounds, but are well worth it. Look, why don't you come down to our place, and I'll show you mine. It really is the best investment I ever made. Saves hours of work.'

'That's terribly kind of you.' David looked up at Melissa.

'I'm sure we'd be imposing, and you've taken so much trouble already. But we're meeting the Grippenheimers for lunch in Arenal at half past twelve.' It was just past noon.

'Ah. Well, come down tomorrow, if you like. We're here tomorrow, aren't we, Donald?'

'Oh, yes. Right oh, old man. Meanwhile, I would say your pool is going to be crystal-clear by tomorrow morning. Oh, by the way, don't go in it for at least six hours after adding the chlorine. It affects the eyes, you know.'

'No chance of us going in until it's blue again,' David assured him. 'Right, Liss?'

But Melissa was no longer looking at the pool. She was looking at the road, up which two vehicles were slowly climbing; leading was a Guardia Civile Land Rover, containing four of the picturesquely dressed and heavily armed civil guards; following was a Peugeot 506 Estate, also driven by a policeman. 'It's our car!' she shouted. 'It's our car!'

Barking loudly, Fred came tearing round the house to investigate, followed by an enthusiastic Corky. David went to the pool gate and stepped through on to the drive. 'So it is. Well, there's a relief.'

'You'd better wait and see what damage has

71

been done to it, before getting too excited,' Barton suggested.

The Guardia swept up the hill and parked with a flourish; the estate car was parked beside the Land Rover. '*Señor* Lytton?' asked the sergeant, looking at Barton, who replied in Spanish. The sergeant looked at David instead, and spoke very rapidly, in Spanish. '*Lentement, señor, lentement*,' David requested.

'That's French, goofball,' Melissa reminded him.

'Ah ... *habla Ingles?*'

The sergeant frowned. 'If he does speak English, he won't,' Barton said, and took over. 'He wants to know if you are the Englishman who had a car stolen in Girona Province on Thursday,' he translated after a lengthy conversation.

'Yes. And this is it. Tell him I'm very pleased, and congratulate him most heartily.'

More chat. The sergeant did not look terribly excited about the hearty congratulations. 'He wishes to know if you can identify the vehicle.'

'Well, of course I can. Those are my number plates.'

Chat. 'He says you had already seen the number plates when he asked the question. He wishes to know if you can give him the engine number.'

'Oh, for God's sake, Donald, he can't be serious.'

'He probably is. The Guardia are a law

72

unto themselves.'

Not for the first time since crossing the Spanish border, Melissa began to feel anxious about David's blood pressure.

'I can see the suitcases. Tell him there are two suitcases. If he will look at the name tags he will see that they are ours. There is also a mobile phone in the glove compartment.'

Chat. 'He says, you are absolutely prepared to admit this car is yours.'

'Admit? Of course it's ours.'

'Then he wishes you to explain this.'

The sergeant opened the passenger door and gestured at the seat. David and Melissa stared at the discolouration on the fabric upholstery. 'What on earth is that?' David asked.

'*Sangre*,' the sergeant said. Even Melissa knew what that meant.

Three

'What am I to say, Big Sam,' Salvador asked. 'The Tarragona police found the car before I got back to it. They have taken it back to Girona.'

'You can say that you are a cretin. Can they connect you with the car?'

'No, no. They cannot do that. But what are we to do? There was a bloodstain on the front seat. Do you think the police will investigate?'

'Of course they will investigate.'

'If they search the car...'

'You had better pray they do not find anything. But I do not believe they will, because they will not know for what they are looking, if anything. And if they do find a card, they will just think it is a credit card belonging to the English people. Now listen very carefully. These English people will deny any knowledge of what has happened, so it is possible that the car will be returned to them. In any event, their belongings, which will include everything found in the car not obviously connected to the bloodstain, will be returned. The card will still be there. Only, like the police, they will not know what it means.'

'But these people...'

'Are you not their friend? Did you not help them in their trouble? Go to them. Be friendly.

74

Get into their house. Do whatever you have to. But find that card before Barton does.'

'Blood?' Melissa shouted. *'Blood?* Oh, my God!' Her knees felt weak, and Fred, seeing her discomfort, nuzzled her leg.

The sergeant was still speaking. 'This could be serious,' Barton said. 'There is a great deal of blood. He wishes to know how it got there.'

'How the hell do I know?' David snapped. 'The car was stolen. He knows that.'

Chat. 'Unfortunately,' Barton said, 'he only knows that you *reported* it stolen. He says you must go with him and the car to the police station.'

'You mean I am under arrest?'

'No, no, he just wants to talk with you, and get to the bottom of this business.'

'Oh, hell. How long is this likely to take?'

'How long is a piece of string? Tell you what we'll do. I'll come with you to the police station and see what we can sort out. Lucy will drive your wife to Arenal and meet up with the Grippenheimers, and we can rendezvous down there.'

Melissa was watching the sergeant, who was showing signs of agitation. 'I think you'd better go,' she said.

The Grippenheimers were waiting, somewhat impatiently, Hans's left hand ostentatiously bandaged, although he took great

75

care to pat Fred on the head, and they sat down to have a drink together, even if Melissa got the feeling that Lucy didn't care for the Grippenheimers all that much. Well, neither did she. However, the sun was shining, and although the dogs were not allowed on the sand, they enjoyed sitting on the restaurant patio, leashes secured to the table legs, engaging passers-by in conversation, while the beach itself was filled with nubile, and topless, young women. But Melissa had observed this last summer; it didn't matter when she didn't actually know the people involved. However, Lucy felt obliged to tell the German couple what had happened, and their response, predictably, was a mixture of consternation and sympathy, with, however, a distinct flavour of, well, it *was* your car, you must somehow be involved.

To her relief, David and Barton arrived after only half an hour. 'It's all rather a mystery, actually,' David explained. 'Seems the car was found in the hills inland from Tarragona. So they don't seem to have got very far before running into, well, whatever they ran into.'

'But they understand that you – we – couldn't have been involved?' Melissa asked.

'Absolutely. The car was actually found by the Tarragona police on Thursday afternoon, but they hung on to it until some kind of bulletin was circulated about stolen cars, then it was sent up to Girona. Which is why, when we telephoned, we got no change out of the Barcelona police, as no one in either Tarragona or Girona thought to bring them up to date.'

'For God's sake!' Melissa exclaimed. 'And it's taken them two days to get it back to us?'

'Well, I suppose they had to run forensic tests and what have you.'

'Then why the palaver if they knew we weren't involved?'

'Well,' Barton said. 'You know what the Spanish police are like. When it finally got here, the Jàvea lot felt obliged to stick their oar in.'

'Do they have any idea who the thieves were?' Grippenheimer asked.

'Not really,' Barton said. 'Apparently a car has been found abandoned up in Girona, not far from the beach where the Peugeot was stolen. This abandoned car was full of bullet holes and had run out of petrol. The police theory is that, having had to leave their car, these men were perhaps prowling the beach looking for a replacement, when they saw the Peugeot, sitting vacant, as it were. But they have no idea who the people were.'

'Whatever they were, or are,' Carrie pointed out, 'you were most awfully lucky. Is the car damaged in any way?'

'Not so far as I can see, and the police went over it very carefully.'

'Apart from the bloodstains,' Melissa said.

77

'What about our things?'

'They're in the car,' David told her. 'Would you believe that absolutely nothing has been stolen? Not even from your handbag, which was in the glove compartment with the mobile. You'd think they'd have taken the mobile. The really odd thing is that the police found the handbag was open.'

'Then something must have been taken.'

'I had a look inside, and it seemed all right to me. All your credit cards, two hundred euros in cash, your passport ... I got mine back as well.'

'That is incredible,' Carrie said.

'Well,' Grippenheimer concluded. 'All is well that ends well.' He signalled the waiter. 'We will have champagne. And the menu.'

The afternoon faded into an alcoholic haze, as the champagne was followed by several bottles of wine, and then glasses of a sweetened brandy called Poncho, which was served on ice. It was nearly five when Melissa looked at her watch. 'Oh, good lord! The furniture! If they come up again and we're not there...!'

'Gotta rush,' David slurred. 'Gotta rush.' He got uncertainly to his feet and staggered along the promenade.

The other four were showing no signs of moving, so Melissa waved to them, rescued Fred, who had lunched as well as any of them and was disinclined to move, and

78

hurried behind her husband, who was managing to trip over the raised stone parapet that separated the esplanade from the car park. Then he leaned heavily on the car while he fumbled for the key. 'Dave, I don't think you are fit to drive.'

'Rubbish,' he said. 'Rub— Got it.' The door swung open and he fell in. 'Put the dog in the back.' Melissa opened the door, and Fred climbed in with his usual grunts and groans. She surveyed the passenger front seat and the dark stain and got in beside the dog. 'Squeamish,' David remarked.

'The seat is torn.'

'Well, they cut some of it off for a blood sample. We'll get it cleaned up.'

They reached Montgo without mishap, and were climbing up their tortuous road when they encountered a *meubles* van coming down. 'Oh, no.' Melissa leaned out of her window to wave vigorously, and the van stopped.

It was *Señor* Garcia. 'Your house is locked up,' he pointed out, somewhat acidly.

'I'm terribly sorry. We were delayed. We're going to open it now. Do bring the stuff back up.'

Garcia looked at his driver, who shrugged. 'We will turn and come back,' Garcia said, magnanimously.

'Oh, thank you ever so. Get this thing moving,' she muttered at David.

The next hour was gloriously exciting for Fred, as he chased back and forth while each article of furniture was carried in. 'There,' David said when the van was departing again. 'That looks a little more civilized. And just look at that pool. It's all blue. Good enough to swim in.'

'Bedclothes, and pillows. We forgot all about them,' Melissa said.

'Oh, shit. Is it back to the Grippenheimers'?'

'Yes, but only to borrow a duvet and some pillows for tonight and tomorrow. We'll get ourselves sorted out on Monday.'

The Grippenheimers, when they came home both very drunk, were quite happy to lend them all the bedding they could possibly use, but it took some time for Melissa and David to persuade them that they really wanted to sleep in their own house tonight, and also to refuse the drinks which were thrust at them. It was seven thirty before they got home. Melissa fed Fred, unpacked the suitcases, and checked her handbag, which, as David had said, seemed amazingly untouched. Then why had it been opened at all? The idea that some drug addict had pawed through her personal belongings made her quite angry. Then the realization that one of those drug addicts had actually been shot and perhaps killed while sitting in her seat made her feel quite sick. She made the bed, and prepared supper, while David turned off the pool circulating pump and opened a bottle of wine. 'Are you sure you want any more of that stuff?' she asked.

'This is for medicinal purposes. And to keep out the cold.'

'Um.' Because, now she had stopped working, she was discovering that since the sun had gone down it was distinctly chilly – the Grippenheimers had had that roaring fire, both last night and tonight. 'All these tiled floors. And no curtains.'

'Shall I see if I can gather some firewood?'

'In the pitch dark? You'll break your neck or something. We'll use these three electric radiators, and tomorrow we'll order some wood.' The electric radiators were plugged in and switched on and the house warmed up rapidly. 'Now, I intend to have a hot bath,' Melissa said.

There was a solid three-bar electric fire in the master bathroom, situated above the door, and this Melissa switched full on. She turned on the hot water before undressing, throwing her pants suit on the floor in the absence of a laundry basket. She stretched, considered herself briefly in the mirror, put up her hair, turned to test the water ... and the lights went out. So did the fire. And the water stopped running; although they were officially on mains, the water only got as far as the tank by the gate, and had to be pumped up to the house. 'David!' She opened the bathroom door, looked at stygian gloom. Every light in the house had gone phut, and it was deathly still; the fridge had also stopped. She tripped over Fred, and bumped into David in the gloom. 'Just our luck to have a power failure.'

'The Grippenheimers' lights are still on. It must be a fuse. The box is right here.' She heard him scrabbling ... and the lights came on again. The fridge started to hum and she could hear the sound of running water. 'That's very odd,' he commented.

'We'll work it out later,' she said, and went back to the bathroom. The bath was nicely hot, so she turned on the cold tap as well, got in and sank to her haunches to allow her body to get used to the heat ... and it happened again. Lights, fire, water and fridge went off. 'Oh, for Jesus' sake!' she shouted.

But the water was hot, and she could find the soap in the darkness, so she sat and soaked, and after a few minutes the lights came on again. At the same moment, David appeared, with Fred, who stuck his head over the rim of the bath and began to drink the water. 'It must be something you're doing.'

'Oh ... bugger off.' Melissa climbed out of the bath and towelled vigorously. 'It's these goddamned lights. The entire electrics. They ... it's done it again! David...'

'Now keep your cool. It's obviously a dicky fuse. Let's see ... what's that? Oh, shit...' There was a thump and a gurgle.

'David?' Melissa shouted. 'Are you all right?'

'I fell over the fucking dog.'

Fred pushed a wet nose into Melissa's hand. 'You knew he was there. You should be more careful. Poor Fred.'

Muttering to himself, David regained his feet, and the lights came on again. 'See?' Melissa asked, and turned off the fire over the door. 'I'm going to bed, before they go again.'

She waited for him, and he joined her a few minutes later. 'The lights are still on.'

'Did you turn off the heaters in the lounge?'

'Yes.' He snapped his fingers. 'Overload.'

'Oh, really, Dave; four electric heaters?'

'I must find out what the total wattage is. But it certainly sounds like an overload. Now the heaters are off, no problem.'

She snuggled up to him. 'We'll have to have something done about that, too, on Monday,' she murmured, drifting off into a deep, dreamless sleep, which ended in a nightmare of being chased by a million sheep. 'Oh!' she said. 'Oh!' Because her eyes were opened, and she was still submerged beneath a continuous 'baaa, baaa, baaa'. She blinked at the curtainless windows; it was just daylight outside. And the house was being attacked by sheep! 'David!' she gasped, digging him in the ribs, and leaping out of bed to run to the window. And gasped again, because the garden was indeed filled with sheep. They might not be attacking the house, but they were nibbling at the plants and the trees, jostling against one another, and bleating.

'Eh?' David was sitting up, rubbing his eyes.

'Sheep,' she told him. 'All over our property. Sheep and ... oh, my God!' She was looking at the shepherd, and he was looking at her, and she was standing at a curtainless window with nothing on. She dived back into bed. 'There's a man! David! Do something!'

'I'll get Fred. Why isn't *he* doing something?'

'Oh, you know Fred. Once he gets his head down it takes an earthquake to wake him. Just explain to the shepherd that this property has been bought and we do not want sheep on it.'

David was pulling on his pants. Now he checked. 'How do I do that? He's not likely to speak English.'

'Stick to basics. *Vamoose.* That's a Spanish word, isn't it?'

David dragged on a shirt and headed for the back door. Melissa got up again and pulled on her dressing gown, listening as she did so. *'Buenos dias, señor.'* That was the shepherd.

'Ah ... *buenos dias,*' David replied. Melissa raised her eyes to heaven; that was no way to discourage trespassers. *'Habla Ingles?'* David was asking.

'*Non.*'

'Ah, Well...'

Melissa headed for the back door herself, ran into a very sleepy looking Fred, who had spent the night in the bathroom. '*Este* ... ah ... private property,' David was explaining. 'No ... ah ... no *cordero*. Right? Savvy?'

The shepherd replied, unintelligibly, while his sheep meandered on their way up the mountain, munching and bleating. Melissa reached the back door and encountered David, returning. 'I can't get through to him,' he said.

'I wish I had Grippenheimer's gun,' Melissa snapped. 'I'd show him whether or not he can cross our property.'

'Now, darling,' David said soothingly. At this moment Fred reached the back door, went outside and raised his leg against the nearest bush, and then realized that he was surrounded by sheep. Fred had never encountered the ovine species before, had only ever seen them from the back of a moving car. For a moment he was too surprised to react. Then the blood of some long-forgotten ancestor seethed through his veins. 'Woof,' he remarked. 'Woof-woof!' And then surpassed himself with a 'Woor-ah-woor-ah-woor-ah-woof!' at the same time baring his teeth and pawing at the ground with his front feet as if about to charge.

The sheep fled for the safety of the upper slopes, jostling each other and even falling over in their haste, and the shepherd, caught in their midst, was knocked sprawling in the stampede. By the time he regained his feet, Fred had properly gotten into the act, and was bouncing up and down, still not actually advancing on the enemy but continuing to give a good impression of being about to do so, and uttering the most bloodcurdling barks. The shepherd also left in a hurry, although as he reached the pine trees at the top of the property he stopped to turn and shake his stick and shout what sounded like both threats and imprecations. 'I think Fred may have put up a black,' David remarked.

'Nonsense! It's our property.' Melissa dropped to her knees beside Fred to give him a hug and a kiss. 'You were absolutely magnificent!' Fred licked her cheek and wagged his tail.

As there was not much they could do on a Sunday, they spent a quiet day, apart from calling Gerry on the mobile to tell him he could cancel all the arrangements he had been making – which did not go down very well – and trying their own pool, which was delicious. But next morning they loaded Fred into the back of the estate car, and went down the hill into Jàvea, Melissa driving the Peugeot and David the Seat. David had done his best with the upholstery, and now there was only a dull brown stain, but Melissa still spread a towel over it.

They dropped the hire car at the local depot, then went to the estate agency. *Señor* Martinez was in his office, all smiles; he was a chubby fellow with what could best be described as a chubby moustache, and a chubby head – he was quite bald. '*Señor* Lytton,' he said, looking about to embrace David. '*Señora* Lytton,' he added, actually embracing Melissa, and then hastily stepping back as Fred, having determined that survival in this strange country lay in the direction of being as macho as any Spaniard, gave a low growl.

'Fred,' Melissa explained. 'He's not dangerous.'

'Except when roused,' David added.

Martinez retreated behind his very large desk. 'Sit down. Sit down. I am sorry about your car.'

'Oh, we got that back,' David said. 'On Saturday morning. Your police are very efficient.'

'It is gratifying of you to say so, *señor*. Now, as for the rest, there were problems, you see. But once the *fiesta* is over, *Señor* Alvarez will resume work, and bingo –' he snapped his fingers – 'the work will be done.'

'What work is this?' David asked.

Martinez frowned. 'Why, in the guest apartment, *señor*.' David looked at Melissa; they had had neither the time nor the inclination to investigate the guest apartment, so far. 'Is there something else?' Martinez

87

asked.

'There is no telephone,' Melissa said.

'No telephone? Oh, it is terrible. But what can you do ... your name is on the list.'

'So are several hundred other people, we understand.'

'I know, *señora*, it is very difficult.'

'Well, it's not so important now we have our mobile back,' David said. 'But we will chase it up. Now we want to talk about the pool. No one has been near it for the past six months.'

'Oh, *señor*. I gave out the contract...'

'And paid for it, I suppose,' Melissa said grimly.

'It is customary to pay in advance, *señora*.'

'Well, thanks to a friendly neighbour, we have got it right, but it needs cleaning, desperately. You tell whoever we paid we want it done, free of charge, and immediately.'

'Of course, *señora*. Of course.' Martinez wrote vigorously on his pad. 'They will be up within a week, I promise you.'

'That's immediately?' Melissa inquired.

Martinez looked at David, his expression suggesting that it might be a good idea for him to exert marital authority over his wife from time to time. David decided to move on. 'Then there's the electrics. Last night the lights kept going off.'

'And the water, and the fridge,' Melissa added.

'Ah, there was an overload, *señora*.'

'What, with four heaters and a fridge?'

'And an immersion heater. It is the wattage, you see. The houses where you are have only five kilowatts capacity.'

'*What* did you say? Five kilowatts?' David demanded.

'I'm afraid so, *señor*.'

'No one can live with only five kilowatts of electricity,' Melissa told him. 'Surely it's possible to get more?'

'Well, it is possible to be upgraded to eight...'

'We would like it upgraded to fifteen, right away.'

'Eight is the maximum for private houses, *señor*.' Martinez wrote busily. 'I will contact Hydroelectrica right away. The matter will certainly be adjusted within a fortnight.'

'A fortnight?' Melissa moaned. 'I thought your *fiesta* was over?'

'This day is no *fiesta* here in Jàvea, yes. Only tomorrow. But the electricians come from Pedreguer, and the *fiesta* starts today for several days.'

'Well, next there's the garden,' David said, before Melissa could explode. 'This morning some idiot shepherd drove his flock of sheep right through our garden.'

Martinez nodded. 'Carlos. Yes. He has grazing rights on Montgo.'

'On Montgo, maybe. But surely not on our land.'

'Oh, no, *señor*. He has no grazing rights on

your land.'

'Well, he was there this morning. With his sheep.'

'Carlos, *señor*? He would not do that. Perhaps he would walk his sheep *through* your land...'

'Well, he won't do it again.' Melissa patted Fred on the head. 'Fred saw to that.'

Martinez looked appalled. 'Your dog attacked Carlos?'

'No, no! He didn't touch him. He chased him off. With his sheep.'

'This is a serious matter, *señora*. You had no right to do that.'

'No right?' Melissa demanded. 'He was on our property with all of his goddamned sheep. Eating everything. They might well have eaten Fred if he hadn't got aggressive.'

'Your property is not fenced,' Martinez almost wailed. 'There is no law of trespass in Spain, upon unfenced property.'

'Do you mean,' David asked, 'that until it is fenced, anyone can walk across it, with his sheep, and we can do nothing about it?'

'Right,' Melissa said. 'Put fencing top of the list.'

'He can put a *denuncia* on you,' Martinez said dolefully.

'For trespassing on our property?'

'For attacking him with your savage dog.'

Melissa looked down at Fred, and Fred yawned. 'We want a fence around our property just as quickly as it can be done,'

David said.

Martinez wrote it down. 'I will arrange for it. Alvarez the contractor also does fencing. You wish him to do this before he finishes the guest apartment?'

'Yes,' Matilda said.

'It is an expensive business, fencing. More than a thousand euros. Much more.'

'Tell him to start just as soon as he can,' Melissa said.

Martinez nodded. 'Friday morning.'

'Friday?' Melissa cried. 'Why not today? Or at least tomorrow? OK, tomorrow is *fiesta*. Why not Wednesday?'

'Alvarez' men will not work Wednesday or Thursday, *señora*. Bad head because of the *fiesta*.'

She sighed. 'Then I suppose that will have to do. Is that everything, David?'

'Everything that's on my list. If you'll put those matters in hand, Mr Martinez, we're off down to Alicante to see Telefonica.'

'Do you think there'll be trouble about Fred and this chap Carlos?' Melissa asked, as they headed for the motorway.

'I doubt it,' David said. 'I'm sure Carlos has been seen off half the properties on Montgo.'

'But they're all fenced,' Melissa pointed out, and leaned over the back of her seat to ruffle Fred's ears. 'If anything was to happen to Fred...'

91

'We'll get the Grippenheimers as character witnesses,' David suggested.

Alicante has a fair claim to be the most beautiful seaport in Spain. The city grows, continuously, and the mound on which the castle now known as Santa Barbara sits – it was built by the Moors several hundred years ago – is well within the huge sprawl which has linked the suburbs of San Juan and Campello into one vast conurbation. Yet the Alicante waterfront, with its mosaic-tiled, palm-lined Ramblas and its yacht-filled pontoons of the Real Club Nàutico, its big ships moored alongside the outer docks and its rows of bar/restaurants, its crowded beaches and equally crowded streets, remains always fascinating and compelling.

Everyone in the Telefonica building was most helpful, forms were signed and additional requirements noted – David wanted a separate line for the Internet – but no one could say precisely when the lines would be installed. 'It is the poles, you see, *señor*,' the young man explained in perfect English. 'We do not put up the poles ourselves. We give the installation of the poles to a sub-contractor.'

'Well, at least you can tell us when the poles will be installed up our road,' Melissa suggested.

'Unfortunately, *señora*, that I cannot do. I do not have the sub-contractor's schedule for delivering and installing the poles.'

'So you have absolutely no idea when we might have a telephone?' David demanded.

'Well, *señor*...' The young man peered into his screen. 'You are on the computer. You will definitely have a telephone. But when ... This I cannot guarantee.'

'Let's go do some shopping,' Melissa said, as David began to show signs of blowing a gasket.

David went along with the idea, but she could tell that he was simmering on the edge of an explosion, and equally that Fred was becoming bored, and after indulging herself by buying a large, floppy pink hat, allowed herself to be persuaded that it was time for lunch. 'This place is starting to give me the pip,' David grumbled, as they sat at one of the outside tables under the green and white awnings of an apparently very popular bar/restaurant. 'One large gin and tonic,' he told the waiter.

'I'll have a small gin and tonic,' Melissa said. 'Do remember we're probably still carrying quite a load from yesterday,' she muttered.

'It is quite impossible to get tight in this place. There is always something frustrating going on to sober you up.'

Melissa hoped he was right. They ordered a very good lunch, with a bowl of water for Fred to wash down his scraps, and, as she was beginning to accept was inevitable, consumed two bottles of wine, or at least, David consumed a bottle and a half, and she the remainder. He then had a brandy with his coffee, and that felt like two, apparently. 'I'll drive home,' she volunteered, as they weaved their way back along the Ramblas to the car park.

'We're using the motorway,' he said.

'I can drive on a motorway.'

'Not in Spain.' She sighed, wondering if she had ever known him as well as she had thought she did, watched with alarm as he threaded his way out of the car park and into the stream of traffic, to the accompaniment of much horn-blowing and arm-waving.

She breathed another sigh, this time of relief, as they left the traffic behind and reached the first *peaje*. But it took David several seconds to extract the ticket from its slit, and the teller in the adjacent booth was clearly interested, especially when David stalled the car on trying to leave the gate. 'It is not possible to stall an automatic car,' Melissa remarked.

'It must be, because I just did it,' David giggled. 'Wheee!' And they shot away at fifty miles an hour, which rapidly increased to seventy-five.

Melissa did a hasty calculation; the speed limit on Spanish motorways was a hundred and twenty kilometres an hour. Divide by eight makes fifteen, multiply by five makes seventy-five miles per hour. She looked at the speedometer. Which was now registering over eighty and climbing. 'We really are in no hurry,' she suggested tactfully.

'Wheee!' he shouted, as they hurtled past a service area. Melissa supposed she had better just sit back and enjoy it – David had, after all, had a frustrating and annoying day; she thrust her hand over the back of the seat to give Fred a reassuring stroke, but Fred was not a nervous traveller. 'Goddamned twit!' David growled. 'There's this idiot sitting right on my bumper.' He rolled down his window and thrust out his arm, two fingers spread and extended, as he moved the hand up and down.

Melissa turned her head to see how the Spanish driver was taking it. 'Oh, my God! David! It's a police car!'

Which, having sat behind them long enough to establish the speed, was now overtaking and flagging them to a halt. 'Oh, shit!' David commented.

'Be polite,' Melissa recommended.

David was braking and pulling on to the shoulder; the police car was immediately in front of him. Now two heavily armed uniformed men got out and came back to the Peugeot. One of them addressed David in Spanish. 'Sorry. *No comprendo. Habla Ingles?*'

'Will you get out of the car, please, *señor,*' the policeman suggested, in good English. David released his belt and got out. 'You

95

were breaking the speed limit, *señor.*'

'Oh. Well ... doesn't everyone?'

'We are talking about you, *señor.* Have you been drinking?'

'I may have had a glass or two of wine with my lunch.'

The policeman nodded to his companion, who produced the dreaded bag. 'Will you blow into this, please, *señor.*' David cast a despairing look at Melissa, then blew into the bag. It was actually changing colour long before he filled it. 'Do you agree, *señor,* that you have about twice the legal limit of alcohol in your blood?'

'Perhaps it was three glasses of wine.'

'May I see your driving licence and green card, please, *señor.*' David looked at Melissa, who took them from her handbag, also getting out of the car. The policeman looked her up and down – she was wearing pants and a loose shirt – and then inspected the documents. 'This man is your husband?' he asked.

'Of course he is.'

The policeman muttered at his colleague in Spanish. Then he turned back to Melissa. 'You do not deny that your husband is unfit to drive?' Melissa looked at David, who gave a Fred-like smile. 'In view of your misfortune,' the policeman said, 'I will not place him under arrest. But he cannot drive.'

'I'll drive the rest of the way.'

'No, no, *señora,* have you not also been

drinking?'

'Not as much as him. I mean, you can't expect us to walk, can you? It's nearly a hundred kilometres to Jàvea.'

'Jàvea,' the policeman said thoughtfully. 'It would be a long walk. *Señor –*' he glanced at the licence – 'Lytton, there is a service area two kilometres back along the road.'

David nodded. 'We saw it.'

'Well, I would like you to walk back there, go into the bar, and have three cups of black coffee. Then I wish you to walk back here.'

David goggled at him. 'You wish me to walk four kilometres in the afternoon sun, without a hat?'

'Yes, *señor.* And do not forget to have the coffee. It is either that, or you walk to Jàvea.'

'Shit!' David commented.

'I think you had better do as the man says, darling,' Melissa suggested. 'You can borrow my hat.'

'Then what about you?'

'The *señora* will remain here with us,' the policeman said.

'No way,' David declared.

'Oh, don't be a dummy,' Melissa begged. 'They're not going to harm me. Besides, Fred is here. He'll look after me.' And seeing he was still hesitant, she added, 'The sooner you start, the sooner you'll get back.'

'Wearing that stupid thing,' he grumbled, gazing at the floppy pink. 'I'll probably be arrested all over again.'

'No, no, *señor*,' the policeman assured him. 'We are the only patrol car on the road this afternoon.'

Melissa watched David disappear along the shoulder; at least there were no hills between them and the service station. 'How long should it take?' she asked the policeman.

He shrugged. 'An hour, maybe. The important thing is that he will be considerably more sober when he returns.'

'He'll also be in a very bad temper,' she commented, and got back into the car. To her consternation, the policeman opened the driver's door and sat beside her; she knew she was being stupid, but one did read and hear of Englishwomen being raped by Mediterranean policemen, especially if they were suspected of some kind of criminal activity.

Of course, they could hardly be in a more public place; every few moments the Peugeot trembled to the wind of some other car passing at speed. One or two even slowed, but they were clearly only interested in the presence of the police car, not her. She did not suppose there would be any help forthcoming if two brawny policemen decided that she had to be strip-searched for drugs. On the other hand, the English-speaking policeman's colleague had got back into the patrol car, and was smoking a cigarette. On the *other* hand, Fred had obviously decided there was going to be no action for a while, and had retired to the very back of the estate car to go to sleep. 'You are on holiday?' the policeman asked.

Melissa looked straight ahead, out of the windscreen. 'No. We have come here to live.'

'In Jàvea?'

'We have a house on Montgo.'

'It is very pretty there.'

'We think so.'

'Tell me about the car. How was it stolen?'

'Well, you will think we're a couple of nerds ...You know it was stolen?'

'The report was circulated to all branches of the traffic police, and the Guardia. Tell me, *señora*,' he went on, 'have you searched the car since getting it back?'

'No. Searched it? What for?'

'I do not know what for.'

'The Guardia said they had searched it, very thoroughly. I suppose they were looking for drugs.'

'Why should they do that, *señora*?'

Melissa realized she might be getting into deeper water than she had intended. 'They said something about the thieves being drug addicts.'

The policeman considered this, then he asked, 'Do you use drugs, *señora*?'

Oh, lord, Melissa thought. 'No, I do not,' she replied.

He grinned. 'But you would hardly tell me if you did, eh, *señora*?'

'No, I don't suppose I would.' She turned her head to gaze at him.

He grinned some more. 'But you do not look like a drug user.' He opened the door and got out. 'We will leave you now, *señora*. Your husband will be back in half an hour. But he must watch how much he drinks, eh? Englishmen do not have the capacity for too much alcohol. One day he could find himself in serious trouble.'

Four

'*Let me get this straight,*' Donald Barton said into the telephone. '*You are saying that Raoul and Dominic are dead?*'

'*The police think so,*' the woman replied. '*Their car was found abandoned, with several bullet holes in it, and some bloodstains.*'

'*But not their bodies. So how do they conclude they are dead?*'

'*The car was abandoned just south of Girona. It had run out of gas. That must have been some time on Thursday morning. And on that Thursday morning, a car was stolen, from an English couple who were swimming on a beach, again just south of Girona. That is too much of a coincidence.*'

'*Good God! An English car? What make?*'

'Well, I believe it was actually a French car. A Peugeot. The point is, this car was found by the police late that afternoon, abandoned in the mountains behind Tarragona. Again, there were bloodstains. But no bodies. Now they seem to have disappeared, at least one of them bleeding very heavily. It looks very bad.'

'Good God!' Barton said again.

'This can only be Big Sam's doing,' the woman said. 'We know he was close. Or his people were. It must have been them shot up Raoul and Dominic, and then followed them, and caught up with them when they were in the English car. So...'

'You say this all happened last Thursday. If Big Sam had obtained the combination,' Barton said. 'He would have used it. One of my people works in that bank, and he says no one has attempted to get at that box. So his people did not find the card on our boys. They must have hidden it in the car.'

'The police searched the car.'

'But they did not know what they were looking for, or even if they were looking for anything.'

'You think the English couple have it?'

'They may do. They may have it without even knowing they have it.'

'And they could be anywhere in Spain. Or on their way back to England.'

'Dolly,' Barton said. 'The English couple have a house here in Jàvea, and it is not a kilometre from where I am sitting. I had lunch with them on Saturday. And it never occurred to me ...

101

God, what a fool I am.'

'Holy shit! Then...'

'No rough stuff, at this stage. You will have to take care of it.'

'Me?'

'You know I cannot be involved. As far as anyone in Jàvea is concerned, I am a respectable retired businessman. You will make friends with these people, gain access to their house, and to their confidence ... and find that card.'

'Just like that?'

'You can do it. Pull your crazy countess act. They are very simple folk. Wow them. Go right over the top. They'll eat out of your hand. Don't fail me, Dolly. Remember what is at stake.' He replaced the phone, looked at his wife. *'We have to get moving, just in case she fucks up. Thursday! Ask them to the lunch party.'*

'Do we have to?' Lucy asked. *'They're terribly boring.'*

'Just think what they may be carrying around with them.'

'Bloody swine!' David growled, as he staggered up to the car and slid behind the wheel. He was clearly very hot and very tired, and very irritated. But he was also comparatively sober.

'Now, David,' Melissa said as soothingly as she could. 'You know you were lucky. He could've run you in.'

'Ha!' He drove home in silence, ignoring even Fred's overtures to the back of his head.

Melissa decided it was best to remain silent too. But as they drove up their road, past the Grippenheimers' ... 'There's a note stuck in the gate!'

'Well, tear it up,' David recommended, braking. 'I've had all the bad news I can stand.'

Melissa got out with the key, and at the same time noticed a car parked a little further along the road. It was a small Spanish Seat, and for that reason was unexceptional ... save that the road didn't go anywhere after their house, just ended in the bushes. She unlocked the gate, removing the piece of paper as she did so. 'Drive up and I'll lock it.'

'Do you think that's necessary? Anyone can walk round it, like that shepherd.'

'There's not much point in having a gate if you don't shut it,' she said.

Grumbling, he drove up the slope, while Melissa read the note. 'It's from the Bartons,' she called. 'They want us to go to lunch on Thursday. That's sweet of them.' She started to close the gates, and saw the Seat driving slowly down the slope, to come to a halt at the foot of the drive.

A woman got out, tall and slim, dark-haired and very well dressed in a blue suit with a white shirt, a string of pearls and several expensive-looking rings; her earrings brushed her shoulders. Melissa estimated she was about forty, and extremely good-looking in an aquiline fashion. 'You are the new residents here,' the woman remarked.

'Well, yes. My name is Melissa Lytton. My husband and I have just moved in.'

'I am the Countess Dolores Angelique de Soto y Florida de Bihar de la Jara.' The countess waved her hand. 'This is my land,' she announced.

'You own this land?' Melissa asked in consternation. *'This* land?'

'I own all of the Montgo,' the countess said.

'Good lord! You'll have to speak to my husband. David!' she shouted, while her brain spun. Martinez had assured them that everything, including their land title, was in order. But then, Martinez had assured them of so many things. Fred emerged round the corner of the house, barking excitedly as he bounded down the slope of the drive. The Countess de la Jara hastily stepped back behind Melissa, who was embarrassed. 'Down, Fred,' she admonished severely, totally confusing Fred. 'I'm sure the countess is friendly.' She forced a smile. 'You are friendly, aren't you, Countess?'

'Well, I hope so,' the countess conceded. 'That is a very fierce dog.'

'He isn't really,' Melissa protested. 'It's just his way of saying hello.'

David emerged. 'What's the trouble now? Oh, good lord!'

'I must warn you,' Melissa said. 'My husband is not in a very good mood. He has just been done by the police for speeding.'

'They are infuriating,' the countess agreed. 'I remember how angry dear Annie was when she was banned for speeding.'

'Annie?'

'The Princess Royal, dear. Surely you know her.'

'We've never met,' Melissa said. Annie?

'You'd like her,' the countess said. 'I should like to see your house. If that dog will permit it.'

'This is the Countess de la Jara,' Melissa announced to the now goggling David. 'My husband, David Lytton.'

'Oh, I say,' David said. 'My pleasure, Countess. Liss, do open the gate and let the countess in. My wife is very shy,' he confided.

'There is nothing wrong with being shy,' the countess conceded.

David reached past Melissa and pulled the gate in. 'The countess claims to own this land,' Melissa told him before he actually kissed the ground at her feet.

'Do you really?' David asked.

The countess stepped inside and went up the drive, David at her heels. Melissa gazed after them in disbelief, then at Fred, who was still totally bemused. Then they followed. 'My family,' the countess was saying, 'once owned the entire Costa Blanca. My name is Bihar. I am a descendant of El Cid. You have heard of El Cid?'

'Oh, indeed,' David said.

'I saw the film,' Melissa said, determined to be as obstructive as possible. 'Do you mean you are a relative of Charlton Heston, or this old Spanish whatnot?'

The countess gave her a pitying smile. 'You are very young, my dear,' she remarked. 'But very pretty,' she added, condescendingly. 'You remind me of Diana.'

'Don't tell me: you're speaking of Princess Diana?'

'Poor child. She was too tall, of course. I often told her this.'

'You knew Princess Di?' David asked.

'Of course. I would like a cup of tea.'

'Right away,' David said. 'Liss...'

Melissa was on the verge of an explosion. 'My husband is a restaurateur,' she explained. 'Mention the word food, and he becomes servile. Would you like a cup of tea, Countess?'

'That is what I said,' the countess reminded her.

Melissa stamped into the house to put the kettle on. The countess and David, and Fred, followed more slowly. 'It's a shame, to lose the land,' David said.

'I did not lose my land,' the countess said. 'It was stolen from me.'

'Not by us, I hope.' He ushered her on to the upstairs *naya*, allowed her to look at the view. 'I mean, we have full title.'

The countess sat down. 'It was stolen from

me by my brother. I would like to kill my brother.' David looked anxiously at Melissa, who was emerging from the kitchen with a laden tray. 'Unfortunately, he is already dead,' the countess remarked.

'Well, you can't win them all,' David said. 'You mean you have no land left at all?'

'It is all mine, really,' the countess said. 'I have explained this to Juan Carlos, but the silly man says he cannot go against the law, and apparently what my brother did was legal. I ask you, what are kings for, if they cannot break the law?'

'Do you take sugar?' Melissa inquired.

'I do not, thank you.'

'I didn't think you would.'

'Have you no relatives left?' David asked, solicitously.

'I am all alone,' the countess said.

'Oh, that is bad luck.'

'Well, I have my friends, of course. Annie, and there was poor dear Maggie.'

'Which Maggie would that be?' Melissa asked.

'You probably knew her as Margaret Rose.'

'I thought you meant the other one. And then I suppose there's Lizzie and Phil, and Charlie, not to mention Juan Carlos and Sophie. Not to mention Andy and Eddy. But not Fergie. But of course, Tony and Cherie.'

'Well, of course, my dear. But I live such a busy life I seldom have the time to see them.'

'Absolutely,' David agreed. 'Still, I suppose

you live in a castle?'

'My brother sold the family castle.'

'That's going it a bit. Have a biscuit.'

The countess munched. 'My grandparents were killed in that castle.'

'Good heavens! When?'

'During the Civil War. It was besieged by the Reds. All this district was full of Reds. They besieged the castle and blew it down. My father was lucky to survive. He was only a boy then. He never repaired the castle.' She looked about to burst into tears. 'But he left it to my brother and I when he died, and then, my brother sold it when I was out of the country. He said it was a ruin, and we did not have the money to repair it.'

'Dashed bad luck,' David muttered.

'He sold it to an American!' The countess made this seem the very last straw. 'The American had the money to repair it. Americans,' she growled, 'always have money.'

'Some of them,' David reflected, remembering the bad cheques he had had to cope with at the Pantry.

'I explained to George,' the countess said. 'Senior, of course. He was President then. I went across and stayed at the White House, and complained. But he said he could do nothing about what goes on in Spain.'

'I'm surprised you didn't take the matter up with Bill,' Melissa remarked.

'Oh, I did. But he was no better. One day,' the countess said thoughtfully, 'I am going to kill that American.' David again looked anxiously at Melissa, who returned his gaze with a cold lack of expression: he had invited this nutcase into the house. The countess finished her tea. 'I must go. But first, may I use your bathroom?'

'Certainly. It's just along the passage to your left.'

The countess departed. 'Of all the—' Melissa began.

'Sssh ... She'll hear you.'

The countess was actually gone some time. Melissa was just considering looking for her, when she re-emerged. 'Now I must go,' she said. 'You will come and have dinner with me. I will send you an invitation.'

David was on his feet. 'We would like that very much. Where do you live?'

'I have an apartment in the *puerto*,' she said, and looked down at Melissa. 'You are very pretty,' she said again. 'I think you are actually prettier than Diana.'

Melissa stood at the balustrade and stroked Fred as David walked the countess down the drive to her car, waited for him to rejoin her on the *naya*. 'Of all the creepy-crawlies,' she remarked.

'I thought she was rather a romantic figure. Tragic, but romantic.'

'I was talking about you, not that pseud.'

'Pseud? How can you say that?'

'Descendant of El Cid? Friend of Princess

Di and Annie? Countess de la Jara? There's a village called La Jara just along the road from here.'

'Well, then...'

'I am pretty damned sure it doesn't have a countess.'

'I could tell you didn't like her,' David said, heading for the bar. 'I think she could tell it too. But she was very polite.'

'So was I. Well, I can tell you one thing: tomorrow we are going to have Martinez's lawyer check out those deeds again.'

'You're contradicting yourself.' She glared at him. 'If she's a pseud, then she can't possibly ever have owned this land. I tell you what: I wouldn't like to be that American who bought her family castle. I wouldn't be surprised if she did mean to do him in. I think we should ask the Bartons about her. They'll know if she's genuine or not.'

'That's a good thought,' Melissa agreed. 'I'm going to have a shower. And you could do with one too.'

'You go ahead.' David was mixing drinks. 'I have the most outrageous thirst. I shouldn't wonder if I have sunstroke.'

Melissa went into the bedroom, began to strip off her sweat-soaked clothes, and stopped, slowly looking around her. 'David!' she called.

'What now?' He carried his drink along the corridor.

'That woman was in our room.'

'She went to the loo.'

'The loo isn't in here.'

'Well ... what makes you think she came in here?'

'That jewel case was on the right side of the dressing table. Now it's in the middle.'

'Oh, really, Liss. You're not accusing her of being a jewel thief?'

Melissa opened the box. 'There's nothing missing.'

'Well, then...'

'But she looked inside. That's why she put it back in the wrong place. And...' She opened a drawer. 'My undies are rumpled.'

'Darling, you're imagining things. You're hot, sticky, and overtired. Listen, have your shower and I'll mix you a drink. Everything will look brighter after that. And who knows, Martinez may get his finger out and be up tomorrow to get things done.'

Martinez had apparently got his finger out, for the next morning they were awakened by the arrival of the pool maintenance man, who apparently came from the neighbouring town of Moraira, which was not *en fiesta* today, and who immediately commenced vacuuming and giving advice, in Spanish. 'That's all right,' David told him; he had slept off both his hangover and his sunstroke, and was his more usual cheerful self. 'We're going to get a Barracuda.' That went down like a lead balloon.

★ ★ ★

They went out at ten with their shopping list, stopping at the Bartons' on the way down the hill. David and Fred stayed with the car while Melissa went in, and had her breath taken right away ... not to mention her nose becoming distinctly disjointed. The average size of a plot on Montgo was two thousand square metres; this was at least six. Being on a slope, it was arranged in a series of terraces, but these were not mere flower beds. Arches led to quiet grottoes and secluded lawns; even the pool was on two levels, the upper flowing constantly, via an artificial waterfall, down to the lower, from whence it was pumped back to the upper. The place made the Eyrie look like a country cottage, and Casa Sagittarius an outhouse. To top it all, it possessed telephone wires.

Yet Melissa found Lucy, wearing a very dirty pair of overalls, proceeding cautiously along one of the lower paths armed with a huge can of Baygon. 'Processionary caterpillars,' she explained in a whisper. 'They're an absolute menace.'

Melissa peered over her shoulder at what appeared to be a long piece of thick string, save that it was moving, very slowly. When she bent lower, she saw that the string was actually composed of a line of tiny caterpillars, each about an inch long, and each touching the ones in front and behind it. 'Don't get too close,' Lucy told her. 'They

112

shoot their hairs like a porcupine, almost like invisible darts which get into your skin and can be most irritating. They're absolutely dreadful, and they can destroy a plant in a morning. But our big problem is Corky. That's why she's locked in the house until I've dealt with this lot; a dog who's been sprayed by these can go almost mad, especially as it usually happens around the nose and eyes.'

'Good heavens!' Melissa commented. 'I thought there weren't any animal nasties in Spain.'

'There are nasties everywhere,' Lucy commented. 'Stand back.' She sprayed the Baygon on to the caterpillars and jumped back. Immediately they began to curl up and separate, until there were some fifty little creatures scattered around the path. Lucy waited a few minutes and then carefully trod on all of them, squishing them as hard as she could into the concrete.

Melissa felt quite sick. 'Do they grow up to be butterflies?' she asked. 'I mean, if they grow up?'

'No, they turn into dull-looking moths,' Lucy said, squishing away. 'Which are just as big a menace, when it comes to eating things. Do keep an eye out for them at your place. They completely kill off pine trees.'

'Oh, I shall,' Melissa promised. She would, she knew, take deep offence at any creature which might try to harm Fred, but she wasn't at all sure she could set about it in such a cold-blooded, matter-of-fact fashion. 'I really stopped by to say thank you very much for the invite,' she said, as Lucy began to stroll back up to the house, mission accomplished.

'I'm terribly sorry it's such short notice, but as we are having the party anyway, I thought it'd be an ideal opportunity for you to meet some of the more interesting people in and around Jàvea. Our crowd is nearly all English, of course. One or two Dutch.'

'There seem to be a lot of Brits in this area.'

'Well there are. Or there were. A lot of them are packing it in now. But a few years ago ... You must have heard the famous story about Prime Minister Gonzales meeting Mrs Thatcher, back in the eighties, to discuss various matters of mutual interest, and the talk naturally got on to Gibraltar. Oh, you can keep Gibraltar, Gonzales is reputed to have said, if you will give us back Jàvea.' Melissa laughed politely. 'But as I say,' Lucy went on, 'that's all changing. Still, there are enough of us left to enjoy ourselves, and now that you and David are here as well...'

'We're looking forward to it.'

They had reached the foot of a curved staircase – one of several – leading up to the *naya*. 'You'll have a cup of coffee?' Lucy asked.

From above them Melissa could hear Corky barking, as well as the hum of a vacuum cleaner, to indicate that Lucy had a maid.

'I mustn't, really. Dave and Fred are waiting in the car.'

'Well, bring them in.'

'That's very kind of you, Lucy, but we have an awful lot to do. As usual. There's one thing, though ... have you ever heard of a Countess de la Jara?'

Lucy threw back her head and gave a shriek of laughter. 'You mean the famous Dolores has been to see you?'

'Last evening. Is she, well...?'

'Mad as a March Hare. Yes. In her fashion. I suppose she told you your land is really hers.'

'Yes, she did.'

'She tells everyone that.'

'But what about her being a countess?'

'Oh, she made that up. Did she tell you about her castle?'

'Oh, indeed. Do you know where it is?'

'Haven't a clue. Somewhere in the mountains. If it exists.'

'Then you don't think we have to worry about the title to our land.'

'Good lord, no. Just mention her name at the *ayuntamiento* and they'll have hysterics.'

'That's a relief. Well, thanks very much, Lucy. Will the countess be at your party?'

'Not on your nelly.'

'I'm glad about that. Oh, there's one more thing: can you tell me which days are garbage collection?'

'Garbage collection? There's no garbage collection up here. Or anywhere, except in the centre of Jàvea.'

'But ... what do we do with our rubbish?'

'You put it in a plastic *basura* bag, just as you would at home, then you put the bag in the back of your car, and you drive down to one of the main roads and you look for one of the big garbage skips; they're always about. Then you toss the bag in there.'

'That sounds rather primitive.'

'In many ways, Spain is a primitive place. If you're going to live here, you just have to like it or lump it and go home.'

'Ah. Yes.' Melissa wasn't at all sure, yet, which it would be. 'Well, thanks again for inviting us, and we'll see you on Thursday.'

'That place is a palace,' Melissa told David as they drove into town. 'I didn't actually get inside, but the outside...'

'Oh, come now, and he drives that beat-up old van?'

'There were two Mercedes in the garage. His and hers, I reckon. I just never put them down as being rich. I mean, they don't act rich.'

'Which makes a very pleasant change, doesn't it?' he grinned.

They bought their Barracuda – the trade name for the automatic pool cleaner – from a store in Teulada and several other household items, stocked up on food and drink, and decided to go home for lunch. They returned along the Jesus Pobre Road just after twelve, and at their turn-off saw a pantechnicon parked by the side of the road, while two youths in sweatshirts and jeans leaned against it and smoked cigarettes. 'Conway and Company!' Melissa cried, as they read the name. 'Hoorah!'

David pulled in beside the huge van. 'Looking for someone?'

'Yeah,' said one of the men in English, and took a grubby piece of paper from his pocket. 'Lytton. Casa Sagittarius.'

'That's me. Us. We're up the hill. You'd better follow us.'

The pantechnicon climbed the hill with much groaning, steam coming out of its radiator, and the cargo was unloaded. This meant that lunch was very late, but at last David could get at his books, and soon the living room looked like a second-hand bookshop after a bomb blast. Melissa was concerned with siting her standard lamps and ornaments and pictures, and the music centre and television; one thing which had been completed was the installation of the aerial, although of course all the network programmes were in Spanish – but that was surely the way to learn the language, she thought. For real news and entertainment there was always the satellite dish.

An hour later she tipped the delivery men and they drove off with much blowing of horns. 'Now we can start turning this place into a home,' she announced, and was distracted by the sound of more car engines, and loud barking from Fred, who had remained in the yard. She hurried out of the back door and goggled at the sight of another Guardia Land Rover. But these were different Guardia from the ones who had returned the car, and they were not getting out of their vehicle, merely regarding Fred through the window with most hostile expressions. 'Oh, Fred, do be quiet!' Melissa called as she went towards them. *'Buenos tardes, señors. Habla Ingles?'*

'Su perro?' asked one of them.

'Si.' She smiled.

'Malo. Malo.' He scowled.

'Oh, no,' Melissa said. There were people to whom she wanted Fred to appear fierce, and others she did not. *'Bueno. Bueno.'*

Slowly the Guardia opened his door and thrust a booted leg down, then slid to the ground, only to recoil against the car as Fred advanced wagging his tail, but also puffing to reveal his magnificent set of snow-white teeth. 'He's just saying hello,' Melissa explained helplessly, as the policeman's hand dropped to his revolver holster.

'Muy grande,' the young man remarked.

'He's horribly overweight. Is it something to do with the car?' The Guardia looked mystified. 'Our car,' Melissa explained. 'It was stolen. But your other officers brought it back.'

The expression on the Guardia's face indicated that he didn't have a clue what she was talking about. He felt in the breast pocket of his shirt and took out a piece of paper, which he slowly unfolded. '*Una denuncia*,' he announced.

'Da ... David!' she called. If only they spoke English.

A string of rapid Spanish followed, from which she recognized only '*denuncia*' and '*usted*'.

'Against me?'

The Guardia looked at his paper. '*Señor Daveed Lytton*.'

'That's me.' David had joined them. 'A complaint about what?'

'*Porque su perro...*' He looked warily at Fred, and then proceeded to read a whole page of incomprehensible Spanish. Only one word registered: *Asalto*.

'Assault? I've never heard such nonsense in my life,' Melissa exploded.

'Assault who?' David asked.

The Guardia shrugged. '*...necessario ... usted ... judicature ... Lunes ... Denia...*'

'Christ!' David exclaimed to Melissa. 'It's something about appearing in court in Denia on Monday.'

'*...y,*' the man continued, '*ahora, su perro...*' He took a muzzle from the back seat of the

119

vehicle and held it towards David. The intent was obvious: they wanted to take Fred away.

'Why?' Melissa demanded furiously. *'Porque?'*

'Si la denuncia es correcta...' As she obviously didn't understand Spanish, he interpreted the remaining words with a sharp gesture, moving the side of his hand across his throat.

'Destroyed?' David was shouting now.

'Over my dead body!' Melissa snapped, dropping to her knees and throwing both arms round Fred's neck. Fred licked her cheek.

The policeman scratched his head. 'Look,' David said, frantically trying to think of the vital words in Spanish. *'Perro con nos a ... judicatura. Si?'*

The Guardia looked at each other, and both shook their heads. *'Non. Non possible.'*

David pressed on. 'I know who it was denounced us. *El...'* he turned to Melissa. 'What's the Spanish for shepherd?' She shook her head, trying hard to stop her lower lip from quivering, *'El hombre con ...* ba-aaa,' he bleated. *'Pero mi perro –'* it was not easy to pronounce the distinction between the Spanish for but and for dog – 'no, a-a-ah...' He demonstrated a vicious bite on his own hand. *'Non. Soliemente* woof! Woof!'

'El pastor es herida,' one of the men argued, striking his leg.

Melissa was indignant. *'Quando todos los*

moutons vamoose. No perro.' In any other circumstances she would have been quite pleased with her linguistic achievements.

David and Melissa held their breaths while the two policemen conferred. But their hearts sank as the two impressive black bicornes shook slowly from side to side. *'Senores...'* The spokesman began to sound quite sympathetic. *'No possible el perro queda acqui.'*

'David,' Melissa said, still hugging Fred. 'You're not going to let them take Fred, are you?'

David was looking extremely worried. 'What can we do?'

'Then they'll have to take me as well,' Melissa declared.

'Now, Liss, that would be going over the top. I'm sure they'll look after him.'

'If he goes, I go.' Melissa stood up, hanging on to Fred's collar.

The Guardia understood. *'Non!'*

'Then it's a stand-off, isn't it? Because I am not letting go of this collar.'

The Guardia had another conference with his companion, then turned to David. *'Usted dicha ... su espose...'*

David lost track, but the meaning was clear. He looked at Melissa. 'You dare,' she said.

'Liss, these chaps have authority. And guns and things. You don't want them manhandling you, do you?'

121

'I expect you to stop them doing that,' Melissa told him. 'And if they lay one finger on me, I am going to have them up before the European Court of Human Rights.'

The Guardia looked at David, and David looked at the Guardia. The situation was suddenly tense, neither man quite sure of how far the other would go, when there was the sound of a blaring horn, and into the park there drove a very battered looking car 'I 'ad trouble finding zees place,' Salvador said, leaning out of his window.

'Salvador!' Melissa screamed, releasing Fred to hurry forward. But Fred was also hurrying forward.

Salvador got out, embraced her, and kissed her upon each cheek. ''Allo, Meleessa. 'Allo, Daveed.' He shook hands, and then stooped to pat Fred. *'Bien?'*

'Salvador?' inquired the Guardia.

'Juan?' Salvador correctly pronounced the name, *Hwan.* And followed with a torrent of Spanish, after which he embraced both the Guardia.

'You mean you know each other?' Melissa asked.

'Juan ees *mi* couseen,' Salvador explained.

'Oh, please can you help us?' Melissa begged. 'He wants to take Fred away.'

'Take Fred?' Salvador addressed his cousin, and a long conversation ensued, with the cousin producing his piece of paper for Salvador to study, while Melissa resumed hugging the dog, more tightly when the conversation became very agitated, with much waving of arms and gesticulations. But at last the Guardia folded up his paper again, replaced it in his breast pocket, and climbed back into the Land Rover, which drove off in a flurry of dust and exhaust fumes.

'Oh, Salvador!' Melissa said. 'However did you fix it?'

''E ees *mi* couseen,' Salvador reminded her. 'And I 'ave told 'eem I weell be responsible. I breeng you to court on Monday. Weez Fred.'

'Oh, Salvador, I am so terribly grateful. But ... they're threatening to have Fred destroyed, for attacking a beastly shepherd and his sheep. You know Fred wouldn't attack anybody.'

Salvador patted Fred on the head. 'I know zees. You no worry, Meleessa. I feex thees too.'

'Don't tell me the shepherd is another cousin?'

Salvador laughed. 'Zat Carlos? No, no, Meleessa. 'E ees not *mi* couseen. 'E ees *mi* brozzer-in-law.'

Melissa didn't know whether to laugh or burst into tears. 'I think this calls for a celebratory drink,' David said. 'Come on inside. And don't forget that we owe you some money.'

'Money, Daveed? I do not take money for 'elpeeng my frien's.'

123

'Oh. But what about giving us that lift?'

'Leeft?'

'Taking us into Barcelona.'

'Well, maybe...'

'Let's have that drink,' Melissa suggested, and led them into the house. 'Beer, or wine?'

'You 'ave no brandy?'

'Brandy. No, I'm afraid we haven't bought any yet. We're just settling in.'

'Zen I weel 'ave wine.' Salvador strolled on to the *naya*, and looked out at the view. 'Zees ees *muy bien.*'

'I'm glad you like it.' Melissa poured a glass each for herself and David, gave Salvador his.

'I think, well ... what about twenty euros,' David suggested. 'For the ride.'

'Zat ees too generous, Daveed.'

Melissa thought so too, for the ride. But she would have paid him anything for getting Fred off the immediate hook. 'I think it's fair.' David handed over the money.

'About Monday,' Melissa ventured.

'You must go to zee court. Eet ees een Denia, *comprende*? You must be zere before ten o'clock. You must carry your passports, eh? I weell come weez you.'

'Will you? How splendid! But ... we can't ask you to take time off work to help us.'

'*No trabajo semana próxima,*' Salvador explained. 'Next week, *mi pueblo* ees *en fiesta.* Zat is why I am 'ere.'

'Why?' Melissa had supposed he had come

124

for his money.

'You are *mi amigos*,' Salvador said. 'Fred ees *mi amigo*.' He patted an appreciative Fred on the head. '*Semana próxima en my pueblo, mucho celebraciones*. You come and eat weez *mi familia*.'

'Well ... that would be awfully nice...' Melissa glanced at David. 'What day?'

'You come *Lunes*, from Denia. I show you, *la carretera*. You come behin' *mi camione con su coche*.'

'With Fred?'

'Oh, yes, weez Fred.'

'You mean we'll still have him?'

Salvador grinned, and patted Fred again. 'You weell always 'ave Fred, Meleessa.'

Salvador had a few more glasses of wine, then declined an invitation to stay for lunch. He went out the back and surveyed the Peugeot. 'Zees is *un grande coche*. *Zee hombres* who stole eet, zey deed not 'arm eet?'

'Not really,' David said. 'They left blood on the seat.' He opened the door. 'There.'

'*Sangre!*' Salvador said in an awed tone. 'But zat ees terreeble.'

'Oh, we'll get it out eventually.'

'But zees *sangre* ... 'ow it get zere?'

'The police think one of the men was shot, or knifed, or whatever. But they don't know, because both of them have disappeared.'

'You 'ave searched zees *coche*?'

'You mean for drugs? The police did that. I

125

don't think they found anything.'

'I theenk you should search eet.'

'Search it for what?'

''Oo knows, Daveed? 'Oo knows what zeese men were doeeng, eh? Let us search eet now. I weell 'elp you.'

David scratched his head and looked at Melissa, who shrugged. Salvador had already begun, most efficiently, raising the two rows of rear seats, looking under them and between them, sliding his hands down the backs inside the cushions, trying all the compartments. Then he produced a screwdriver and unscrewed the large plate beneath the chassis holding the spare wheel, hunting in that compartment as well before restoring it. Finally he turned his attention to the engine, before standing back with a perplexed expression. 'Zere ees nothing zere.'

'Well, frankly, we didn't think there was,' Melissa said. 'Or I am sure the police would have found it.'

'Eet ees strange. But I must go. *Lunes*, eh? I see you een Denia.'

Melissa stood on the *naya* to watch his car bouncing down the hill. 'He's a funny chap, but sweet.'

'And full of surprises,' David said. 'He took the car apart as if he were a mechanic.'

'Maybe he is. Anyway, I think we have made a friend.'

'Wouldn't you say we've made several friends?' David asked. 'What about the Bar-

126

tons? And the Grippenheimers?'

'I'm not *too* sure about either of those. But I must go to Spanish classes as soon as possible. One feels so helpless with people like those Guardia. And anyway, I want to make friends with Spanish people. And I don't mean nutcases like the countess. I mean people like Salvador.'

'I thought you went for the Bartons?'

'Well, I did. Until I saw their place,' Melissa admitted honestly. 'I didn't feel they ... belonged in that setting.' She sighed. 'Maybe it is just jealousy.'

'Anyway, all Salvador is really interested in are your legs.'

'He also likes Fred,' Melissa pointed out, accepting his observation as a compliment.

'What time is this party?' David asked, as they swam up and down the pool after breakfast on Thursday. They had spent a restful Wednesday after the traumas of the previous week; Melissa had taken Fred for a walk up the mountain and David had pottered in the garden. They had been able to relax, even the looming thought of their court appearance on Monday alleviated by the knowledge that Salvador would be there to look after them.

'Twelve o'clock,' Melissa replied, climbing out and towelling herself. 'But I don't suppose we want to get there much before half past. Mustn't appear overanxious.'

'Do you suppose it's a jacket and tie job?'

127

'Well, it wouldn't do any harm, as it's our first Spanish party. I'm going to wear that pretty frock I bought in Barcelona.'

'What about Fred?'

Melissa ruffled Fred's head. 'I'm afraid you're going to have to stay here and guard the house, Fred. We won't be long.' Fred heaved one of his monumental sighs; he had heard that one before. 'But I don't think we should mention anything about Monday to anyone.'

'Oh, quite. I wonder how many people will be there?'

Well over fifty, Melissa calculated, as they tried to find somewhere to park in the narrow lane outside the Bartons' house. There were cars everywhere, and they wound up walking almost as far as if they had left the car at home with Fred. The noise level, even in the open air, was enormous, and seemed to be rising. On finally reaching the front gates Melissa and David were met by a white-jacketed waiter who presented them each with a champagne cocktail, and then indicated that they should descend to the lower garden.

They checked at the foot of the steps, appalled by the mass of unfamiliar faces, but Lucy hurried forward. 'David! And Melissa! But where's Fred?'

'Oh, we didn't feel we could bring him.'

'Of course you should have; he's so

gorgeous. Now come along, who haven't you met?' Introductions whirled about their heads, names which were either not properly heard or instantly forgettable. One thing was obvious from the first moment: they were both hopelessly overdressed. Most of the women were in pants, and some in shorts; most of the men were in shorts, and all wore open-necked shirts. Melissa looked in vain for the Grippenheimers, but they had either not yet arrived, or, more likely, she supposed, they had not been invited.

'Lytton. Lytton,' said one rather stout man with a florid complexion. 'Knew a fellow named Lytton, once. Owned a London restaurant.'

'That's my husband,' Melissa explained – she and David had become separated. 'You must come and say hello. He's just over there.'

'Oh! Ah! When I say I knew him, of course, I meant I had eaten in his restaurant.'

'I'm still sure he'd like to make your acquaintance.' Melissa unloaded him, stepped back to find the waiter at her elbow presenting her with a second champagne cocktail – and the first was doing quite well – and overheard some blue rinse she had not yet met confiding to another, 'My dear, I have eaten there. The food was quite dreadful.'

One didn't have to be Sherlock Holmes to deduce which restaurant they were talking

129

about. Melissa turned away, and was relieved by the banging of a gong. 'Come and get it!' Donald shouted.

It was a buffet luncheon, but quite the most splendid buffet Melissa had ever seen, ranging from prawns, lobsters and crab through to barbequed pork chops and T-bone steaks, with lashings of bread and salad and copious quantities of home-made sangria. Melissa found herself behind an Englishwoman who, to her surprise, appeared to be younger than herself, quite unexpected in this distinctly middle-aged community. 'Let's find somewhere to sit. I know, the pool area.'

The girl, a genuine redhead, judging by her pale, freckled skin and green eyes, led the way up the steps, plate in one hand, glass in the other. She was short, and inclined to plumpness, but was quite attractive, and wore her curly hair loose and long. 'I'm Janey Trewit,' she said over her shoulder.

'Melissa Lytton.'

'I knew that.' Janey kicked off her sandals and sat on the pool edge, allowing her bare legs to dangle in the water. 'You're famous. Well, your husband is.'

'Did you ever eat at the Pantry?' Melissa curled her legs beneath her dress.

'Good lord, no. Too pricy for me.'

A unique situation, for this crowd, Melissa thought. 'But you live in Jàvea?'

'I don't, actually. I'm out here spending

Easter with my mum. She's the one with the frizzy blue hair.' The one who didn't like David's food, Melissa noted. 'Isn't this an appalling place?' Janey asked.

'Jàvea? We've just come to live here.'

'No, no, I meant this house. These gardens. Talk about *nouveaux riches*.'

That was no way to refer to one's hosts, but Melissa was curious. 'Are they *nouveaux riches*?'

'They must be. No one has ever heard of them.'

'Is it important to be heard of?'

'Isn't it? Everyone's heard about you.'

'About my husband, you mean.'

'No, no, you too. About how you were skinny-dipping and had your car stolen, and had to walk into Barcelona in the nude. And about how you were arrested by the Barcelona police for indecent exposure.'

Melissa decided she did not like Janey very much. Or the people who had been spreading the gossip, which could only be either the Grippenheimers or the Bartons themselves. She got up, plate in one hand and glass in the other. 'I think I'll go and see how David is getting on.'

'Aren't you coming for a swim? I am.' To Melissa's consternation, Janey also got up, removed her shirt, dropped her shorts and briefs – she was wearing nothing else – and dived into the water. She was even plumper naked than dressed.

Melissa looked left and right, but the other people around the pool seemed to be enjoying the view, and several of them were beginning to undress as well, to a rising level of chatter and laughter. She hurried down the steps, and encountered Lucy. 'My dear! You've hardly eaten anything! Don't you like it? Let me get you something else.'

'Oh, I ... ah ... I'm just not hungry.' Hurriedly she drank some sangria, then said, 'I'm drinking and talking too much.'

'Oh. Well ... aren't you coming for a swim?' Lucy made for the steps and the laughter.

'I'd rather not.' Melissa put down her half-full plate on a vacant table and hurried into the throng of suntanned guests who were still in the lower garden, saw David some distance away, chatting to several people.

'Liss!' he said as she approached. 'Let me introduce you.' Once again the names swirled round her head.

'My dear, you are absolutely charming,' declared one of the women, as if she didn't really exist, Melissa thought.

'We're just going up for a swim,' announced the man, who appeared to be her husband. 'Going to join us?' His gaze wandered up and down Melissa's body as he spoke.

'No,' Melissa said shortly.

'Sounds like a good idea to me,' David said.

'I think we should be off.'

'Eh?' he asked, bewildered.

'Home,' Melissa said. 'Think of Fred. There's Donald.'

He was leaning on the balustrade which surrounded the pool area, wearing only a towel, but at least there was a towel. 'Coming in?' he asked, as she approached the steps.

'I'm sorry,' she said. 'We'd simply love to. But we have to go.'

He frowned. 'You're not going home already?'

'Well ... yes. There's Fred, you see.'

He looked at his watch. 'You've only been here just over an hour.'

'I know. It's been lovely, but...'

Barton looked past her at David, who shrugged. 'Must do as the boss wishes.'

Barton looked as if he would have liked to protest some more, then changed his mind. 'Well, it's been nice having you. I'm sure we'll meet again.' He turned away, removing the towel as he did so, and a moment later there was a splash and a chorus of screams.

'I think we may have put up a black,' David remarked, as they drove up the hill; the noise from the Bartons still blaring through the pine trees. 'I think they genuinely want to be friends.'

'Ha!' Melissa went into a brood. She supposed she was getting old. Ten years ago she might have just enjoyed cavorting in the nude with total strangers. But right now ... and with Fred in trouble with the law! The temptation to cut and run was enormous. But she didn't know if David would go along with that. And whatever the faults he was uncovering – mainly, she was sure, the effects of having suddenly ceased work – she loved the bastard. Equally, she loved her new house, and indeed, Spain itself.

'So what are we going to do with our evening?' David asked. 'Watch TV?'

'Get drunk,' she suggested. 'All by ourselves.' Then she looked up the last steep stretch of road. 'David! The gates are open.'

David braked. 'So they are. I was sure we'd locked them.'

'We did lock them.'

'Then what...?'

Melissa got out and peered at the lock. 'This has been picked. There's somebody in there. Dave...!'

'Now, take it easy. Get back in the car.'

'Fred!' She ran up the drive. David released the brake and followed her. As the car pulled into the parking space, Fred began to bark. 'Oh, Fred!'

David got out of the car, peered at the back door lock. 'This seems all right.'

'Open up.' Fred was still barking. But when the door swung in, he galloped at her for a hug and a kiss. 'He's all agitated. And look at those tyre marks. They aren't ours, and they're over the others. Someone has been here.'

'OK. And when they discovered we weren't

in, they went away again.'

'After picking the gate lock to get in?'

'You quite sure we locked it?'

'We always lock it. Dave, we have to go to the police.'

'We need to think about that. We've already been involved with the police, twice. And neither time has turned out very well. I think we need to sleep on it.'

'Dave, it's two o'clock in the afternoon.'

'That's just what I meant. Things will look better after a siesta.'

Five

'Did you get away in time?' Barton asked.

'I never even got into the house,' the woman replied. 'There was no problem with the gate. But they'd left their goddamned dog behind.'

'That great hulk? He's a golden retriever. He's harmless.'

'I met him the other day. And they told me how fierce he is. Do you know they have to go to court next week because he attacked a shepherd? As soon as he heard me starting to pick the lock he set up a tremendous racket. I'm surprised you didn't hear it.'

'There was quite a racket going on here at the time.'

'Well, the first thing we have to do is get rid of that dog. Do you want me to go back? I could take some poisoned meat.'

'Leave it with me, for the time being. Meanwhile, go on being friendly. Get them out of the house, if you can. At night. We'll work on it from our end. But remember, no rough stuff until I say so.'

Things certainly looked better when they awoke. They went for a swim, Fred joining in, and Melissa towelled him while David mixed drinks. Then they sat together on the *naya*, eyes rolling over the distant hills, thoughts drifting over the day. 'We could go out for a meal,' David suggested.

'Do you want to?'

'I feel kind of flat.'

'I don't like the idea of leaving the house. Or Fred.'

'We'll make sure we lock the gate.'

'Meaning you think we forgot to do that this morning. Listen, that lock was picked. I'm sure of it.'

'Tell you what. We'll ask Salvador about it on Monday.'

It was odd how reassuring that sounded. 'I'll go put on a face,' she said.

But she was only halfway to the bathroom when a car came up the hill. 'A Mercedes,' David commented.

Melissa hastily reached for her pants and blouse. David reached for his clothes, then opened the back door. 'Mind if we come in?' Lucy Barton asked. 'The gate wasn't locked.'

'Please do,' David said, but he looked somewhat uncertainly over his shoulder at Melissa.

Who arranged her features into a smile. 'Did we forget something?'

'See?' Lucy asked her husband. 'They *are* upset.'

The Bartons were both fully dressed and, remarkably, appeared quite sober. 'Upset?' Melissa demanded.

'The way you left our party.'

'Well, we were worried about Fred, and—'

'What time did it break up?' David asked, before she started about their intruder, if he, or she, had actually existed.

'Six-ish. Par for the course, with a good Jàvea lunch. But we really didn't mean to upset you two.'

'You did not upset us,' Melissa insisted.

'Then how about having dinner with us?'

'We were just talking about dinner,' David said.

'With you?' Melissa was suspicious.

'There's so much food left over,' Lucy explained.

'Everyone else has gone,' Barton added.

'And you can bring Fred,' Lucy invited. 'Corky is dying to meet him again.'

Melissa knew she was trying desperately to be friends, and she didn't want to be rude, or upset them, after they had been so helpful.

But she had gone right off the idea of partying, certainly for tonight. She even thought she might have gone right off the Bartons. So she said, 'It's terribly kind of you, Lucy, Donald, but we really have had an exhausting couple of days, and we do need our sleep. Do please excuse us.'

As usual, the Bartons looked inclined to argue, but then exchanged glances and changed their minds. Melissa and David stood together to watch them driving back down the hill. 'So much for dinner,' David said.

'You think I'm a nerd.'

He hugged her. 'I think you're probably right. Come along. I'll scramble some eggs, al la Lytton's Pantry.'

Melissa sat up in bed with a start. 'Fred!'

'What about Fred?' David asked drowsily.

'Rabies! We've been here a week, and he hasn't got his certificate. He must have it before Monday.'

David put his arms round her waist and pulled her back down beside him. 'We'll do it today. It is today, isn't it?'

'Any moment now.'

It was a busy Friday. Martinez himself arrived, together with Alvarez the builder. They tramped around the property, deciding where the posts for the fence would go. 'You understand that before he can start he must obtain the permit from the *ayuntamiento*,' Martinez explained.

'What's the *ayuntamiento*?' Melissa had forgotten.

'The town hall, *señora*. He must have a permit before he can put up any fence.'

'How long will it take to get this permit?'

Martinez shrugged, hands held out with the palms facing up.

'Well, you'd better get to it, *Señor* Alvarez.' Melissa nodded to the Spanish builder.

Señor Alvarez, who spoke no English, was looking thoroughly bemused, but Martinez continued interpreting in rapid *Valenciano*. Melissa and David prepared to go out. They drove to the vet's surgery, which was situated on the front, overlooking the sea. 'Now, Fred,' Melissa said. 'Please be a good boy.'

Fred gave a lecherous grin, and was soon in the midst of a toy poodle, an Alsatian bitch, a Rottweiler and three cats, in the waiting room. 'I don't like the look of this,' Melissa muttered, as they went in.

'They all seem peaceful,' David said.

Melissa sat at the end of the row of chairs, keeping a tight grip on Fred's leash. The Alsatian and the Rottweiler seemed to be fast asleep. The poodle unfortunately was not, and appeared to fall in love with Fred at first sight, leaping around the place and yelping, while its owner, a nervous young woman with horn-rimmed spectacles, shortened her grip on *its* leash.

Fred was prepared to ignore this, and follow the big dogs into slumber, but for the cats. Two of these were in closed carriers, the other was on its owner's lap. This was a stern-faced woman of fringes, in blouse and skirt and hat – she looked like a refugee from *The Last of the Mohicans* – and obviously did not like golden retrievers; both she and the cat arched their backs, and the cat hissed. 'He's perfectly harmless,' Melissa explained.

But Fred let her down. His had been a relatively catless life, until his encounter with Antoinette. That had caused him to rethink his attitude to the species, deeply. Now here they were again, and one of them was actually hissing at him. Fred put his nose close to the tasselled woman. 'Woof,' he remarked. 'Woof-woof-woof.' And then went into his party piece. 'Woor-a-woor-a-woor-a-woof!'

This awoke the Alsatian, who sat up and also began to bark. This in turn awoke the Rottweiler, who took one look at Fred and remembered that he didn't like goldens either. 'Aaagh!' Melissa screamed, as the Rottweiler lunged, all snapping teeth. She stuck out her foot as Fred made a dive beneath her chair, and got the Rottweiler in the snout. It yelped, and sat down, while its owner, a pimply youth, joined the fracas, leaping to his feet and tugging on his leash and shouting in Spanish. 'Don't you speak English?' Melissa inquired.

'Yesa, I speaka Inglis,' he answered with pride.

'Then bugger off and take your dog with you.'

The youth sat down again, clearly wondering if his mastery of English was as good as he had supposed. The Alsatian, who apparently didn't like the Rottweiler either, began to puff happily. Fred re-emerged from beneath the chair, prepared to take on the Rottweiler if his mistress was going to be beside him.

'Your dog attacked my cat,' declared the fringed lady.

'Rubbish! Your cat hissed at my dog!' Melissa riposted.

'She did not. Did she?' The fringed lady turned to the poodle mistress for support.

'Well...'

'Damned cats,' remarked the owner of the Alsatian, who from both his military moustache and his choice of words appeared to be English.

The Rottweiler snarled at Fred, who joined the Alsatian in a contented puff. The inner door opened, and a pretty young nurse appeared, apparently oblivious to the previous racket; perhaps every day was like this, Melissa thought. *'Próximo?'* the nurse asked brightly. The young man with the Rottweiler went in.

'Thank God for that,' Melissa remarked to David, who had been a scandalized spectator, uncertain when he was going to be required to go into action himself.

'Geoffrey Banning,' remarked the military gentleman. 'Lieutenant-Colonel, retired.'

'Melissa Lytton. This is my husband, David.'

'Lytton. Lytton ... That is vaguely familiar. Have we met before?'

'Not in Spain.'

'Still, it's a pleasure. Living here, are you?'

'Attempting to,' Melissa said.

'You'll get used to it. Jàvea?'

'Montgo.'

'Pretty spot. Telephone?'

'I'm afraid not.'

'Ah. Must meet the wife. Lytton. Lytton. Knew a general named Lytton, once.' He looked at David.

'Sorry. No generals.'

'Ah.' The colonel's expression indicated that not everyone could be a winner. 'Well...'

The inner door opened, and the Rottweiler emerged. Melissa had no idea what his problem was, but the treatment had done his blood pressure no good at all. With a huge snarl, he again lunged at Fred, who was just nodding off while still sitting up. Melissa leapt to her feet as the young man lost his grip on the leash. Once again she kicked as violently as she could, but missed altogether and got the Alsatian instead. The bitch fell over with a yelp, carrying her master with her in a welter of chairs and paws. Fred, by now moving backwards at speed, took Melissa with *him*, and she fell over her chair. The fringed woman climbed on to her seat, hugging her cat and screaming. The woman with the cat baskets did the same. And the Rottweiler continued its advance, teeth bared. 'David!' Melissa screamed. He was the only one of them still intact, as it were. Now he stepped forward. 'Be careful,' Melissa begged, as the Rottweiler noticed him and turned a mouthful of fangs in his direction.

David lowered his head, hunched his shoulders, bared his own teeth, and went 'Grrrr!' in a low and most menacing growl emanating from the back of his throat. The Rottweiler looked absolutely stunned, and then assumed an expression rather like Fred when he knew he had done something reprehensible. David took another step forward. 'Grrrr,' he said again, hunching his shoulders even more and giving a very good impression of being about to charge. The Rottweiler bolted for the door, followed by his master.

Melissa scrambled back to her feet. So did Fred, shaking himself. So did the Alsatian, watching David, distinctly apprehensive. Melissa helped the colonel up. 'I'm sorry about your dog,' she said. 'I didn't mean to kick *her.*'

'Think nothing of it, my dear. But I say, old chap –' he beamed at David – 'where did you learn that party trick?'

'Dogs only attack people who are afraid of

143

them,' David explained loftily, adding, 'usually,' under his breath. He was looking quite pale.

Melissa kissed him on the cheek. 'I think you were just marvellous,' she said. 'And Fred does too.' Fred gave his lecherous grin.

They lunched on the front in Arenal, Fred now the proud possessor of a blue tag on his collar, which announced to the world that he was immune from rabies. Not all the meeting with the vet had been quite so satisfactory. 'Of all the cheek!' Melissa growled as she drank her wine. 'I know Fred has a slight weight problem, but to say he suffers from *obesidad* ... really! He is *not* fat.'

'Is that why you didn't ask the vet to be a character witness on Monday?' David inquired.

'Well, I didn't think he'd be appropriate, after that fuss in the waiting room. Oh, Dave, I'm so worried.' She held his hand.

'Have faith in Salvador,' he told her.

Martinez and Alvarez had still been measuring when they had left; when they returned, neither agent nor builder, nor builder's labourers, were to be seen, but parked behind the house was a small Seat. 'Oh, lord,' Melissa muttered. 'She's the last person I want to see at this moment.'

The countess was walking to and fro in the car park. 'Every time I come to see you, you are out,' she complained.

Melissa decided against another tart reply. 'Moving in is an exhausting business. And how are you today?'

'I am always well,' the countess announced, and eyed Fred, who was just getting out. 'That dog does not like me.'

'Of course he likes you. Fred likes everybody. Except burglars.'

She did not look convinced. 'You will come to dinner with me tonight? Yes?'

'Tonight? We had rather a heavy day yesterday.'

'I am talking about night, not day.'

Melissa looked at David, who was, as ever, looking about to lick the countess's hand. 'We'd love to come to dinner, Countess,' he said. Melissa glared at him.

'Then you must call me Dolores. Tonight is the running of the bulls.'

'That's in Pamplona,' Melissa objected.

'Pah! We run the bulls in Jàvea also. At eight o'clock. We will watch the running of the bulls, and then we will have dinner. Yes?'

'Sounds entrancing,' Melissa murmured.

'Now, Liss, you know you've always wanted to watch the running of the bulls,' David said. 'What time would you like us, Dolores?'

'We will meet in the car park at seven thirty,' Dolores said. 'The main streets will be blocked off, so you must come round the back way.'

'Seven thirty?' Melissa asked. 'Isn't that

rather late? What time will we eat?'

'The usual time, my dear child. Half past ten.' She got into her car. *'Hasta la vista.'*

'Are you sure we're doing the right thing?' Melissa asked.

'Sounds exciting.'

'I'm not talking about watching the bulls run. I mean, should we be accepting an invitation from her?'

'Why on earth not?'

'Well, we know she's as nutty as a fruitcake. And we know she went through my things when she was here before. And she doesn't like Fred.' The ultimate test of friendship. 'And if we go to dinner at her place, we'll have to ask her back.'

'In due course.'

'And what about eating at half past ten? We won't get home until some time tomorrow.'

'As I said, it sounds rather exciting. I mean, we haven't been here a week, and we're being taken up by the Spanish aristocracy.'

'You reckon?' Melissa remarked.

They had a siesta, in view of the approaching long night, and then Melissa brooded on what to wear. The countess had been as chic as ever, and that seemed to indicate a dress. On the other hand, getting mixed up with a lot of bulls seemed to indicate pants. Finally she settled for her pants suit, and they set off just after seven, leaving Fred to look after

146

Casa Sagittarius, with all the lights on and a large rawhide bone.

Jàvea was even more humming than usual, and it took them some time even to find a parking slot in the central park. 'I thought you were not coming,' Dolores said, emerging from a group of several elegantly dressed people. 'Now let me introduce you.' All of the women were in dresses, and Melissa began to feel like a tramp. 'This is the Marques de Santa Longa, and the Marquesa, of course, and Victoriana de las Pordos, and...'

As usual the names swirled around Melissa's head, leaving her quite dazed. David, of course, was lapping it up; he had enjoyed this sort of thing at the Pantry, whereas she had always been on the organizing side of her PR business and had established who was what long before the festivities had begun.

'Now!' Dolores announced. 'The bulls!' They walked to the Ronda Norde, and down to the square, where elaborate barricades had been erected, including high trestles laddered with heavy wooden staging for the spectators. The square was crowded with people – men, women and children of all ages from about three to ninety, chattering excitedly in Spanish and clambering up and down the trestles, while the children played underneath, pushing their heads through gaps in the staging to shout, 'Boo!'; chic or not, Melissa was glad to be wearing pants, if

147

she was going to be required to do any climbing. In the square itself, a few young men lounged, leaning on the cars which had remained parked there.

'You are very beautiful,' someone said, and Melissa's head turned sharply. He was at least a member of Dolores' party, but was the sort of man Melissa instinctively distrusted, from his slicked-back black hair through his pencil moustache to his flawless double-breasted blue blazer, white pants and two-tone shoes. Not to mention the cigarette drooping from his mouth.

'You're very kind,' she said, and looked for David. But David, predictably, was chatting up the best-looking of Dolores' female friends. 'What exactly is going to happen?'

'Well, you see –' her admirer held her arm to usher her out into the square, beyond the barricades – 'the bulls are released up there –' he pointed along the street to the west – 'and they come galloping down here ... well, they are supposed to gallop. They come down here, anyway, and then they go down there.' He pointed to the street leading south-east, the exits from which were also barricaded.

'But what about the cars?' Melissa asked. Every parking slot was filled.

'Oh, the bulls do not bother with the cars. They do not bother with anything. These are very young bulls. Not like the ones in Pamplona. Here they are.'

There was a fanfare on a trumpet, and Melissa turned to see half-a-dozen horned animals clattering down the street towards her. 'Liss!' David bellowed. He was mounted on the trestle barricade, a woman to each side. 'Get up here!'

'We'd better go,' she muttered to her escort.

'I have said, there is nothing to be afraid of with these bulls,' he insisted.

Melissa looked at the bulls, and had to agree with him. The six animals were advancing very reluctantly, having to be driven by several small boys, who poked at their rumps with branches and sticks. In front of them the younger men of the town lounged, tapping them on the head as they came close. She waved at David. 'Take my photo!' she shouted. Melissa in the midst of the bulls. That would be one in the eye for Audrey. Then there was a sudden shout, and both Melissa and her escort turned together, to see a seventh bull, altogether larger and more ferocious-looking than the others, advancing at speed along the line of the barricades.

'Liss!' David bellowed, doing his knight in armour bit again as he leapt down from the trestle on to the road beside her. She willingly let him grab her arm and push her back against the slatted wood. Her friend was not so fortunate. Either totally bewildered or unable to believe one of the bulls could actually have aggressive intent, he merely

149

gazed at the huge beast as it charged up to him and into him with a terrifying crunch.

'David!' Melissa screamed, throwing both arms round one of the staging planks while women and children dragged her up. David was left trying to cope with the bull. But the bull was not interested in David. Melissa's Spanish friend having collapsed, the animal stood above him with head lowered and horns thrusting into his twisting body. 'David!' Melissa screamed again, having a vision of him also on the ground being gored.

By now the entire square was in an uproar. Small boys pulled the bull's tail and thumped its buttocks. Young men hit it on the head and grasped its horns to pull it round. Policemen and Guardia Civiles approached with stately tread, bellowing instructions. And, the bull having been driven off, a small army of eager youths, wearing green uniforms but with red crosses on their sleeves, took over. Melissa joined David. 'Are you all right?'

'I'm fine. But this chap...'

Her friend was groaning dreadfully, and his blazer would never be the same again, even if the laundry did manage to remove the bloodstains. 'Is he going to die?' Melissa asked.

One of the Red Cross men grinned. 'No, no, *señora*. But 'e 'as broken several reebs.'

Bells clanged and an ambulance appeared,

the policemen hastily dragging a barricade aside to let it through. The injured man was placed on a stretcher and taken inside, and the bell started clanging again. 'I feel so guilty,' Melissa said. 'He was explaining what was going to happen, when it happened.'

'Duarte is always showing off,' Dolores said, having joined them. 'Well, he will miss dinner. Shall we go?'

'To the hospital?'

'No, no, my dear child. To dinner.'

'But we can't just abandon ... did you say his name was Duarte?'

'Means Edward,' David muttered. 'Actually, I'm starving.'

'Of course you are,' Dolores said. 'It will soon be ready. Come along. I will come with you, to show you the way.'

The entertainment was apparently over. The bulls had disappeared to be rounded up lower down in the town, the crowds were dispersing to the bars, and Duarte, having given everyone something to talk about, had been removed. Melissa felt terribly guilty at just going off and leaving him, but no one else seemed to be the least concerned, as Dolores' party wandered back to the car park, chatting amongst themselves. 'At least the Red Cross were prompt and efficient,' Melissa remarked. 'I've never seen such a turn-out. Does that mean you often have accidents?'

'No, no,' Dolores said. 'It takes an idiot like Duarte to have an accident. There are always a lot of *Cruz Rojas* about. They are national servicemen, you see.'

'I don't see.' They had reached the car, and David was unlocking it. 'Your Red Cross is part of national service?'

'Of course.' Without a by-your-leave, Dolores got into the front beside David, leaving Melissa to wrestle with erecting the first row of rear seats in the estate car, which had been flat for the comfort of Fred.

'Want a hand?' David asked, when she was finished, puffing.

'Get lost,' Melissa snapped, before she remembered that he had behaved rather splendidly in jumping to her rescue in the face of a rampant bull.

Dolores ignored the domestic crisis. 'When a young man is called up for national service,' she explained, 'he is given the option of joining the Army or the Red Cross.'

'What a brilliant idea,' David commented, as he drove out of the park.

'You must turn right,' Dolores commanded. 'Of course, most of them choose the Red Cross.'

'I'm surprised you have an army at all,' Melissa said. 'You wouldn't, in England.'

'Oh, there are always young men who like to play with guns,' Dolores said. 'Young women, too. I was a soldier, once.'

'Come again?'

'I volunteered. You can turn left at the next corner, then go to the *puerto*.'

'Why did you wish to be a soldier?' Melissa asked, imagination boggling at the thought of this elegant creature sharing a barracks or attempting an obstacle course.

'I like to shoot guns,' Dolores explained simply. 'If the Communists ever try to gain power again, I will shoot them.'

'Absolutely,' David agreed.

'In here,' Dolores said. David obediently swung the wheel.

'What rank did you attain?' Melissa asked. 'Sergeant-major?'

'I was a captain,' Dolores said. 'Here we are.'

They had driven through an archway into a courtyard behind a large block of flats, where the rest of the party were already disembarking. There was an elevator to whisk them to one of the upper floors, where Dolores' flat was situated. This was very grand, with modern steel and plush furniture, surrealist paintings, and a splendid view over the harbour from the *naya*.

'She can't be a complete fraud,' David whispered.

Open bottles of wine were waiting for them, and the men made themselves useful. Delightful smells were coming from the kitchen. 'We are having *paella*,' Dolores explained. 'Do you like *paella*?'

'I'm not sure,' Melissa confessed.

She was taken through the kitchen on to a rear *naya*, where two maids were busy with a huge shallow cooking pan arranged over a gas burner fuelled by a butane bottle. One was frying pieces of meat while the other sliced peppers and more meat. Dishes of raw chicken joints, shrimps and mussels stood waiting, with a bowl of olives, jugs of broth and a big bag of rice.

'In another hour, it will be ready,' Dolores said.

'Another hour!' Melissa felt as if she were starving already. So it was back to the wine, and the conversation, which was almost entirely in Spanish. She did hear the name Duarte mentioned several times, however, so she understood they were discussing the events of the evening, and when one of the men spoke to her she replied, 'I was beside him. I was scared stiff.'

'Ah, the bulls,' her acquaintance said.

'Thank heavens you speak English. I was beginning to feel a little lonely.'

He gestured her to a seat and sat beside her; he was a man of about sixty, and looked cuddly. 'Do you like the bulls?'

'After tonight, I think I prefer them from a distance.'

'Have you been to the bullfight?'

'No. Do you think I should? I'm not into blood sports.'

'The bullfight is an art form,' he said, apparently seriously. 'You must go. One must

154

experience everything in this life, do you not agree?'

'Well ... within reason. I mean, if the bull had a chance, it might be different.'

'You think the bull has no chance? I will tell you a story about the bullfight. There were these two *touristas*, American ladies, both, shall we say, middle-aged. Very respectable. They are in Spain on a holiday, so they go to the restaurant, but the menu is in Spanish, and they do not know what to order. So they look at the table beside them, and there the man is sitting down to what look like two huge duck eggs. So they ask the waiter, what are those? And the waiter replies, *cojones*.' He paused, peering at Melissa, but Melissa had not the slightest idea what he was talking about. 'Well, the American ladies ask, are they good? Oh, very good, replies the waiter. Very tasty. Then that's what we'll have. Alas, says the waiter, but those are all we have, tonight. However, if you can come back next week, I will promise to keep a pair of *cojones* for you. The ladies are intrigued, and return the following week. We have come for our *cojones*, they tell the waiter. But of course, he says, and serves them. The ladies are surprised, and very disappointed, for instead of the huge meal they anticipated, they are each served with a tiny circular piece of food, smaller than a boiled egg. What has happened? they demand. Why are we being given *cojones* only a fraction the size of those you served last week? Ah, *señoras*, the waiter replies, the matador does not always win.' Whereupon he began to roar with laughter.

Melissa smiled politely, and went off to find David. 'What are *cojones*?' she whispered.

'*Co*—? Who's been talking to you about *cojones*?'

'That chap over there. What are they?'

'Darling, it's the slang word for balls.'

Fortunately, dinner was then served, and the party became jollier yet. Melissa looked at her watch; it was midnight, and the evening seemed to have a very long way to go. And Fred was waiting at home, with a dreadful threat hanging over him, and...

'Why do you look so sad?' Dolores asked.

'Was I? Sorry. I am most terribly tired. I do think we should be getting home.'

'If you are tired, then you must go to bed. It has been an exhausting evening for you,' Dolores said sympathetically. 'Come into my bedroom for a minute.'

'What for?' Melissa asked suspiciously.

'There is something I wish to show you.'

'Oh? Oh, there's David.'

'I will show him too. Come in here, David.'

David looked at Melissa, eyebrows arched.

'I said we should be going home, but she wants to show us something,' Melissa hissed.

David led her into the bedroom, and paused in consternation, not so much at the decor, which, with its accent on purples and

156

deep reds, perhaps mirrored the countess's personality, but at the guns which were everywhere. They varied from Berettas small enough to be concealed in a woman's evening bag to long-barrelled rifles, not to mention three Kalashnikovs – 74s, not out-of-date 47s – and three magnums. They were suspended from hooks on the walls, lying on the top of the dresser, balanced on the window sills.

'I told you, I like guns,' Dolores explained.

'You look about to fight a war,' Melissa remarked.

'Who can tell? If the Communists—'

'Don't you think Communism is a bit passé? At least in Europe.'

'One must be prepared. One must always be ready. I am a very good shot. I will show you.'

'We'll take your word for it,' Melissa said. 'David, we simply must be going.'

'David,' Dolores commanded. 'Open the window.'

'David...' Melissa tried a bit of commanding herself, but David was already opening the jalousie, to admit all the very loud noise emanating from both the *puerto* and the *pueblo*.

'Now place that onyx ashtray, on end, on the outer sill,' Dolores said.

'Oh, don't do that,' Melissa begged. 'It's such a lovely thing. It might fall and be smashed.'

David set the ashtray on end. Dolores turned to face the inner wall, and from it took one of the magnums. She held it in both hands, but continued to face the wall, drawing deep breaths. 'Stand aside, David,' she said.

Melissa grabbed David's arm and pulled him against the side wall. 'She's absolutely dotty,' she whispered. 'David...'

'*Santa Maria!*' Dolores shrieked, at the same time whirling round and levelling the revolver, squeezing the trigger in almost the same action. The sound of the explosion filled the room, and the onyx ashtray disintegrated.

'My God!' Melissa screamed. 'Suppose you hit somebody?'

'That window overlooks the sea,' Dolores said, breaking the revolver and reaching for her cleaning materials.

'Are they all loaded?' David asked.

'There is no point in having guns which aren't loaded.'

'We have to rush,' Melissa said, dragging David to the door. 'Before the police get here,' she muttered.

Not softly enough. 'The police will not trouble me,' Dolores said. 'They know I like to shoot out of that window.'

'That is some woman,' David remarked, as they weaved their way home.

'The next thing you'll be wanting a gun of

your own,' Melissa remarked.

'Now that is an idea.'

'God, give me strength,' she moaned.

They actually got home without hitting anything, to face a wide-open gate. 'Oh, my God!' Melissa cried.

'How very odd,' David agreed, braking.

The lounge light was still on, and the house looked perfectly normal. But ... 'Do you think there's someone up there?' Melissa whispered.

'Well...'

'David! Melissa!' They looked out of their windows to see Hans von Grippenheimer striding up the road from his house. 'Someone tried to break into your house tonight.'

Melissa got out of the car. 'Not again!'

Hans came up to them. 'It has happened before?'

'We think so. Fred! Is he all right?'

'I would say so. I heard him barking. However...'

David also got out. 'How do you know all this?'

'I knew you were out for the evening. So when I heard this car coming up the road, quite early, I looked out and saw it stop at your gate. I assumed they had come to see you, and would go away again when they realized you were not at home. But instead, to my surprise, I saw two men get out and start fiddling with the gate, and then it opened and they drove up behind the house.'

'What did you do?'

'Well, there was only one thing I could do. We are neighbours, are we not? I came up to investigate.'

'You came up here, in the middle of the night, to challenge two strange men? What did Carrie say?'

'Carrie went to bed. She does not like it when I start using my gun.'

'What did you say?'

'Well, I was not coming up here unarmed. *They* were armed.'

Melissa had to hold on to the car to stop her knees giving way. 'What happened?' David asked.

'I inquired what they were doing, and they told me – well, they used a very indelicate expression which I will not repeat in front of a lady. So I drew my pistol and told them to leave. Whereupon one of them drew a gun of his own.'

'Oh, my God!' Melissa said. 'Oh, my *God*!'

'But what *happened*? David shouted. 'Were you hurt?'

'Oh, good heavens, no. I shot him before he could squeeze the trigger. I,' Hans added proudly, 'was the best pistol shot in the German navy.'

'You shot a man, in our garden?'

'Actually, I shot him in the chest.'

Now Melissa's knees did give way, and she

found herself sitting on the ground. 'Is he there now?' David asked.

'No, no. His friend got him into their car and they drove off.'

'And you have contacted the police.'

'You don't want to involve the police in something like this. That way lies endless trouble.'

'But that man could be dead.'

'Which is what he deserves to be. Come, I have something to show you.' He went up the drive. David helped Melissa to her feet, and they staggered after him. Hans went round the house to the parking area, produced a flashlight, and shone it on the ground by the back door. 'There.'

'That looks like a lump of meat,' David said.

'It *is* a lump of meat They dropped it when they were getting away. I would say it is poisoned. It is the oldest trick in the business. They force the door, your very fierce dog rushes out, they throw him the meat, he stops to eat it, he collapses in agony...'

'Fred!' Melissa screamed, grabbing the keys and unlocking the door.

'And they loot the house at their leisure,' Hans continued, unperturbed.

'Fred!' Melissa got the door open, and Fred was in her arms. 'Oh, Fred! Don't go near that meat,' she snapped, as his nostrils twitched.

'Wasn't he barking while all this was going

on?' David asked.

'I think he was, at the beginning,' Hans said. 'Then he stopped.'

'Because you fired a gun,' Melissa said, massaging Fred's head. 'He's terrified of guns.'

'But isn't he a retriever?'

'He's never retrieved anything in his life.'

'I don't know how we can ever thank you for interfering,' David said.

'I am your neighbour. And your friend.'

'Absolutely. But what do we do about this?'

'I would recommend that you buy yourself a gun.'

'Ah. Perhaps you're right. But, I mean, you think we shouldn't report it to the police?'

'Definitely not.'

'Suppose someone heard the shot?'

'It is unlikely. But if anyone did, they will just think there is some idiot firing at a rabbit. Now I must go back to Carrie. She will be worried.'

'But why do people keep trying to break into our house? Have you ever been burgled?'

'I imagine they regard you as a sitting bird, eh? You have the reputation of being a wealthy man, you have just arrived from England, you do not know the ropes, eh? I have never been burgled, because it is well known that I have a gun. You get one for yourself. Good night, dear lady. Good night, Fierce Dog. Good night, David. I would get rid of that meat.'

'I have a suspicion that he was taking the mickey,' David suggested, as Hans disappeared into the darkness. 'But wow! What a character.'

Melissa stood up. 'David! What are we going to do?'

'He said to do nothing. He's probably right. As he said, he knows the ropes.'

'I meant what are we going to do about us. This whole situation. I think we should go home.'

'Home? You mean to England? Why should we do that?'

'We just seem to be attracting trouble down here. Someone may have been killed in our car, now a man has been shot in our garden, Fred's in trouble with the law...'

'You're not going to let a few things like that chase you away, Liss. Not you. We have a lovely home here, good neighbours ... people do get burgled in London, you know. And sometimes they get shot. At least in Spain you can get on with defending your property. Listen, come to bed and have a good night's sleep. Tomorrow it'll all look a lot brighter.'

'What the fuck is going on?' Donald Barton demanded into the phone. 'Do these people live in a goddamned fortress? They weren't even there, for Chrissake.'

'Maybe, boss,' said the man on the end of the

line. 'But they had some kind of a trigger-happy watchman. He shot Ricardo.'

'Ricardo is dead?'

'No. He's going to be all right. But he won't be doing anything physical for a while.'

'And you just ran off.'

'You said it'd be simple. You said that dog would eat anything offered to it. We didn't even get to see the dog. You don't think Big Sam—'

'If Big Sam had the card he'd have used it. I'll be in touch.' He replaced the phone and looked across his desk at Lucy. 'These people are beginning to get my goat.'

'They got my goat from the start,' Lucy remarked. 'That simpering little goody-two-shoes and that oaf of a husband.'

'They've cost me three of my best people, either dead or badly wounded. We're going to have to handle them ourselves, Lucy. Just like the old days, eh?'

'Make my day. Just tell me I can get my hands on that little bitch.'

'All in good time. There's a possibility the card may still be in that car. We'll start on that, and get around to them later.'

Melissa actually did feel better when she awoke, at least partly because it all seemed like a dream in the light of day. Alvarez's workmen were on site at half past seven, despite it being a Saturday, to Fred's annoyance, as he was still fast asleep when they appeared. The necessity of waiting for a

164

permit had apparently been forgotten. And they started work with great gusto, unloading concrete blocks and shovelling cement while they sang out of tune to their transistor radio. At nine thirty, they knocked off for breakfast, which consisted of a litre of wine per man, caught expertly in the mouth from a double-necked container, and a huge *bocadillo*, or sandwich roll, made from very hard bread and containing slices of salami. Then they went back to work until one. Lunch was a repeat of breakfast, wine-wise, but they collected dry pine twigs to make a fire and cooked a meal of fresh sardines, following which they took a siesta for two hours, scattered around the garden under the trees, before resuming work at half past three.

Melissa found it fascinating, because it was so unlike the English work pattern, but the court case lay like a grey cloud across both of their minds, and Sunday was a deadly day, with neither of them feeling like doing anything save brood on the morrow. Melissa kept telling herself that no one could justly call Fred vicious, but she couldn't convince herself that the Spanish would necessarily agree with her. Fred himself was of course oblivious of his own danger, and thought the idea of going out early the next morning and driving round Montgo to Denia a brilliant one. Melissa determined to pull out all the stops, and wore a dress and high-heeled shoes, as well as make-up. They were already over the hill when she suddenly remembered ... 'Oh, shit! I've forgotten my handbag!'

'Well,' David said, 'we can't go back now. We have to be at the court by ten, and it's a quarter to. Where is it?'

'On my dressing table.'

'Then it'll be quite safe.'

'Suppose someone tries to get into the house again? There isn't even Fred.'

'I don't think that's likely, with friend Grippenheimer on the loose. Stop worrying.'

David parked on the avenue, having secured the required ticket, and they walked along to the court, joining the considerable crowd outside. There was no one they immediately recognized, but Fred, with Melissa holding his leash, was in the best of humours, merely grinning when people trod on his feet. 'There's Salvador,' Melissa said. 'Thank God!'

Salvador was pushing his way towards them, from the direction of the court. 'You come,' he said, and led them round the building, where there were less people. Waiting for them was Carlos, smiling ingratiatingly. He even stooped to pat Fred, to Melissa's annoyance. 'I 'ave spoken weez 'eem,' Salvador explained, 'and 'e ees weelleeng to weez-draw zee *denuncia*.'

'Oh, great,' David said. 'Well, then, shall we shake hands and call it a day?' He held out his hand, and Carlos took it.

'But zere ees one small matter,' Salvador went on.

'I didn't doubt it for a moment,' Melissa remarked.

'To make a *denuncia*,' Salvador told them, '*primero* eet ees necessary to place a deposeet. Zees ees to be certain eet ees a serious *denuncia*, and not a feud, or *frivolo* ... stoopeed. Zee money ees returned when zee case ees proved. Eef not, eet ees kept by zee court. You *comprende*?'

'Ye-es,' David said slowly.

'Carlos 'as given zees deeposeet. Now, eef 'e weezdraw zee *denuncia*, 'e must lose zees money.'

'How much is it?'

'Seven hundred and fifty euros.'

'That's five hundred pounds! You want us to give Carlos five hundred pounds, to drop the utterly absurd charges he brought against us?' Melissa wanted to get the facts absolutely straight. 'That's daylight robbery.'

'What's the alternative?' David asked.

'Well, Daveed, eef Carlos no 'as zee money, 'e weell not drop zee *denuncia*.'

'And you don't think we can win our case?'

'Well, Daveed, eet ees zee *perro*.'

'Fred wouldn't hurt a fly, and you know that,' Melissa said.

'Eet ees not zee fly we are talking about. Carlos' sheep are not 'appy, by zee barking and zee teez.'

'Oh, really! Fred can't help having teeth.'

167

'Zere ees mucho talkeeng about zee barking and zee fighting een zee surgery on Friday.'

'He was set upon. He had to defend himself. Actually, all the barking and the fighting was done by David.'

'Daveed?' Salvador looked at David admiringly.

'All right,' David said. 'I'll pay the money. There's just one problem: I don't have it.'

Salvador's expression indicated disbelief. 'You, Daveed, not 'ave five 'undred pounds?'

'Well, I do have it, of course,' David said. 'But I haven't opened the account with the local bank yet. You will have to wait until I can do that and our funds have been transferred. It's in hand.'

'Zat ees all right,' Salvador said. 'We weell trust you, Daveed. You pay us zee money when you go to zee bank.'

'You do realize that you are being robbed just as if you had a gun stuck in your ribs?' Melissa asked her husband.

'Do you have any better idea?'

Melissa looked down at Fred, who looked up at her, and winked. She sighed. 'No, I don't have a better idea. Now, if you don't mind, I will go back to the car. Are you coming?'

''E must sign zee paper,' Salvador said.

'Right. You do that. Fred and I will wait for you on the avenue.' She felt like a stiff drink.

'But you are comeeng to zee *fiesta*,' Salvador said. 'Eet ees all arranged.'

Melissa looked at David, who gave a crooked grin. 'When in Rome...'

'Don't *ever* say that to me again,' Melissa snapped. 'Come along, Fred.' She stalked through the crowd, waited by the odd lamppost as Fred had had an exciting morning, and regained the avenue and the neat little blue-lined space in which David had left the Peugeot ... but the space was now occupied by a Volvo.

For a moment Melissa could not believe her eyes. She went right up to the Volvo, decided that she must have been mistaken about the advertisement stand in front of which they had parked, and walked the length of the next block. But there was no other stand and no blue Peugeot estate. And all the time the realization was growing on her that it had been removed. Again! Judging by his expression, Fred had clearly known all the time that this was going to happen. She retraced her steps towards the court, and watched Salvador's car weaving towards her; David was sitting beside him. They were talking so animatedly they didn't immediately see her, and she had to wave her arms before Salvador pulled up, a line of traffic immediately building behind him. Both men looked at her inquiringly. 'You won't believe this,' Melissa said, 'but our car has been stolen.' They clearly didn't believe it. 'It's not there,'

Melissa insisted. 'It is gone. Vanished. Disappeared.'

'Zees ees very strange,' Salvador remarked. 'Do you not zeenk eet ees strange, Daveed?'

'You don't mind if we go have a look?' David asked.

'You don't mind if Fred and I get in?' Melissa countered.

Back to square one, she thought, as Fred huffed and puffed himself on to her lap – she thought he might have put on weight during the week he had been in Spain. She also began to regret wearing a dress, as it rode up and Salvador couldn't avoid looking at her legs. However, he retained sufficient concentration to drive down to the avenue. 'It was parked just there, on the far side,' David told him.

'Where that Volvo is,' Melissa pointed.

'Zees ees an unlucky car,' Salvador suggested.

'Or there is something funny going on. Will you drive us to the police station?'

Salvador shrugged.

The police sergeant stroked his chin and regarded the particulars he had taken down. Then he turned round to a shelf filled with packed files, and began sifting through them. He selected one, placed it on the desk before him, and opened it. 'Peugeot 506 Estate,' he said. 'Dark-blue with blue interior. Registered in Great Britain.'

'That's the one,' David said.

'This car was reported stolen Thursday before last,' the sergeant pointed out. 'Why have you come here to tell me about it now?'

'Because your police got it back for us, last Saturday.'

'Then this file is out of date.'

'I'm afraid it is.'

The sergeant scratched his head. 'Then why are you reporting it again?'

'Because it has been stolen again.'

The sergeant gave David a very severe stare, then turned the stare on Melissa, then on Fred; he obviously hadn't liked the look of Fred from the start. Salvador spoke rapidly in Spanish. Apparently he was supporting their story, for the sergeant's look softened, slightly. 'You are a careless man, *Señor* Lytton.'

'Not this time, I swear. The car was locked. Here.' He held up the keys.

'It's some kind of a conspiracy,' Melissa said.

'Drugs,' Salvador suggested, unhelpfully.

'You have drugs in your car?' the sergeant snapped.

'No, no,' David protested. 'There is nothing in the car.'

'We would like to get it back,' Melissa said, changing the subject.

'I understand. But you must realize that you have to explain about the drugs, when the car is found.'

'I am going mad,' Melissa muttered savagely. 'Stark raving bonkers.'

The sergeant looked apprehensive. 'I weell explain,' Salvador volunteered.

'No,' Melissa said. 'I think you've done enough already.'

But he was in full flow, with the sergeant replying in kind. This went on for ten minutes, with a great deal of gesticulating. Fred yawned and lay down, chin on paws. He was becoming used to the interior of police stations. 'Eet ees feex,' Salvador said at last. 'We go now. When zee car is foun', zey bring it to you.'

'Oh, great.' David stood up. 'Do you think you could drop us home?'

'No, we need to go to a hire-car company,' Melissa objected.

'But you come to zee *fiesta*,' Salvador protested.

'I'm afraid that neither of us is really in the mood for a *fiesta*, Salvador,' Melissa told him.

'But eet ees all feex. My family, zey wait for to meet weez you.'

'What about the money we owe your friend Carlos? Shouldn't you take us into Jàvea to see if our transfer has turned up?'

'Carlos ees not my frien', Meleessa; 'e ees my brozzer-in-law. 'E can wait until tomorrow for 'ees money. My family weell be very sad eef you do not come to zee *fiesta*.'

Melissa looked at David, who opened his

mouth, his lips forming the words, 'When in Rome.'

'If you say it, I shall hit you,' she warned him.

'There's just one thing.' David turned to Salvador. 'How do we get back from your village?'

'I weell drive you back.'

'That will leave us without any means of transport tomorrow morning,' Melissa pointed out.

'I weell come for you and drive you to zee hire-car people, and to zee bank for Carlos' money. Zees week I am *en fiesta*.'

They drove out of Denia, through the tunnel beneath the motorway, and headed for the mountains. Melissa reckoned she might as well endeavour to enjoy herself; things could not possibly be worse. Save if they had lost the case against Fred, and that had been avoided. The sun was hot and beads of sweat were forming down the sides of her face, under her hair and across her neck. With both hands she scooped the hair back and up, letting the draught from the open window dry her skin. 'You weesh a dreenk, eh?' Salvador suggested. He might have read her thoughts.

David looked at his watch. 'Good lord, it's past eleven.'

'Zee bottle ees under zee seat,' Salvador explained. It was a wine bottle, to Melissa's relief. And if she could not help but think about things like AIDS, and chewed tobacco juice, she was too tired and depressed to care. She took a swig and passed it to David, who drank and gave it to Salvador, who also drank, expertly, at the same time steering round a horse and cart with one hand. 'Wow!' Melissa commented. But the mere act of swigging by the neck while belting along in this tatty old car began immediately to lift the cloud of gloom that had been enveloping her. They were well away from civilization now, the road was increasingly narrow, running beside a deep dry river bed filled with stones and small boulders and assorted rubbish. 'Is there ever water in that *barranca*?' David asked.

'When eet rains in zee mountains, zat reever comes over zee road,' Salvador asserted.

'I find that hard to believe,' Melissa said. 'I ... oh, my God, look out!' A car came round the bend at speed. There was a frantic blaring of horns, on both sides, and Salvador's car crashed through several bushes before regaining the road. 'If you'd been holding the bottle, we'd be dead,' Melissa gasped.

'I drive better weez zee one 'and,' Salvador said, waving the free one in the air before reclaiming the bottle from David and then handing it to Melissa. She hastily took another drink, if only to finish the bottle before Salvador could get at it. He glanced at it in disgust. 'T'row eet out of zee window,' he commanded.

'That's litter.'

'Een Spain, leeter is *basura*,' Salvador pointed out. 'Zey say you must put eet een zee beens. But when zere are no beens, zen you must put eet somewhere. Zere are no beens 'ere.'

'But don't you have bins in your village?'

'Zey weell all be full. Eet ees *fiesta*.' His logic was devastating. Melissa threw the bottle as far away from the car as she could, and managed to get it into the dry river, where it shattered into a thousand pieces. 'Zere ees anozzer bottle under zee seat,' Salvador said.

They hadn't got very far into the second bottle when there was a fusillade of what appeared to be gunfire from in front of them. Fred promptly put his head out of the window to bark, then brought it back inside and tucked it under Melissa's arms. 'Zey are just starteeng,' Salvador said, with some satisfaction. It was noon. Rockets exploded as they rounded another bend and found themselves on a hillside looking down into a small secluded valley, where there was, at first sight, a sea of television aerials. But these were supported by an equal number of very old tiled roofs. 'You like my veellage?' Salvador asked.

175

'I think it's very ... very quaint. You must watch a lot of television.'

'Zere ees not much to do at night, een zee mountains, eef you 'ave no woman,' Salvador remarked philosophically.

The road dipped down and down, and grew narrower and narrower, and a moment later they were driving through a street barely wide enough for the car, between white-painted houses with bead curtains over the open doors. There were few people to be seen, although there was a great deal of human noise in the near distance, but they hadn't got very far when there was a blaring of a horn, and the front bumper of a car emerged from an alleyway between two of the houses, and began to turn towards them.

Salvador promptly placed his fist on his own horn, and the other car stopped, before lurching forward again. Salvador blew even more, while braking, and now the driver of the offending car could actually see the street, and Salvador's car. He gave a few more toots on his horn, and backed up. Salvador drove by. 'Must be a stranger,' David commented.

'No, no, 'ee 'ees my couseen. 'Ee leeves 'ere.'

'Then you'd think he'd know better than to turn up a one-way street.'

'Zees ees a two-way street,' Salvador explained. Melissa hugged Fred tighter.

The car debouched from the street into a

central square, which included the church and one or two other largish and official-looking buildings. Round the sides of the square were a continuous line of trestle tables, backed by benches, while in the area surrounded by the tables was a mass of people, shouting and laughing; as they arrived, a fresh barrage of firecrackers exploded. The noise was tremendous, and Fred promptly dived off Melissa's lap on to the floor of the car, and thrust his head under the seat. "Ee ees a gun dog, no?' Salvador inquired.

'No,' Melissa told him. 'You're thinking of one of his ancestors.'

Salvador opened his door and stepped down, and Melissa and David did likewise. Melissa left the door of the car open, but Fred was showing no immediate desire to emerge. Which was just as well, she supposed, because mingling with the people were several dogs, apparently unaffected by the explosions. No doubt they were used to them. The arrival of Salvador's car had been observed, and almost the entire party converged on them. David and Melissa were surrounded by men, women, and children of all ages, who wished to kiss and hug them and shake their hands. They discovered that Salvador was related to nearly everyone in the village, and had difficulty in identifying his actual mother and father and brothers and sisters, but gathered that his father's name was Julio – pronounced Hulio – and his mother's Encarna.

Glasses of wine were pressed into their hands, and someone made a speech. Melissa realized that the speaker, a small, wizened fellow with only one arm, was indeed Salvador's father, and also that he was relating the exciting story of how his two *amigos Inglesi* had this very day escaped the clutches of the *policia*, thanks to Salvador. He earned tremendous applause, while Melissa wasn't sure whether or not they were having their legs pulled. 'Means every word of it, ma'am,' said a voice behind her, and she turned, and started to look up and up and up, as well as sideways. Had she not been surrounded by so many people, she would have run for her life. It was not merely that the man was very tall – hardly less than six feet eight inches – and quite enormous – she put his weight at twenty stones, mostly concentrated in the vicinity of a bulging belt which was trying to restrain a buttonless shirt – he also hadn't shaved in several days and as a result had almost as much hair on his chin and revealed by the inadequate shirt as on his head, which was nearly bald. He reminded her irresistibly of Popeye's arch-enemy Bluto come to life, and she didn't have a can of spinach handy.

'People allus look't me that way, the first time,' he remarked. 'Ah get used t' it.'

'You're an American,' Melissa asserted.

'Yuh got it. Folks round here call me Amigo.'

'That means friend, doesn't it?' Melissa was hopeful.

'Sure thing. Ma real name's Sam Guichard. But ma friends call me Big Sam. And Ah'm right pleased t' meet yuh.'

Six

'Thank you,' Melissa said. 'I'm Melissa Lytton. This is my...' She looked round, but David had been hurried off by several men towards the table on which the beer, wine and brandy waited. 'Well, I suppose he'll be back.'

'When he's had a drink,' Sam suggested. 'Say, who's the lil' fella?' Fred was pushing a cautious nose out of the car door, the fireworks having for the moment ceased.

'My dog,' Melissa explained. 'He doesn't like loud noises, especially when they sound like guns.'

'Sensible fella,' Sam agreed. 'Come on down, dawg. Ah'll see they don't get yuh.'

Fred looked at Melissa, and she nodded. He scrambled down, and as Sam bent to pat him on the head, seized the enormous hand between his teeth, his jaws stretched to their

179

widest. 'Fred, let go,' Melissa said. 'It's a gesture of affection, really.'

'Sure 'tis,' Sam agreed, and with the thumb and forefinger of his other hand, inserted against Fred's teeth, opened the jaws even wider and removed his hand. Fred looked scandalized; no one had ever done that to him before.

Salvador's father was making another announcement, and people were taking their seats at the tables, while the young men hurried away with the remains of the firecrackers. *'Comida,'* Sam said. 'Yuh-all have reserved places.'

Melissa and Fred were escorted to the very centre of one of the trestle tables, Fred occasionally pausing to pass the time of day with one of the village dogs; the dislike appeared to be mutual, from the guttural growlings. Melissa's place was with Salvador's father on her right, and Salvador's mother on her left. David sat on the left of Salvador's mother, with one of Salvador's sisters next to him, and then Salvador himself. On the right of Salvador's father was another sister, and then Sam. Fred lay under Melissa's bench and did some more throat-clearing when a village dog came too close.

The young men now produced several portable wood-fire barbecues, and an equal number of enormous paella pans. The young women, supervised by their elders, began to work with great speed and precision, as the

180

fires were lit, and brought to the right temperatures, and the meat and fish and peppers were prepared, as well, of course, as the rice.

Melissa realized that none of Salvador's immediate family were taking any part in the cooking; she hadn't realized they were so important. 'Why should they?' Sam asked, leaning back on his bench to look at her. 'He's the *alcalde* round here. What we'd call a mayor, Ah guess. Head man.' So that's why Salvador carries so much weight, she thought.

Meanwhile innumerable jugs of red wine were set before them, and her glass was filled. 'Yuh don't wanna drink too much of that stuff,' Sam warned. 'Jalón wine has a kick like a mule.'

Melissa tasted the wine, and tried not to flinch. Sharp and raw, it certainly was unlike anything she had ever drunk before.

'Once upon a time, eet was good wine,' Julio said. 'Now eet ees rubbeesh.'

Melissa hadn't realized that he spoke English. 'I suppose things have changed a lot, here in the hills,' she commented. 'Over the years.'

'Oh, *si*, zey 'ave changed. Zee Fasceestas, zey shot all zee people.'

Melissa gulped, and looked past him at Sam for help. Sam grinned. 'Sure thing, M'lissa. This part of Spain was Republican. You ask old Julio how he lost his arm.'

"Eet was shot off,' Julio said proudly.

'Shot off? Good lord? But ... you were surely too young to fight.'

'I was a boy,' Julio agreed, more proudly yet. 'But zey gave me zee machine gun, and I fire zee bullets, all zee time. Zen pow-pow, an' I am een zee 'ospital.'

'What a terrible experience. But ... how did you survive?'

'Zey cut eet off.'

'I meant, how did you survive the Fascistas?'

'Zey no shoot me. I am a boy, yes?' He emptied his glass and refilled it, and Melissa's; absentmindedly she had finished hers as well. 'Zey shoot *mi padre.*'

'Oh, gosh. You must hate them very much.'

"Ate? I don't 'ate nobody now,' Julio said, a trifle sadly. 'What for I am to 'ate people now? Now we 'ave plenty of everyzeeng. Eet was a long time ago.' He gave a crooked smile. 'Anyway, I shoot a lot of zem.'

'A sound philosophy,' Sam remarked.

'I had no idea you had had such an exciting life,' Melissa confided to Encarna, who merely smiled politely.

'She no speak zee Eengleesh,' Julio said. 'Anyway, she ees not born when zees happening.'

'Oh. Ah.' Melissa smiled in turn.

While the most attractive smells were arising from the paella pans, dishes of mixed salads were placed on the tables, together with trays of tiny hot pasties filled with savoury sauce, and individual quiches. There were baskets of bread and bowls of *aioli* – garlic mayonnaise – green olives, black olives and roasted almonds. Leaning forward, Sam noticed Melissa suspiciously eyeing a dish of snails. 'Lil' land snails in garlic sauce,' he explained. 'Use one of them toothpicks to dig 'em out the shells.' He demonstrated. 'D'licious.'

Melissa spooned a couple on to her plate and took some bread. The sun had steadily got hotter and she consumed several more glasses of the wine, and watched David doing the same. She reflected that at least they didn't have to drive home, and then remembered that Salvador did, and he was drinking as fast as anyone. 'These guys sure know how to enjoy themselves,' Sam remarked, round the back of Julio.

'Are you a resident in Spain?' Melissa asked.

'Sure thing. Ah live here.'

'Here? You mean, in this village?'

'Well, pretty damn close. Up there.'

He pointed up the hillside, and she saw a ruined castle perched some distance above the road. 'You live in that?'

'Sure. It looks better when yuh get close to't.'

'Don't tell me, you designed it and built it yourself.'

'No way, honey. Rebuilt it, maybe. It was

183

falling down. But it was what Ah wanted. If we ever get out of here alive, Ah'll show it t'yuh. Say, it's ready.'

A heaped plate of paella was placed before Melissa by a pretty smiling teenager. Having already made a meal of snails and salad and pasties, Melissa didn't actually feel like eating anything more, but she supposed she had to, and once she tasted the paella her appetite re-emerged. Fred was sitting up and taking an interest by now, and was very pleased with the titbits she passed down to him. 'This is absolutely marvellous,' she told Julio. 'Do please congratulate the cooks for me.'

'My mozzer made a good paella,' Julio said. 'But zee Fasceestas, zey shot 'er.'

Melissa couldn't think of an adequate reply to that, and her plate was being refilled. 'No, really,' she protested.

'Eat up,' Sam recommended. 'It's gonna to be a long day.'

When the paella was finally cleared away, great baskets of fruit were placed on the table, as well as refills for the wine. 'How're you doing?' Melissa asked David round the back of Encarna.

'Some spread. Are you as tight as you look?'

'Worry about yourself,' she recommended, and watched all the younger men, including Salvador, leaving the table to hurry down one of the narrow side alleys between the houses. 'Do they do the washing-up?' she giggled at Sam.

'Floor show time,' he said. 'Moors and Christians. All the villages in this part of Spain re-enact the old battles between the Moors and the Christians, in their own peculiar fashion. Prepare for a lot more noise.'

He was right there, too. A moment later there came the measured beat of several drums, and then a volley of what sounded like musketry. Fred sat up. The drums came closer, and there was another volley. Fred stood up. Melissa patted his head. 'There's nothing to be afraid of, Fred. They're just playing a game.'

Fred did not look convinced. The drums were now upon them, and into the square marched a line of young men, red tabards decorated with white crosses worn over their shirts and jeans. 'Zeese are zee Chreesteans,' Julio told Melissa, just in case she was confused.

From her point of view, they were relatively harmless, as they carried swords and shields. The swords looked lethal enough, but the only noise they made was a clang when they were whacked against the shields, or against each other as the men slowly marched round the square, in time to their drummers, while the crowd cheered. Then the drums fell silent, and into the square came three more figures. These consisted of two men wearing what looked like long, heavily embroidered nightshirts, and fezzes, and dragging between them a young woman, as spectacularly blonde as Melissa herself, and wearing only a black and gold leotard. These advanced into the very centre of the square, the girl writhing between the men most sensuously, and then she was thrown away from them. She fell to the ground and continued her writhings and posturings, rapidly becoming covered in the dust which clung to her sweat-wet body, while the cheering grew ever louder. 'She ees zee Chreesteean slave,' Julio interpreted, and looked Melissa up and down. 'Perhaps next year you weell be zee Chreesteean slave.'

'Not bloody likely. I mean,' she added hastily, 'perhaps.'

'She's a pro,' Sam said. 'Acts in all the Moors and Christians on the Costa Blanca. Makes good money.'

The girl rose to her knees, still flailing her hair to and fro, and one of the young men hurried forward with a glass of wine for her to drink. Meanwhile, the drums started again, now increasing their tempo, and into the square there trotted the most magnificent white horse, mounted by an equally magnificent rider, who wore white breeches and a flowing white cape, embroidered with gold thread. His burnous was also white embroidered with gold, and he wore kid boots.

His elaborate turban was crowned with a crescent moon and above his head he waved a scimitar which flashed in the sun. He coaxed his mount to rear on its hind legs, the better to show off his horsemanship, and the onlookers cheered more loudly than ever. ''Ee ees zee Sultan,' Julio informed Melissa. The Sultan backed his horse out of the line of fire, as it were, very slowly. For behind him into the square there came a double line of men in embroidered nightshirts and fezzes, and every man was armed with some kind of firearm, from blunderbusses through shot-guns to rifles and revolvers. 'Zeese are zee Moors,' Julio explained.

'Oh, my God!' Melissa muttered, as they all pointed their guns at the sky.

'Zere ees nozzeeng to be afraid of,' Julio reassured her. 'Eet ees all blank shot. Not like in zee old days,' he reminisced.

Melissa turned round to find Fred. But it was too late. With an enormous rippling boom, the guns exploded. Melissa caught a glimpse of Fred's tail disappearing down an alleyway behind her. She leapt to her feet, almost knocking Julio off the bench as she swung her legs over, and ran behind the dog, tripping in her high heels and landing on her hands and knees before regaining her feet. She turned a corner, but the alleyway was deserted. 'Fred!' she shouted. 'Fred!'

She heard a distant woof. It came from inside one of the buildings, but as nearly all the doors were open, she had no idea where to start looking. Heavy footsteps sounded behind her, and Sam arrived, somewhat out of breath. 'That dawg *sure* don't like guns,' he remarked.

'He's never had anything to do with them,' Melissa explained. 'He's lived all his life in Central London, and really, we don't see a lot of guns there.'

'He should try Miami,' Sam suggested. 'Dawg!' he bellowed. 'Where are yuh?'

'Woof,' Fred replied.

'That one.' Sam pointed and led the way across the street.

'Can we go into someone's house, un-invited?' Melissa asked.

'They won't mind, long as yuh don't take anything.'

Melissa braced herself for an unpleasant experience as Sam parted the bead curtain; she had got the impression that although the villagers were putting on a great display for what was a special occasion, they were desperately poor, and she feared the worst. And checked in consternation as she followed Sam over the raised threshold and found herself standing on a beautiful mosaic floor, partly covered with thick rugs, on which there stood two straight chairs which would have earned a fortune in any London antique shop. The hallway itself was small, and dark, but beyond was a door with stained glass panels, which gave access to a drawing room in which, again, the furniture was antique, the walls hung with tapestries and the window drapes with thick folds of red velvet.

Flowers stood in deep vases against the walls, and beyond, more double doors opened on to a central patio, in which there was a sparkling fountain, the pool containing several goldfish. Off the patio were more doors, while the roof above the fountain was a trellis laden with vines, both to keep out the sun and to ensure privacy from the neighbours. 'Is this Julio's house?' Melissa asked in amazement.

'No, no,' Sam said. 'Julio's house is a lot more grand. He's the *alcalde*, remember.'

'But this is rather nice, don't you think?'

'Sure 'tis. It's all a point of view. These people in the mountains, they don't spend their money on flash cars or holidays to Flor'da. They have all the sun they can stand right here. They put it into the house and the furniture, and the food and the drink. They know how to live. There's the lil' fellow.'

Fred was showing his nose from one of the inner rooms. 'Oh, Fred!' Melissa said. 'You really are a goofball. What am I to do with him, Sam?'

'Bring him back to the tables. If he's gonna live in Spain, he may as well get used to the noise.'

The afternoon was well advanced, and Melissa realized that, as the wine had not stopped flowing during her absence, no one, not even David, had noticed her departure at all. When she thought that she had been all alone in an empty house with a very large and very strange man with only a terrified Fred for company, and no one had thought about her ... then she realized that she had to pull herself together. This was Spain, not England. These people only wanted to enjoy themselves; she doubted there was a sex maniac in the entire crowd, which was more than she could possibly have hoped in a corresponding English gathering. 'How long does this go on?' she asked.

'It ain't even started yet. Now we're gonna dance. Yuh care to?'

Melissa realized that in her absence the Moors and the Christians had departed, and in their place was what appeared to be a youth orchestra, composed of both sexes, wearing black skirts or pants and white shirts with black bow ties, all very smart, quite tuneful, and dominated by a Hammond organ. It must have just arrived, because people were slowly making their way into the central square. 'We don't have to do something special?' she asked anxiously.

'Anything yuh like,' Sam said. He only knew a one-two one-two anyway, and they jogged amiably around the square. While she tried to discover David, and found him dancing with a very short, large-bosomed Spanish lady who was chattering away non-stop in her native language.

'And the best of luck,' she murmured as they brushed against each other.

'Say, yuh folks living here?' Sam inquired.

Melissa told him about the house; it helped to pass the time as his dancing grew increasingly boring. But when she persuaded him to take her back to her seat to make sure that Fred was still relaxed, she discovered that indeed her evening was just beginning. There was quite a queue lined up, and head of the list was Julio. His dancing was of the hand-pumping, up and down variety, which, with his single arm, kept throwing her off balance. 'Tell me about Sam,' she panted.

'Sam?'

'Ah ... Amigo.'

'*Si, Amigo.* 'Ee ees Amereecano.'

'Yes. Has he lived here long?'

'Oh ... many years.'

'He's retired?'

'Retired?' Julio shrugged, in time to the music. ''E is one of us.'

Melissa wasn't sure whether or not she was any further ahead.

Dancing with Julio left her exhausted, but Salvador was awaiting his turn. She could at least rest on Salvador, because he held her very close, pinned against his large, solid stomach, and hardly moved his feet at all. But she wasn't sure she wanted to rest on Salvador, as his hand kept sliding up and

191

down her back, hovering just above her bottom, before drifting back up to her shoulders. She thought of the cat in the adage so beloved of Shakespeare and Wodehouse, and wondered just what she was going to do if 'I would' got the better of 'I dare not'. 'It's a splendid party,' she suggested.

'Zee night ees young,' he said, nuzzling her neck.

'Yes, but I'm afraid we will soon have to be going.'

He moved his head back, just far enough for their noses to touch. 'Why? Eet ees not yet dark.'

'Well, there's Fred's dinner...'

''E weell eat 'ere. I weell see to eet myself.'

'Oh. Well, I suppose our car has probably been brought back by now...'

'Not so queeck. No, no. You weell stay, for zee eveneeng, Meleessa. You weell 'ave a good time.'

Feeling somewhat crushed, physically and mentally, after being pressed against Salvador for ten minutes, Melissa went in search of David, who was dancing with Encarna. But when Encarna saw his wife waiting for him, she willingly handed him over. 'Wheee!' David commented.

'You're as pissed as a newt.'

'Aren't you?'

'Dave, we have got to get out of here.'

'Why?'

'Well, because we're both tight, and because we're going to get tighter, and because
there are about fifty young men waiting to
get their hands on me, and because Sam
wants to show me his castle.'

'Has he really? A castle?'

'Then there's Fred. He's had a traumatic
afternoon. My God! That's him.' There was a
very loud noise coming from beneath where
she had been sitting. Unfortunately, Fred
had left his tail sticking out, and someone
had trodden on it. The woman was most
apologetic, and Melissa stroked Fred into a
reasonable calm. 'See what I mean?' she
asked David, but David had wandered off to
dance with some other dark-haired beauty.

'Feel like a break?' Sam asked. 'Come'n up
to ma place for a rest.'

'What?'

'Say, you can bring the dawg. We'll introduce him to my girls. They'll be tickled pink.'

His girls! Yet she didn't want to be rude to
this huge, friendly man. She looked for
David, but he was now dancing Spanish
fashion, his hand sliding up and down the
back of his *señorita*, and he wasn't stopping
above the backside, either. Of course, he was
drunk, but that didn't mean he wasn't being
a lecherous bastard. 'Well,' she said.

'Ma car is just over there.'

He set off into the gloom, and Melissa
hesitated a last moment before pulling Fred
to his feet. 'I may need you,' she told him. It

was growing darker by the second, but there was a glare of headlamps on the far side of the square. Melissa and Fred hurried towards it, and found it was an enormous American-made car. 'This is yours?' Melissa was astounded.

Sam pushed his head out of the window. 'Gotta have headroom, see? And leg and shoulder room. And butt room,' he added. 'The dawg can get in the back.'

Melissa pushed Fred into the cavernous interior, and sank into deep leather cushions beside Sam, gazed at a dazzling array of lights and signals. 'What is this thing?'

'Cadillac.'

She secured her belt, watched in horror as he headed for the same narrow street down which Salvador had brought his car, with difficulty; here goes an entire block, she thought. 'Did you buy it in Spain?'

'Nope. Shipped her over,' Sam explained, gradually increasing speed. 'Cheaper.'

Melissa had been sinking lower and lower in her seat, bracing herself against the coming impact and the shattering of glass that would follow. Now she sat up again. The houses were behind them, unscathed. 'Don't you find it a little large, for Spain?'

Sam guffawed. 'Ah guess Spain finds me a little large for it, Lissy.'

Melissa wasn't sure she liked the diminutive, but she was too busy trying to remember how much a Cadillac cost, much less

194

shipping it across the Atlantic; she had put Sam down as an inland beachcomber. She grasped the armrest as the huge car turned left and right up a zigzag road without any diminishing of speed, and decided it was a good thing it was too dark to see what lay on either side of the mountain track – she suspected it was going to be nothing, save a very long drop. She gasped, as the headlights picked out another right-angle bend, beyond which was only blackness. Then to her relief they made another sharp right turn and rumbled across what appeared to be a drawbridge set between two stone towers. 'Good heavens!' she cried. 'It *is* a castle.'

'Yeah, well, if yuh're gonna live in Spain, Ah guess it should be in a castle, right?' Sam opened his door and got out, and came round to open Melissa's.

'Right,' she agreed, stepping out and gazing up at the crenellated walls which surrounded her. Fred, also emerging, appeared dumbfounded, and alarmed, as he was suddenly surrounded by six barking dogs, each approximately twice his size. 'My God! Fred!' Melissa sank to her knees beside Fred, who was trying to get back into the car through the closed door, and threw both arms round him.

'Shaddup!' Sam commanded. The barking stopped. 'Clear off,' Sam said. 'Cain't yuh see we got guests?' The Irish wolfhounds slunk into the darkness. 'A dawg likes to know who's t'boss,' Sam explained. 'A dawg's happy when he knows who's t'boss. Like Fred there. He knows who's t'boss. Actually, three of those are bitches. This here is Jose.' Melissa struggled to her feet while hanging on to Fred's collar. The Spaniard was small and bearded. 'Jose kinda looks after me,' Sam explained. 'He and his whole family. His wife comes in and cleans the place up, and his brother does the garden.' He spoke affectionately in Spanish, and Jose replied, equally affectionately.

Fred, realizing that he was confronted by only a human being, growled. 'Fred!' Melissa admonished.

'He's OK.' Sam chuckled. 'Jose can allus fire off a gun. Yuh-all come inside.'

Melissa glanced at the six wolfhounds, sitting in a row, panting, and staring at Fred. 'It's the safest place to be,' she told him.

The house must have been the keep at one stage, Melissa supposed. By now she was past being surprised at the Persian carpets and the huge fireplace, filled with sizzling logs of wood, or, when they had climbed a short staircase to an inner chamber, by the paintings on the walls. 'I hope these aren't originals?' she ventured.

'Naw. Prints. But they look nice.' He led the way into a smaller room, clearly his office, but there was a roaring fire in the grate and a bar in the corner. 'What're yuh gonna drink?'

'I think I've probably had enough,' Melissa suggested.

'Cain't stop now. The night is young. Heck, it ain't even begun. Hey, Jose, we'll have some of that sangria, but go easy on the vodka, right?'

'*Si, señor*,' Jose agreed, going to the bar and starting to mix.

'He puts vodka in it?' Melissa asked in alarm.

'Sure, Ah know most folks use brandy. But Ah find the vodka mixes real good. Now, Jose, he speaks English real good,' Sam explained. 'But yuh know what these people are like. They don't like to let on. Now, say, sit down.' He indicated a settee against the wall. Fred had taken up a position on the hearthrug in front of the fire and clearly considered he had found what he had been looking for all of his life, especially now he had worked out that the killer wolfhounds weren't being allowed into the house.

Jose placed a tray bearing a jug of sangria and two glasses on the coffee table. 'That's great,' Sam said. 'Now, why don't yuh take the boy and give him some dinner? Don't let the girls interfere.'

'Ah ... I'm sure he's had enough,' Melissa said.

'Oh, let him indulge. We're indulging. It's *fiesta*.'

Jose snapped his fingers and gave a little

whistle. Fred looked up. Jose snapped his fingers again. 'You come.'

Fred looked at his mistress. 'Well,' Melissa said. 'You can go with this kind man. But just a little, mind.'

Fred followed Jose from the room. The door closed, and Melissa suddenly felt very lonely. But she knew she was being paranoid. Sam sat beside her, and poured. 'Here's to yuh, and your husband. And Fred. How're you settling in to Jàvea?'

'How do you know we're in Jàvea?' She sipped the drink and discovered that it was the strongest sangria she had yet tasted. Go easy on the vodka, Sam had said!

'Word gets around.'

'Well, we'd be settling in very well if it wasn't for the odd things that keep happening. Like, our car was stolen again today.'

'Shit! I beg yur pardon, Lissy. Stolen from where?'

'We were in Denia...'

'Yeah,' he agreed. He *does* know a lot about us, Melissa thought. 'Now that's real bad news,' Sam went on.

'Oh, I suppose the police will find it and bring it back. They did the last time.'

'I sure hope so. Say, yuh know what's bothering me? Yuh ain't got a handbag. I thought ladies allus had handbags.'

'They're supposed to. I forgot mine at home.'

'There's a pity. But still, Ah'd like yuh to do

198

me a favour.'

'That would depend on what the favour is.'

'No sweat. When yuh get home, Ah want yuh to have a look in yur handbag.'

Melissa stared at him. 'What can I possibly have in my handbag that would interest you?'

'Well, Ah've been thinking, and I reckon yuh could have something belonging to me in that bag.'

'How on earth can anything belonging to you be in my handbag?'

Sam regarded her for several seconds, then he topped up her glass; she had absent-mindedly been drinking. 'Lissy, honey, Ah'm gonna tell yuh a lil' story. But yuh must promise me not to repeat it to anyone. Anyone, right?'

'Well, all right. But if it's that personal, are you sure you want to tell *me*?'

'Ah reckon yuh need to know. There was this guy, a friend of mine. Well, actually, he was ma boss. A fortnight ago he died, in Toulouse, where he was living.'

'Oh, I am sorry. Was he a good friend?'

'The best. He left me something. Something real valuable. Yuh could call it ma inheritance. So, as it's not convenient for me to leave Spain right now, Ah sent a couple of guys to collect. But a real bastard knew about it and sent his people as well. They got there first, and took ma inheritance.'

'Oh, that sounds dreadful.' Melissa drank some sangria.

'Yuh got it. So ma guys gave chase, and there was some trouble. The other guys got a bit shot up.'

Melissa gulped. 'Did you say shot up?'

'These things happen. Anyway, they got across the border, and even as far south as below Girona, before their auto gave up. Then they were in trouble, as they knew ma people were still behind them. So they ditched their auto, and took the first one they could find.' Melissa slowly put down her glass and sat up. 'Yuh got it,' Sam said again. 'Now, ma guys caught up with them again, and shot them up some more.'

'They killed them,' Melissa said in a low voice.

'They had it coming. The point is, ma boy, who isn't the brightest guy in the world, took the bodies away to search at his leisure. It never occurred to him that they wouldn't have the goods on their persons. When he realized they didn't, he went back, but by then the cops had found the car.'

Melissa gulped some sangria. 'You're a murderer.'

'Don't go gettin' hysterical on me, Lissy. Ah cain't abide hysterical women. Now, Ah thought it most likely those guys had hidden ma inheritance in yur car.'

Melissa licked her lips. 'The police searched the car. And then we searched it, with that nice man Salvador. We didn't find anything. And now, I told you, it's been stolen again.'

'Yeah. But now Ah don't reckon they hid it in the car at all. Ah reckon when they saw trouble coming, they hid it someplace else. Like in something belonging to yuh, figuring the police wouldn't search there. It's just a card, see? Same size as a credit card, same shape and feel. It has some numbers on it, just like a credit card, too. Sort of thing anyone might overlook, in her handbag. Now, yuh tell me, yuh wouldn't have found it already, would yuh? Maybe that's why yuh left yur handbag at home.'

'You're a murderer. I'm not going to help you. I'm...' She stood up, and to her consternation had her arm grasped to pull her back down so violently she sprawled against the back of the settee.

'Yuh're gonna do what?' Sam asked, still speaking quietly, almost genially. 'Go to the police? What're yuh gonna tell them that they'll believe? Yuh show them the card, and they won't have a clue what it is. What they will know is that yuh come out here to a *fiesta*, get drunk, and dream up some fancy story. I'm a respected guy around here, have been for years. Yuh're a newcomer who's already had brushes with the law. Get real, honey chil'. They'll laugh at yuh, if they don't lock yuh up. And then yuh'll have me to reckon with.' Melissa found herself gasping for breath as she gazed at him. 'Ah, cain be real nasty, when people try to fuck me. They tell me yuh got nice legs. Let's have a look.' To her renewed consternation he pushed her skirt up to her thighs. She attempted to sit up and swing her hand but he merely put his hand on her breast and pushed her back again. 'Yuh're not gonna fight me, lil' girl. That'd be a mistake. Yeah. Nice. Yuh wanna make sure they don't get broke.' She gasped as he put his hand on the crotch of her knickers and squeezed. 'This would be even worse. Tell yuh what. When yuh find that card, Ah'll come calling, and yuh and me'll have some fun. Right now, yuh need to do some drinking.' He filled her glass.

Seven

Melissa sat up in bed, thrust both hands into her hair, and hastily lay down again. 'God!' she muttered. 'Oh, God!' She slapped the bedclothes beside her, and found nothing. So she sat up again. 'David? David!' Her voice rose an octave.

There were odd sounds coming from the bathroom. Melissa got out of bed, staggered to and fro, thrust her toes into slippers, and stood in the doorway. David was seated on the floor with both arms and both legs wrapped around the toilet bowl. 'How long have you been there?' she asked, pressing the flush. His body gave a heave rather than shrug. 'Did it really happen?' she asked.

Because her memory became very fuzzy after she had gone up to the castle with Sam, much less after the second jug of sangria. Oh, my God! she thought. The liquid had been literally poured down her throat, while Sam had been indecently assaulting her. Assaulting her! Had he...? She clutched at her pubes, only then realizing that she was naked. It certainly felt sore. But that had to be from that dreadful squeeze he had given her; surely she would know if she had been raped. And that man had confessed to having ordered the killing of two men. And then ... She had to tell David. But he was in no fit state for such a story right now. In any event, would he believe her? Sam had said no one would, and David certainly considered that she had overreacted before.

He was muttering something, but she couldn't catch it. 'I'll mix something up,' she promised, and then thought of Fred. If Sam had done anything to Fred ... 'Fred!' she shouted, and raced along the corridor into the lounge. Fred was there, lying on his side, his tongue lolling. When she came in, he opened one eye, yawned, and went back to sleep. Fred had always hated late nights. Melissa made some black coffee, drank half a cup herself, and went back to the bathroom with the other. David had not moved. 'Drink this,' she suggested.

'Ugh! I'd start throwing up all over again.'

'You have to take something.' She returned to the kitchen, mixed up some sugar and orange juice; she didn't have any glucose. He drank the juice, and she helped him back to bed, where he sprawled on his back, eyes shut, breathing heavily. At least, she presumed he had brought up all of the alcohol, and if that was the only problem, the rest could be left to time. She had to think, to remember, to decide what she was going to do. But her brain was going round and round. She showered, standing for several minutes beneath the flowing cold water, with her face turned up to the jet, then went down to the pool, and swam up and down several times. She wondered if Salvador had got home in one piece? Fred joined her, to sit on the coronation and regard her with reproachful eyes. 'You're all right, Fred,' she pointed out. 'You don't have a hangover.' She heard the sound of engines, and voices. Splashing up the steps, she grabbed a towel and made the house as Alvarez's men began work.

She got dressed, in shorts and a shirt, thrust her toes into sandals, and surveyed David. He was asleep now, his breathing quieter. Obviously he wasn't going anywhere today. But then, was she? She had no transport. She went down to see how the men were getting on. They were doing very well, were already halfway round the property, cementing stakes into the earth with great expertise. Alvarez was there himself, checking things over. He chatted to her in Spanish, and, not understanding a word he was saying, she smiled and replied, '*Si, señor. Si.*' She breakfasted on the *naya* with Fred, looking down the hill, and watched Salvador's car climbing up.

'Salvador!' she shouted from the back door as he parked. 'Am I glad to see you. How do you feel?' Because he looked the same as always.

'Feel? What I should feel?' he inquired, regarding her legs with a thoughtful expression.

'Nothing. It was a long night. What time did it finish?'

He shrugged. 'Feeneesh? Eet no feeneesh. Steell zey fire rockets. You enjoyed see *fuegos artificiales*? 'Ow you say eet, fireworks? Beeg show, *si*?'

Vague images pierced her headache. Fireworks! 'Yes. Magnificent!' she agreed.

'Now, I 'ave come to take you into zee *pueblo, si*?'

'Oh, right. Just let me get a few things together. Come in.' She led him into the house. 'I'm afraid David won't be coming with us. He had rather a lot to drink last night.'

'We all drank a lot. Eet was *fiesta*.'

'Some of us are more susceptible than

205

others.' Melissa left him in the lounge while she went to the bedroom and changed into a respectable pair of pants. Then she picked up her handbag, scribbled a note for David, collected Fred, and got into the car.

Salvador drove down the hill. 'Deed you truly enjoy last night?' he asked, clearly recalling dancing with her.

She wondered if he had any idea who Sam was, how he would react if he knew how she had been threatened and assaulted? The very vague memory of what had happened at the castle made her feel there was something very important about what Sam had told her, but she couldn't remember what. In any event, she decided against telling Salvador right that moment. 'It was great fun.'

Jàvea was crowded. 'Eet ees zee market day,' Salvador said. *'Que lata maldito.'*

Melissa didn't understand the words, but easily identified his tone of voice. 'I thought market day would be good for the town?'

'For zee *pueblo, si.* But zee car park ees zee market place. Ah.' He had spotted an opening on the Ronda Sud, squeezed in, led the way up to the bank, and sat down in an armchair, holding Fred's leash, while Melissa sat in front of one of the desks and introduced herself. 'Mrs Lytton!' The clerk might have spent the entire day just waiting for her to appear. 'We have been expecting you. Your husband...' He looked past her at Salvador.

'He is not my husband,' Melissa said. 'He is a friend.'

'I know this,' the clerk agreed. 'He is Salvador.'

'You mean you know him.'

'Everyone knows Salvador,' the clerk said, enigmatically. 'But you do *have* a husband? Because we have some money for him.'

'And for me, I hope. How much?'

He typed rapidly on his computer. 'Fifteen thousand euros. Approximately ten thousand pounds.'

'Oh, good. Will you open a joint current account?' He typed busily. 'We'll need chequebooks.'

'They will be ready in about a week, Mrs Lytton.'

Melissa considered. What with hiring the original car and stocking up the house, they only had about a hundred of Gerald's five hundred pounds left. Of course, she intended to put the new hire car on her credit card, but still ... 'I'll need a couple of hundred pounds in euros right now.'

'I will see to it. If you would just sign here...'

'And another seven hundred and fifty euros in cash.' He regarded her severely, much like the clerk in Barcelona. 'Oh, don't worry,' she told him. 'I'm not going to walk around with that much in my handbag. It's for Salvador.'

The clerk looked more unhappy yet. 'You

wish to give Salvador seven hundred and fifty euros?'

'I owe it to him.'

The clerk looked from her to Salvador, shrugged, and departed to organize the withdrawal of the money while Melissa signed the various mandates presented to her. 'Eet ees all right?' Salvador asked anxiously, when at last she stood up.

She gave him the bundle of notes. 'You'd better count it.'

'Why I should count eet? I zeenk you are good, Meleessa.' Fred puffed happily.

Salvador drove her to a hire-car firm, and she picked up another car, a Fiesta. 'What you do now?' he asked.

She was again embarrassed, because now she had no further need of him. 'I guess I have to say thank you. I can't really tell you how grateful I am,' she hurried on, as she looked at his expression. 'We both are. We *all* are...' She patted Fred's head. 'For all you've done.'

'Eet was nozzeeng,' Salvador said. 'You are my frien'. Daveed ees my frien'. *Fred* ees my frien'.'

'Look...' She took a long breath and made the decision. 'You and your father and mother must come up to Casa Sagittarius for a meal.'

'You do not 'ave to do zees for us, Meleessa. You are reech Inglesa. We are poor peasants. You do not weesh to 'ave us to deenner.'

'I do. David does. He said so,' she lied desperately. 'Not dinner. Lunch. That's it. Lunch. You come and have lunch with us. When would suit you? Tomorrow?'

'Tomorrow I must go back to zee *trabajo*,' Salvador explained.

'Oh, I'm so sorry,' Melissa said, trying to conceal her relief.

'So we come *Domingo*.'

'Ah ... yes, that would be splendid. Sunday.'

'And Meleessa ... ees possible we bring Beeg Sam?'

'*What?*'

'You no like Beeg Sam? 'E like you very much. 'E say to me thees morning 'ow much 'e like you.'

Melissa drew another deep breath. 'How well do you know him? Big Sam?'

'Well, I no know 'eem. 'E ees very rich, my family ees very poor.' Melissa thought of the house Fred had taken refuge in. Sam had said Julio's house was much grander. But if they considered themselves as poor relative to him ... and he was a self-confessed murderer! 'But 'e ees very good to zee village,' Salvador went on. ''E pay for zee school, and 'e repair zee church...'

Melissa's brain was ticking. Sam had assaulted her and threatened her. She could not remember exactly what he was after, but she was sure he had said he was coming to see her. She didn't know when that would be, but she did want to be rid of him, and see him get his comeuppance. He had said she would get nowhere with the police, and she thought that was probably true. But if she had him in her house, with a sober David and Salvador and his family ... and she could have others. She could have a big lunch party, the Bartons, the Grippenheimers, even that odd woman Dolores. And if in the middle of it she denounced him, well, at least she'd have plenty of protection with gun-toting lunatics like Dolores and Hans about. It was a plan, and she hated being pushed about. 'Well,' she said. 'Of course bring Sam. It'll be fun.'

It was only half past eleven. Melissa put Fred in the back of the car and drove back up Montgo, where Alvarez and his men were still happily pounding in fence poles to the accompaniment of their blaring transistor radio; the noise would surely have awakened the dead. She parked the car, released Fred, went into the house, and gazed at David, who did not appear to have moved; he was snoring. She sat beside him and shook him awake. 'How are you feeling?'

'Bloody awful. God, just leave me alone.'

'It's after eleven.' He rolled over with a grunt. 'I've been to the bank,' she said. 'There are all sorts of things there for you to sign.'

'Oh, do bugger off,' he pleaded. Melissa kept telling herself that she mustn't lose her temper, as she packed Fred back into the car, and drove down the hill, waving cheerily to Alvarez and his people. Presumably all men got blind drunk from time to time, and ill-tempered with it. It was when they started to make a habit of it that they got her goat.

She tried to think – difficult, as her head was still throbbing. Looked at from any angle, their expedition to Spain had so far turned out an unmitigated disaster. And there was no one on whose shoulder she could weep. At home she would have picked up the phone and talked things over with Mary or Jo ... but this was not something she could explain in a long-distance telephone call. As for David, well, when he finally got over his hangover, she would have to put him in the picture, but she had no idea how he was going to react, or even if he would believe her – she had been as drunk as he, even if she seemed to have both a stronger stomach and a stronger head.

She decided to start on her invitations for Sunday, tried the Grippenheimers first, but they were out. So she tried the Bartons. But they also were out. Feeling increasingly dis-gruntled, she drove down to the *puerto*, but Dolores was also out. 'Shit!' she grumbled, and went home. David was still fast asleep. She mixed herself a bloody mary, had a swim with Fred, waved to the workmen, looked at

David, still snoring, scrambled some eggs, and went to bed in the spare room.

She was still suffering from a hangover and lack of sleep herself, and did not surface until David woke her up. 'There's someone at the gate.'

'Eh?' She sat up. 'Are you all right?'

'I'm bloody hungry.'

'I'm sure. Well...' She swung her legs out of bed, and Fred, on the floor beside her, stretched. 'Did you say there was someone at the gate?'

He peered out of the window. 'It's the countess!' He hurried out of the house and down the slope; at least he was wearing pants. 'Good evening, Countess!' His tone was, as always, ingratiating. Melissa wanted to spit. On the other hand ... She dragged on some clothes and went down herself.

'Why, Melissa,' Dolores said. 'You look, well, untidy.' She was, as always, totally chic.

'It happens to all of us,' Melissa said. 'I'm actually glad to see you. I wanted to have a word.'

David looked at her in surprise. But Dolores accepted it as her due. 'Certainly.'

'We're having some people to lunch on Sunday. Would you care to come?'

'That would be very nice.'

'Shall we say twelve? Oh, and I tell you what, bring one of your guns. That magnum. I'm sure our guests would love to see you shoot it.'

Now Dolores did raise her eyebrows. 'If that is what you would like, my dear girl, then of course I will bring a pistol. *Hasta la vista.*' She drove off, while Melissa remembered that she hadn't told them why she had called in the first place.

David was totally bemused. 'I thought you didn't like her?'

'I don't. But I have an idea she may amuse our guests.'

'Guests? What's this about a lunch party? Nobody told me anything about that.'

'You weren't in any shape to be told anything this morning. I tried, and you told me to bugger off.'

'Oh, I am sorry about that, Liss. I felt like death not even warmed up.'

'I understand that, and I forgive you. But we do have a lot to talk about.'

'Right.' He held her hand as they walked up to the house. 'I'll get supper tonight. Like a drink first?'

Melissa realized that it was very nearly dusk: she had lost the entire afternoon. 'Yes, I would,' she said. 'How do you feel?'

'I'm not drinking tonight, if that's what you mean. Scotch or gin?'

'Scotch,' she said, sitting down and then starting up again as the bell jangled. 'David! There's someone else at the gate.'

'I'll just go and see. Come on, Fred. Now you be polite, eh?' Fred bounced up and down enthusiastically.

Melissa followed them on to the *naya*. They were already through the pool door and marching down the drive. She hurried behind them, standing in the doorway to stare into the gathering darkness.

David had reached the gate. 'Who's there?' he demanded.

'It's me, my dear fellow. Hans.'

'Hans?'

'Hans von Grippenheimer. Please, my dear fellow. I must speak with you.'

'Well...' David looked back up the hill at Melissa.

'My dear fellow, this is serious. Terribly serious. I need help.'

'Well, you'd better come in.' David unlocked the gate. 'Do behave, Fred.'

'Ah, Melissa, dear lady,' Grippenheimer said as he came up the drive. 'It is good to see you.'

'Hans seems to have a problem,' David explained.

'Is that a fact? What is it?' Melissa asked, unsympathetically.

To her consternation, Hans burst into tears. 'Caroline has left me,' he wailed.

Eight

'You need a drink,' David said, escorting Grippenheimer up to the house. Melissa supposed she was going to have to be sympathetic, even if she didn't feel it; she didn't approve of December-March marriages, and even less of the Grippenheimers' lifestyle – but he had prevented Fred from being poisoned, and he was an integral part of her plan for Sunday. David showed Grippenheimer into the lounge, sat him down, and gave him a scotch. 'Now,' he invited, 'tell us what this is all about.'

'I told you,' Grippenheimer wailed. He had stopped crying, but was looking thoroughly distraught. 'Caroline has left me.'

'How do you know?'

'She isn't there. And she's taken the car and her clothes. And she's left a note.'

'Do you have it?'

Grippenheimer handed over a crumpled piece of paper.

David studied it. 'This is in German.'

'Well, of course it's in German.'

'I don't read German.'

'It says, "You'll find the car on the front in

Benidorm,"' Grippenheimer translated.

'Did she take the cat?' Melissa asked.

'Yes, dear lady, she took the cat.'

'Then it's serious. Did you have a quarrel or something?'

'I do not think we had a quarrel.'

'You mean you don't know for sure?'

'When one is three times the age of one's wife...'

'Always a mistake.'

'Suppose you tell us exactly what happened?' David asked.

'We were out this morning, lunched at home, then this afternoon Carrie said she was having a hair appointment. She is always having hair appointments. She also wished to take the cat to the vet, she said. So she took the car while I remained at home and had my siesta. I expected her back by six. But she didn't come. And then, a few minutes ago, a taxi arrived, bringing this note. I had to pay him, too.'

'You said she took her clothes,' David said, assuming his Sherlock Holmes expression. 'Does she usually take her clothes to the hairdresser?'

'Or to the vet?' Melissa asked.

'That is the most disturbing thing of all,' Grippenheimer said. 'When I got the note I looked in her closet, and her favourite suitcase and at least half her clothes had gone. She must have packed and put the suitcase in the boot last night, while I was asleep. I often go to bed earlier than she,' he explained.

'But in the same room, surely,' Melissa suggested.

'No, we normally sleep in separate rooms. She says I keep her awake with my snoring. Of course, I know I don't snore.'

'Sounds like a great marriage,' Melissa commented. Perhaps the poor old chap had to exist on voyeurism, she thought.

'She says she's left the car in Benidorm,' David said. 'Then you know where to look. How long is the front in Benidorm?'

'About a kilometre. Finding the car will not be difficult. But Caroline ... Benidorm is a big place.'

'I'm sure you'll find her,' David said confidently. 'I tell you what you do. Stay and have dinner with us –' he carefully avoided Melissa's eye – 'and then have a good night's sleep, and tomorrow you can go down to Benidorm and find her. If she hasn't come back by then.'

'She won't have,' Melissa said with gloomy satisfaction. 'Not if she's taken the cat.'

'You do not understand,' Grippenheimer said. 'I cannot wait until tomorrow. I must find her tonight.'

'Why?'

'Because she's gone off with a man, that's why!' He was shouting.

'Oh, really, old man, do you know that?'

'Of course she's gone off with a man,' Grippenheimer declared. 'Caroline is like that.'

'With the cat?' Melissa asked.

'The man probably likes cats.'

'No man likes cats that much,' Melissa pointed out. 'Three in a bed, great for some ... but they all have to be human beings.'

'Unless you've been married a long time,' David argued.

There was a splintering sound, and from the mixture of blood and whisky dripping on to the carpet, they realized that Grippenheimer had crushed his glass in his hand. 'Oh, my God!' Melissa cried. 'Don't panic! Come with me. I've got some first-aid stuff. Dave, don't let Fred lick that up, will you, there'll be glass in it. He adores blood,' she explained to an apparently dazed Grippenheimer, as she seized his left wrist and led him to the bathroom.

'I must find her,' he muttered. 'Don't you understand? I love her. I adore her! The thought of her with a man ... Ow!'

'TCP,' Melissa explained. 'It's the best. You don't know where that glass has been. Actually, we do. It's been in a box in the back of a removal van, for days. Couldn't be worse.' What in the name of God are we to do? she wondered as she gabbled; this man is on the edge of a breakdown.

'I must find her,' Grippenheimer repeated. 'If I do not find her, I shall kill her.'

'Ah ... yes. Right. I agree. You must find her.' Must be something about the heat, she supposed, that made everyone want to kill

218

everyone else.

He seized her arm. 'You will help me, dear lady. Beautiful lady.'

'Of course we are going to help you, Hans,' she said. 'You have our absolute word.' Though for the life of her she couldn't imagine how. She applied sticking plaster.

'Then we must hurry now, before it is too late.'

'I still think you'd do better to have a good night's sleep,' she said. 'But if you must ... Sure you won't even have a bite of supper?'

'I could not eat a thing. But if you wish to have something, before we leave...'

'Before *we* leave?'

'Dear lady, I have no transport. Caroline has taken the car.'

Melissa gulped. 'David!' Her voice carried a note of warning.

He sighed, and made his way reluctantly along the corridor to investigate the latest problem. 'You'd better explain what you want,' Melissa told Hans. He did so, and David did not look amused. 'What about a taxi?' Melissa asked.

'A taxi? To go looking for my wife?'

'It *would* cost a fortune,' David observed.

'The thing is,' Melissa went on, 'neither David nor I had much sleep last night. We were at a *fiesta*, you see. I don't think we'd be much good to you. As for Fred, he's a walking corpse.'

Grippenheimer's face started to crumple;

219

he looked about to burst into tears all over again. 'Well,' David muttered to Melissa, 'I suppose I have spent almost the entire day in bed.'

'David!' she hissed.

'They helped us,' he hissed back. 'He shot that character.'

'That's what bothers me.'

Carefully examining his cut hand, Grippenheimer pretended not to have heard the exchange. 'I understand,' he said. 'You are very tired. I could not possibly ask you to come out again.'

Melissa sighed in turn. But she knew David was right. 'Of course we'll drive you down to Benidorm, Hans,' she said. 'On one condition.'

'Tell me what this is?'

'That you do not bring your gun.'

He snorted. 'I do not need a gun to deal with that scum.'

Presumably he was not referring to his wife. 'OK, then. Have you a spare set of keys for your car?'

Melissa reckoned, once they found the car, he could be left to get on with it. David of course suggested that she let the two men get on with it, and just go to bed. But she had no intention of allowing David loose amidst the fleshpots and nightspots of Benidorm with a distraught Hans. So she changed into her pants suit, picked up her handbag, they locked up the house, and she and Fred got into the back seat of the Fiesta, Fred's expression revealing clearly what he thought about having two nights out on the trot. 'Do you think it is a good idea to bring the dog?' Grippenheimer asked.

'It might turn out to be a very good idea indeed,' Melissa assured him.

Within minutes of leaving Casa Sagittarius, she was fast asleep, her head on top of Fred's; but then, Fred was fast asleep as well, his head on her shoulder. They both awoke with a start when traffic lights blinked in their faces, and she gathered they were entering the once tiny fishing village which had become Spain's most famous resort. Growth had brought more than mere traffic lights; Benidorm was a glow of hotels and nightclubs and restaurants all advertising themselves as brightly and as noisily as possible. Even the promenade was a kaleidoscope of light, and, at nine o'clock in the evening, a hum of activity as well.

David drove slowly along, while Grippenheimer peered out of the window. 'There!' he announced suddenly.

David braked, and the car behind him blared aggressively. 'I think we need to park,' Melissa suggested. 'There's a space.'

David gave the driver behind him two fingers and pulled into a parking space. He might not have had anything to drink today,

221

but he was still carrying a load of alcoholic aggro from yesterday. Melissa realized that it could be another long night, and then remembered that she also was carrying a load from last night and was also feeling fairly aggressive. She allowed Fred to stand on three legs against a palm tree while David and Grippenheimer went back to look at the BMW. They returned in five minutes. 'Wrong one,' David explained.

'I cannot understand it,' Grippenheimer complained.

'Didn't you look at the number plate?' Melissa inquired.

'I cannot remember the number of my car,' he told her.

'Big deal. I suggest we find someplace to eat. Any place. I'm ravenous. And so is Fred.' Because he hadn't been fed either.

'We must find the car,' Grippenheimer insisted.

'And hope next time it's the right one,' David agreed, pulling out of the parking space and resuming his slow drive. 'What do you think the young couple in that one were saying to us when we left?'

'I do not speak that kind of Spanish,' Grippenheimer said with dignity.

'You mean there were people in the car when you tried to open the door?' Melissa asked.

'A man and a woman, necking,' David explained.

'Then I can translate what they said for you.'

'Really? Are you psychic, dear lady?' Grippenheimer asked.

'Yes. Bugger off,' Melissa told him. 'I mean, that's what they said. In Spanish.'

'I think your wife is unhappy, David,' Grippenheimer remarked.

'Just hungry. Look, there's a nice-looking place.'

'And there's my car!' Grippenheimer shouted.

David braked. 'Are you sure, Hans? This could end in a punch-up.'

'I am certain of it.'

'OK,' Melissa decided. 'Park the car, David, and you, Fred and I will go across the street and start dinner. Join us when you've checked out your car, Hans.' David found a parking space, and before there could be any argument, Melissa and Fred were hurrying across the street and grabbing one of the pavement tables. 'Whee!' she shouted as David joined her. 'It's a Steak House. I will have three T-bone steaks,' she told the waiter. 'Savvy? Understando? *Comprende?*'

'You wanna t'ree steaks? You, lady, wanna t'ree steaks?'

'One for me and two for my dog. And if you do not stop standing on his tail, you will be the first, right?'

The waiter spotted Fred for the first time and hastily retreated round the table; Fred was apparently too exhausted to react. 'Make that four,' David said. 'No, five. May as well order one for Hans. And some red wine.'

'Ow you wanna steaks?'

'Oh ... medium will do.'

The waiter went off. 'Presuming we have found the car,' Melissa said. 'Do you intend to spend the rest of the night on this wild goose chase?'

'I thought we might give him a bit of a hand. Just for a while. We do owe him. And besides, I'm not sure he's fit to be out on his own. I mean, if he catches up with Carrie, and she does have a man in tow, he's likely to kill him.'

'Dave, Hans can't be a day under seventy-five. I would say more.'

'I doubt that has lessened his aggro. He's very fit. Hello, here he comes. And he's smiling!'

'David! Melissa! It is our car.'

'Oh, great. Is the cat in it?'

'No, dear lady. The cat is not in it.'

'Not so great. Sit down and have some dinner. You'll feel better.'

'I do not feel like eating.'

'Well, we do. So if you want any more help from us, you'll just have to sit it out.' The waiter brought the wine, glasses, bread and aioli; Hans immediately started eating. 'Actually,' Melissa said, 'I've had an idea. *Señor*,' she said, as the waiter started to depart again. 'That BMW parked immediately over there. Do you know how long it has been there?'

'Five hours, maybe.'

'You mean you saw it come?'

'I must see eet, *señora*, eef I am 'ere.'

'Absolutely. It was driven by a blonde lady, right?' He goggled at her. 'Yellow hair. Like mine. And she would have had a cat. Miaow. Right?'

'Oh, yes, *señora*.' He looked Melissa up and down, no doubt making a mental comparison. 'Zee lady 'ad zee *gata*, and she was like yours.' Like my what? Melissa wondered, as she had been speaking only of colour; her hair was straight where Carrie's curled.

'That's great stuff, Liss,' David said. '*Señor*, can you tell us where this lady went?'

'She come een 'ere.'

'Here?' Grippenheimer sat bolt upright, looking from left to right.

'She weesh to use zee telephone,' the waiter explained.

'And did she?' Melissa asked.

'Oh, yes, *señora*. Zen she seet at zat table, over zere, and she dreenk a coffee and smoke a cigarette, and zen, maybe feefteen meenutes more, a man come along een 'ees car, and zey drive off togezzer.'

'What sort of man?'

'A young man, *señor*.' Grippenheimer groaned, and drank some wine.

'I mean, was he Spanish?'

The waiter considered. 'I do not zeenk so,

señor. I zeenk 'e was Dutch.'

'What makes you think that?' Melissa asked.

''E was driveeng a car weez a Dutch number plate.'

'Oh, hurrah! You didn't make a note of it, by any chance?'

'Why I should do zat, *señora*?'

'I suppose there was no reason.'

'I go get zee steaks.'

'They'll be burned to a crisp by now,' David commented.

'My Caroline, with some Dutch toy boy,' Grippenheimer groaned. 'Do you know what I am going to do? I am going to cut off his balls and make her eat them.'

'Not before dinner, please,' Melissa protested.

'Anyway, we have to find him first,' David said gloomily. 'They could be anywhere in Spain.'

'I have another idea,' Melissa announced. The waiter returned with the steaks, and Fred sat up, suddenly wide awake. Melissa handed him a T-bone, and he demolished it in a few mighty crunches. The waiter hastily stepped a little further away. 'Señor,' Melissa said. 'Do you have a pay telephone here?'

'No, *señora*.'

'But did not the blonde lady pay for her telephone call?'

'Oh, yes, *señora*. She pay me.'

'Well, then, can you tell us, was it a local

226

call or long distance?'

'Eet was local, *señora*.'

'Well,' she said triumphantly. 'That narrows it down a bit.'

'Do you know how many people live in Benidorm?' David asked. 'Foreigners, I mean?'

'Most of them are English,' Melissa argued.

'But a lot of them are Dutch,' Grippenheimer pointed out.

'You know zees lady?' the waiter asked. 'Zee one weez zee *gata* and zee yellow 'air? Like yours, *señora*,' he added to make sure. 'But weez zee...' he made a rotating movement with his forefinger.

'Curls,' Melissa said. 'Yes. We know this lady. We are trying to find her.'

'I zeenk zees,' the waiter said. 'I tell you...' He paused, hopefully.

'Money,' Melissa muttered. 'Come along, Hans.'

Grippenheimer produced a fistful of bills, reluctantly.

'It's all right,' David assured him. 'We'll pay for the meal.'

'Tell us,' Melissa invited the waiter.

'She go weez Veelhelm.'

'Say that again?'

'He means William,' David explained.

'You mean you know this fellow she went with?' Melissa cried.

'Oh, yes, *señora*. Veelhelm, 'e comes 'ere

often. 'Ee 'as meet zee lady weez zee yellow curls 'ere, often. But before, she no 'ave zee *gata*.'

'The bitch,' Grippenheimer growled. 'Every time she went to have her hair done ... I wondered why it took her a whole afternoon. The bitch! When I catch up...'

'Not now, Hans,' Melissa begged. 'You wouldn't have an address for this character, would you, *señor*? Willhelm?' The waiter looked at the notes on the table. 'They're all yours,' Melissa assured him. 'Cross my heart.'

He looked interested in doing that, but decided against it, in view of the presence of Fred, masticating his second steak noisily, not to mention David and Grippenheimer. So he reached out and pocketed the handful of notes. ''E 'as a cloob.'

'A club? A nightclub?'

'A very bad cloob, *señora*. Zee *policia*, zey speak of closing zees cloob.'

'Drugs, I'll bet,' David said. 'Does Carrie use them, Hans?'

'Well, from time to time. Before she married me, of course.'

'So, will you give us the address of this club, *señor*?' Melissa asked.

'Oh, *si, si, señora*. Eet ees zee Cloob Poorple. You go so...' He gave the directions.

'The Club Purple,' Grippenheimer moaned. 'We must go...'

'No, no, *señor*. Zees cloob, eet does not

228

open unteel eleven o'clock.'

'Eat your steak,' Melissa recommended. 'There's nothing like a lot of protein when the chips are down.'

'But what is my Caroline doing, in an un-opened club?'

'Joining it?' Melissa suggested. 'Oops.'

'Where are the veggies,' David complained. 'Ah!'

Their friendly waiter was returning with a huge platter of fried potatoes. 'What about peas and things?' Melissa asked.

'Pees, *señora*? You wish to pees?'

'Oh, no, you're not going to catch me with that. But I don't have anything green on my plate, save for this piece of lettuce which looks as if it was left behind by Noah. Can't we have some green vegetables?'

The waiter consulted the menu. 'Zere ees green beans weez 'am.'

'Do you think there are more beans than ham?'

'Oh, yes, señora. More beans.'

'Then green beans with ham it shall be.'

'But you already have a steak,' David protested. 'You're going to put ham on top of that?'

'I am going to put green beans on top of the ham,' Melissa said. 'Having inspected the steak, it begins to look like Fred's lucky night.' Fred chomped happily on his third T-bone.

'You sit there, eating and playing with your

229

dog, while my Caroline...' Grippenheimer looked ready to burst into tears again.

'Have some wine,' David suggested, pouring.

They chewed in silence for several minutes. 'How are we going to handle this?' Melissa asked, eyeing the limp, greasy beans which had appeared, infiltrated by a few pieces of chopped ham. 'What I mean is, whatever Carrie is doing, it's what she *wants* to be doing, right this minute.' Grippenheimer blew his nose, loudly. 'It isn't as if she's been kidnapped,' Melissa went on. 'And I assume she's over eighteen.' She conveyed a forkful of beans to her mouth.

'Well,' David said, in that tone of voice she now recognized as meaning he did not have a clue, 'we'll have to play it by ear. Appeal to her better nature.' Melissa was temporarily silent as she drew long green strings out from between her teeth.

They finished eating just before eleven. By then Fred had gone back to sleep. 'Wake up,' Melissa told him, nudging him with her toe. 'We may need you.'

'Now then,' David said importantly, finishing his Poncho. Melissa realized too late that he had abandoned the water wagon. But then, so had she.

Grippenheimer stood up, and commenced to make what appeared to be a speech, although, as it was in German, they didn't

230

know what he was saying. 'I'm sorry about our friend,' Melissa explained to the table next to them – the restaurant was now quite full. 'He's upset. I'm afraid I do not know what he is saying.'

'He is saying,' said a German diner, 'how unlucky he is to be surrounded by fools.'

'Is that what he's calling us? Fools?'

'No,' the German said. 'I am making a free translation.'

'Well!' Melissa said. 'I think...'

David was signalling the waiter. *'La cuenta, por favor.* I think we had better get him out of here. Sit down, Hans, you're making a fool of yourself.' Grippenheimer sat down, heavily.

'I don't think there is anything more we can do tonight,' Melissa declared. 'The club will be full of people. Let's come back in the morning.'

Tears began to trickle down Grippenheimer's face. 'I don't think we can abandon him now,' David said. 'Would you mind settling this, darling? I didn't bring my cards.'

Melissa snorted, opened her handbag, and selected a card. She actually maintained four cards: an American Express, a Diners, a Visa, and a Mastercard, each of which she used for different purposes. The Amex was her travelling card, so this was the one she chose. And then frowned. The waiter took the card ... but she still had four left! Suddenly memory started to stir, of what Sam had said last night. 'You are the only friends I have,'

231

Grippenheimer sniffed, before she could investigate.

'Well, you remember that,' she said severely. There were times, David thought, when she could sound just like her brother.

'OK. Now let's see,' Melissa said, when they had got both Grippenheimer and Fred out of the restaurant – the Germans at the next table had been surreptitiously feeding Fred chips and he had been extremely reluctant to leave. Although she wanted to investigate the card situation, she was resigned to completing Hans's search. 'He said it was a couple of blocks away. First right, and then third left. How many cars are we going to take?'

'We will go in my car,' Grippenheimer announced.

They heaved Fred into the back seat of the BMW, and Melissa sat beside him. Grippenheimer drove in a jerky fashion, but a few minutes after leaving the front they saw a huge blaze of purple ahead of them, and gathered it was a neon sign. There was quite a large car park, presently only half full, and Grippenheimer found a space without difficulty. 'Looks interesting,' David observed, gazing at the poster outside the leather-panelled door, which depicted half-a-dozen topless young women high-kicking.

'Aren't you glad I'm here?' Melissa quipped. 'You ever come here before, Hans?'

'I did not know a place like this existed, in

Benidorm,' Grippenheimer declared.

They reached the door, and a large young man, wearing a lion skin round his waist and apparently nothing else, materialized from the shadows, and addressed them incomprehensibly. 'Try English,' Melissa suggested.

'No dog,' the bouncer explained.

'Haven't you? What bad luck. But *we* have one.'

'I knew it,' David said sadly, remembering. Melissa's weakness for defending Fred, whatever the circumstances. 'This is going to end in a punch-up.'

'No dog,' the bouncer repeated, slightly more aggressively.

'There's no sign,' Melissa argued.

'No dog!' the bouncer said a third time, loudly.

Grippenheimer stepped past Melissa, wrapped two large fists in the bouncer's lion skin, and pulled. The lion skin came away, the bouncer grabbed after it, and Grippenheimer kneed him in the front of his brightly coloured Y-fronts. The bouncer fell to his knees, groaning. 'My God!' Melissa cried. Fred licked Grippenheimer's hand.

'Scum,' Grippenheimer remarked, and opened the door.

David and Melissa hurried in behind him with Fred, leaving the bouncer gasping. The girl behind the desk, in a rather gloomy foyer, was as topless as those on the poster, although somewhat heavily shrouded in

233

bushy black hair. 'Three,' David said, leaning across the counter.

'Twelve euros,' she said, and then leaned across the counter herself, fortunately not exactly opposite David. *'Perro, non.'*

'The chap outside didn't object,' Melissa pointed out. The girl looked puzzled. 'So I suppose it's half price for dogs,' Melissa went on. 'Give the girl fourteen euros, Hans.'

'I gave all my money to that waiter,' Hans reminded her.

'I'll do it,' David produced the money.

'Perro ees no good,' the girl remarked, but she put the extra two euros in her pocket.

'I beg your pardon?' Melissa asked, aggressively.

'Stay cool,' David begged, and parted the curtain. Inside was a typical nightclub scene, with a bar down one side, several tables with adjacent chairs, a stage on which two couples were dancing to a tape, and a cigarette girl-cum-usherette, who could have been the receptionist's twin, only larger. 'This place could grow on me,' David said.

'So *you* stay cool, lover,' Melissa recommended.

The girl led them to a table, quite close to the stage, and then seemed to realize that one of her customers was walking on four legs. *'Perro, non,'* she announced.

'Oh, don't you start,' Melissa told her. 'Look, we have four tickets, right? And there are four of us, right?' She brandished the pieces of cardboard under the girl's nose, and nearly removed a nipple. The girl retreated.

'I have bad vibes about this evening,' David said.

'Nonsense. Just sit down. Fred is going to sit down, quietly, under the table. Aren't you, Fred?' She pushed him out of sight before he could argue.

David also sat down. 'Hans, I have to ask you something. How old are you?'

'I am seventy-nine, dear boy.'

'Good God! Don't you think that's a little old to go round kneeing men in the whatsit? I mean, what are you going to do when he comes in here looking for round two? Am I elected?'

'I do not need anyone to fight my battles,' Grippenheimer announced with guttural dignity.

'So what's your plan?'

'To find Caroline, and take that Dutch toy boy and...'

'David is talking about the bouncer.'

'Oh, him. If he comes back I'll break his arm.'

Melissa gulped, and then nearly jumped out of her pants as she discovered someone standing beside her. 'You wanna dreenk?' the waiter asked.

'Yes,' David said. 'A bottle of red wine. No, make that two, and three glasses.'

'You no wanna champagne?'

'No, we do not want champagne. *Vino*

tinto, right?'

'You no wanna eat?'

'We've had dinner, thank you.'

'You must eat.'

'Bring us some tapas,' Melissa suggested. 'And a bowl of water for the dog.'

The waiter noticed Fred's tail for the first time, and hastily stepped backwards. 'No...'

'Don't say it,' Melissa recommended. 'He's in the mood for tearing legs off people tonight.'

The waiter hurried for the bar. 'Bad vibes,' David groaned.

'Where is my Caroline?' Grippenheimer inquired, loudly. 'We came to this den of iniquity to find Caroline. She must be behind there somewhere.'

'Very probably,' David agreed.

'Well, let us go and get her. And deal with that toy boy.'

'Easy, Hans, easy.' David patted his hand. 'We must do some reconnoitering first.'

'Such as?' Melissa asked.

'Such as sitting here for a while, having a glass of wine, and waiting for something to transpire There we go.' He was watching the stage. The taped music had stopped, and the dancers had returned to their tables. Now there was a blare of sound and a spiel in Spanish, and on to the stage cavorted the chorus to the accompaniment of a piano and drum. True there were only three girls, and none of them was quite in the class of the illustrations outside the door, but they were topless and there was a great deal of movement.

'Caroline, in a place like this...' Grippenheimer moaned.

'David!' Melissa hissed.

'Not now, darling.'

Melissa was looking at the entrance, and watching the bouncer, who had regained his lion skin and been reinforced by another large young man, threading his way through the tables towards them. She sighed. It was too late to do anything now. David was totally lost in the tit show, Grippenheimer was weeping into his wine, and Fred was fast asleep under the table. The bouncer arrived above them. 'You,' he said. 'Out!'

Neither David nor Grippenheimer appeared to have heard him. 'Us?' Melissa inquired, smiling as sweetly as she could. 'We have tickets.'

The bouncer threw two notes on the table. One was a ten euro, the other a two. Both were very crumpled. 'Out,' he repeated. 'Weez zee *perro.*'

David noticed the notes. 'Hello,' he said. 'Have we won the bingo?'

'That's our admission fee being returned,' Melissa explained. 'He wants us to leave.'

David looked up at the bouncer, and then at his friend. 'Ah,' he said. 'Well...'

'You don't think you could take them both on?'

'Perhaps I could, with a little bit of help from my friends, but what about the police, etc, etc?'

'You go,' the bouncer said. 'Or I t'row you.'

Heads were turning from the adjacent tables, although the girls on the stage gallantly kept bouncing away. 'Hans,' Melissa said. 'I'm afraid we have to go.'

'Eh?' Grippenheimer had been sunk in a lachrymose reverie. 'You have found Caroline?'

'No, but these gentlemen have found us.' She collected Fred's leash and stood up. 'Time for home, Fred.'

Grippenheimer also stood up. 'You again,' he sobbed to the bouncer.

'Out, you great geet,' the bouncer said, parading his English, and pointing. This last was a mistake. Grippenheimer simply seized the outstretched limb at wrist and upper arm, brought it down with tremendous and unexpected force, and at the same time brought his own knee up with a similar amount of force. The snap of the bone was so sharp and clear it cut across even the beat of the music.

'Shit!' David commented.

'Oh, my God!' Melissa muttered. *'Hans!'*

'I said what I would do,' Grippenheimer announced.

A woman at the next table screamed. The music stopped, and the girls ran for the stage exit. The bouncer had kept on going down, to his knees, and was making inarticulate moaning sounds. His friend was running for the curtain, parting it, and disappearing. The cigarette girl joined in the screaming, at the same time jumping up and down, both breasts and the contents of her tray flying. Fred woke up and started to bark. The lights went off. The chorus of screams and shouts grew louder. 'We have to get out of here,' Melissa said. 'Fast.'

She pulled on Fred's leash, and Fred lumbered after her, from the noise of scraping wood and shattering glasses and bottles, bringing the table with him. 'We must find Caroline,' Grippenheimer announced, out of the gloom.

'The hell with Caroline. This is going to be a riot.' She pushed bodies to and fro, but was brought to a halt by Fred's efforts to disentangle himself from the table; his leash had wrapped itself round one of the legs. But perhaps this was fortunate. People surged around her, all trying to reach the exits, and by the time Fred was free she was comparatively isolated. 'David!' she called. 'David!'

'Where are you?' He had managed to get in front of her while she was wrestling with Fred's table.

'Here. Where are you?'

He grasped her arm. 'Are you there, Hans?'

'Scum,' Grippenheimer remarked.

'Here's the curtain,' David said. 'Here's the ... Oh, shit!' From outside there came the wail of a police siren.

'Caroline will be the other way,' Grippen-heimer said.

'I think he has a point,' Melissa said. 'There must be a back way out of here.' They stumbled back through the debris of scattered tables and chairs, broken plates and glasses, in the direction of the dim glow which was the stage. From their left there came a high-pitched screaming. 'Really, Hans, to break that fellow's arm,' Melissa said. 'I mean, people just don't do that sort of thing in polite society.'

'I always do what I say I am going to do,' Grippenheimer declared.

'Boy, have I got bad vibes,' David complained.

'Look on the bright side,' Melissa pointed out. 'At least he's on our team.'

They reached the shallow steps leading up to the stage, went up, and through the opening to their right. Here the lights were still on, and they blinked for a few seconds, while there was another burst of screams, and the chorus pushed past them in a great hurry to get out. The noise at the front of the club was now enormous, with people, presumably the police, asking questions at the tops of their voices. Then the door behind them opened again. 'You,' said the newcomer, a hand-some, well-built fellow wearing only a dressing gown, who had obviously been taking a

240

recce out front. 'You come here, with that goddamned dog, breaking up my joint...'

'Don't you like dogs?' Melissa asked, prepared to take offence.

'You must be William,' David said.

'Villhelm,' Grippenheimer said with great satisfaction.

'David Lytton,' David said, holding out his hand. 'There appears to be a spot of bother, but I am sure it is nothing we cannot settle like gentlemen.'

William ignored the proffered hand. 'I am going to bust your ass,' he declared.

'You don't seem to understand,' David said. 'This is Mr Hans Grippenheimer, who thinks you have run off with his wife.'

'Von Grippenheimer,' Grippenheimer corrected.

William looked at Grippenheimer. 'You, are Carrie's old man?'

'Where is she?' Grippenheimer inquired, quietly.

'Old is the word, eh, man? Well, let me tell you something, *old* man. Carrie's through with you. So I am going to bust your ass as well.'

'Oh, please don't do that,' Melissa said. 'I'm sure Mr Grippenheimer wouldn't like it, and he has this habit—'

'And you,' William informed her, 'I am going to kick the teeth out of that bleeding dog.'

'I say, your English is awfully good,' David

commented.

But Melissa had had enough of these people insulting Fred, and she had also drunk several glasses of red wine on top of her hangover... She slipped the leash. 'Get him, Fred!' she said. 'Kill!'

Fred seemed surprised, but William precipitated matters by actually aiming a kick at him. Fred hated being kicked. The only person who had ever tried it had been a postman and Melissa had had to pay for a new pair of blue serge trousers and his medical expenses. Now Fred easily avoided the swinging foot and sank his teeth into what he thought might be William's trousers. But William wasn't wearing trousers, and Fred got his ankle instead. William let out a howl of pain, which ended abruptly, because Grippenheimer had hit him. Again there was that terrible clicking sound, and William disappeared sideways. 'We have got to get out of here,' Melissa repeated. 'Do let go of that foot, Fred. Is he dead?'

'Well, I think his jaw is broken,' David observed, bending for a closer look. 'He needs a doctor.'

'So does his friend out front,' Melissa pointed out. 'I think the next time we take Hans anywhere, we should hire an ambulance first.'

'I need some more of your TCP.' Grippenheimer showed them his cut knuckles. 'But first, we must find Caroline.'

Neither Melissa nor David felt like arguing with him, but the noise at the front of the club was growing louder, and coming closer. They hurried along the corridor, and opened another door, which gave access to a bedroom. And there was Caroline, lying on the bed, and wearing very little lipstick. 'Hans!' she screamed, sitting up and seeking a non-existent sheet.

'Now, Hans, please behave,' Melissa said. 'Don't you have any clothes, Carrie?'

'Clothes?' Carrie asked, vaguely.

Melissa realized she was high. She looked around and saw a heap of discarded female clothing on the far side of the room. 'Get dressed, and hurry, or we are all going to wind up in the calaboose.'

'Woof,' Fred recommended, now thoroughly awake, and possibly disturbed at the thought of prison.

'Do be quiet, Fred,' Melissa recommended. 'We don't want anyone to know we're here. Oh, my God!'

She had forgotten about Antoinette, who had been asleep on another chair. The arrival of several human beings she had merely regarded as an irritation. The presence of a dog she already disliked was too much, however. 'Hissssss,' she remarked, leaping for her mistress's naked bosom.

'Aaagh!' Carrie screamed; Antoinette had her claws out.

'Woof!' Fred bellowed, retreating behind

the chair. 'Woor-a-woor-a-woor-a-woof!'

'Fred! Stop that!' Melissa grabbed at his collar and fell over.

'Antoinette,' Carrie remonstrated. 'You have scratched my boobs. You are a naughty pussy!'

'Is there a back way out of here?' David asked, concentrating.

'There's the window,' Melissa said, having got Fred under control, and opened it. 'Biff the light.'

David switched off the light, which brought a protest from Carrie, who was wrestling with her clothes and the cat. 'And where's Willhelm?' she wanted to know.

'Resting,' Melissa assured her.

'If you've hurt him...'

'I should have broken his neck,' Grippenheimer growled.

'Do you still have the cat basket?' Melissa asked. 'For God's sake shove her in.'

From the miaows of protest, Carrie was obeying. 'Come on.' David climbed through the window and dropped to the ground, which could only have been a few feet below the sill, as his head was still visible. 'We're OK. Everyone's round the front. Pass me the dog.'

'Pass you ... Fred weighs ninety pounds,' Melissa protested. 'At least!'

'Let me.' Grippenheimer stepped past her, put both arms round Fred's waist, and lifted. Fred grunted in consternation, nothing like this had ever happened to him in his adult life, but before he could make up his mind whether to lick Grippenheimer's face or bite his hand, he had been transferred to David's arms, and went down somewhat quicker than he had gone up.

'Oof!' he commented, echoing David.

'You go next,' Grippenheimer told Melissa. 'I will pass Caroline down to you.'

'Don't you touch me,' Carrie said. 'Don't you...'

'Try not to break anything,' Melissa begged, and got one leg through the window. She sat on the sill, surveyed the ground, and Fred, and David, who was sitting in a flower bed, Fred still on his lap. A moment later she was beside them, to discover they were round the corner of the building from the car park, and that most of the racket was now coming from inside, behind them.

'Take the cat,' Grippenheimer said, and threw the basket. David, having just got rid of Fred, caught it.

'You bastard,' Carrie bawled, as they discovered the true meaning of the word caterwauling. 'You could have killed her. Don't you touch me!' she screamed. 'Don't you...' She came through the window in a flurry of arms and legs. Both David and Melissa moved to catch her, David dropping the cat basket to the accompaniment of more hisses from the outraged Antoinette, and also became a flurry of arms and legs, which

245

ended with all three of them falling over Fred.

'Oof!' Fred remarked again.

Grippenheimer joined them, having now clearly taken command. 'We will walk round the corner in a totally orderly fashion,' he announced, 'and get into the car.'

'Suppose someone recognizes us?' David asked.

'Who is likely to do that, in the dark? Come along, Caroline.'

He set off, holding Caroline's arm. David looked at Melissa, who shrugged, and found Fred's leash. David picked up the cat basket, and they followed the Grippenheimers round the building. An ambulance waited outside the entrance to the club, and people were milling about, but no one paid any attention to the four people and the dog getting into the BMW. 'Well,' Melissa said as they drove out of the car park. 'That was quite an adventure.'

'Where are you taking me?' Carrie inquired.

'Home,' Grippenheimer announced. 'To bed.'

None of them awoke until the arrival of Alvarez's men at half past seven, and even then the clanking of the truck and the thuds of the various gear being offloaded only slowly penetrated their consciousnesses; it was not until the transistor radio began to

246

blare that Melissa really registered where she was. Several minutes passed before she recalled the events of the previous night. From the lounge, Fred was giving his gentle, 'I need to lift my leg,' bark, so she let him out, had a shower, and was contemplating breakfast when she heard a more definite 'woof', and went on to the *naya* to see Carrie entering the pool gate and crossing the coronation towards the front steps. 'Hello,' Melissa said, as enthusiastically as she could. But she was curious.

Carrie looked her usual glamorous and immaculate self, and her very short shorts had brought work on the fence to a standstill. And as far as Melissa could make out, all her limbs were intact and she was not walking as though any ribs were broken – Melissa did not doubt that Hans could accomplish that with a flick of his seventy-nine-year-old finger. 'Hello,' Carrie said, in a somewhat subdued voice, as she came up the steps.

'Coffee?'

'That would be very nice.' Carrie sat down and looked at the view, until Melissa returned with a tray. 'I wish to thank you,' she then said. Melissa had no idea what to reply to that. 'I ... I suppose you think I was very foolish,' Carrie went on.

'Oh, no. I mean, I don't know. No one ever does know, do they, about what actually goes on in someone else's bedroom. Or bed.' She searched her brain for something to follow, and remembered. 'Oh, by the way, we're having a few people to lunch on Sunday. Would you and Hans care to come?'

'That's very nice of you,' Carrie said. 'Of course we should.'

'Well, shall we say twelve thirty for one?'

'I shall make a note of that in my diary.' Carrie finished her coffee. 'But I am sure we will see you again before then.' She stood up. 'I must get back for my morning swim. Hans does like to watch my morning swim. Would you like to come?'

'I think I had better see about getting Dave up,' Melissa said firmly, and escorted Carrie to the steps, accompanying her down. She had just remembered that David was not yet in the picture, and he had to be, just as quickly as possible. 'But give Hans my love.'

'Oh, I shall. And again, I can't thank you too much for all you have done. And David, of course.'

'It was our pleasure,' Melissa assured her.

Carrie threw her arms round Melissa's neck and kissed her on both cheeks. 'I shall not forget,' she said.

Melissa accompanied her to the pool door, opened it, and stared at Fred, who was lying in one of the flower beds just inside the gate, on his back, tongue lolling. It was a most unFred-like pose. 'Fred?' she called. 'Whatever are you doing? Fred?' Her voice had risen an octave, because instead of getting up, Fred had moved convulsively, at the same time gasping for breath in a disturbing fashion. 'Fred!' Melissa ran forward, Carrie at her heels, and the two women arrived above the dog at the same time.

Fred rolled his eyes, tried to get up, fell over, and was seized by another convulsion. 'That dog has been poisoned,' Carrie said.

Nine

'Poisoned?' Melissa shrieked, and dropped to her knees beside Fred. Her shout penetrated even the din of the transistor radio, which was promptly switched off as the workmen abandoned their tools and ran to see what was happening. 'Fred!' Melissa cried, attempting to lift the dog. 'Fred! Oh, my God, Fred! Please! Carrie ... do something.'

'I know nothing about dogs,' Carrie confessed. 'I have only ever had cats.'

'But poisoned! How...' One of the workmen held up a half-eaten piece of very high meat, which had apparently been thrust through the gate at some time during the night, and which Fred must have found while rooting around the garden after welcoming Carrie. 'Oh, my God,' Melissa moaned. 'Oh, my God! What are we to do?'

'*El perro finito*,' the workman said, drawing the side of his hand across his hairy throat.

'No! He can't die. Carrie...'

'I'll fetch David,' Carrie decided, and ran up the drive to the house.

It occurred to Melissa that it might be better to fetch Hans. But not even Hans' phenomenal strength was going to save Fred. 'Fred,' she moaned, tears pouring down her face. 'Oh, Fred, my darling Fred.' She stroked his brow, bent to touch his ear with her lips and whisper, 'Please don't die! Fred, don't die, Fred.'

Vaguely she heard the noise of a car engine, became aware of the shuffling of feet amongst the Spanish workmen, all of whom were now standing around. They parted to allow a huge form into their midst. 'What the hell...?'

'Sam!' Melissa screamed. 'Oh, my God! You bastard!'

Sam ignored the comment, knelt beside her. 'What's the matter with the lil' fella?'

Despite considering fetching one of the workmen's pickaxes to hit him with, Melissa responded to the solicitude in his voice. 'He's been poisoned.'

'When?'

'It could only have been a few minutes ago. Oh, Sam...'

'*Si, si*,' said one of the workmen, and broke into voluble Spanish.

Which Sam apparently understood. There was a quick exchange. 'Right,' Sam said. 'Get up to the house,' he told Melissa, 'and mix up a strong emetic. Salt, mustard, and water. Do it.' Melissa scrambled to her feet and ran up the drive, up the *naya* steps, and into the house. She only half heard the voice from the bedroom, where Carrie was apparently disturbing David. What an awakening, for a man who slept naked and had obviously had lascivious thoughts about the blonde bombshell, who would no doubt be sitting on the edge of his bed, holding at least his hand. So what the hell? Right now, Fred's life was far more important.

She filled a jug with water, mixed in salt and mustard, and ran for the stairs again. When she got back, Sam had forced Fred's jaws apart and had his hand inside, his finger poked down Fred's throat. As Melissa watched in horror, expecting him to lose at least the finger, Fred started to vomit. Sam withdrew his hand. 'Good boy,' he said. 'Good boy. Yuh got that emetic? Come along, boy, come along.' He held Fred's head as Fred tried to sit up, forced the jaws open again, and poured some of the liquid on to the back of his throat. Fred swallowed before he realized what was happening, and Sam hastily poured more liquid in. Fred gave a convulsive heave, and a kind of groan, and vomited again. 'We have to get him to the vet,' Sam said. 'Open the back door of ma car.'

It was the same huge American thing he had driven two nights previously. Melissa opened the back door, assisted by the eager workforce, and Sam, lifting Fred as easily as if he had been a puppy, laid him on a rug. 'He's still vomiting,' Melissa said apologetically. 'All over your upholstery.'

'Fuck that. Yuh get in beside him and hold his head. Keep him awake. Keep him moving.'

Melissa got in and lifted Fred's head. Fred's eyes rolled and then shut. 'Oh, no you don't,' she said, and ruffled him awake again. Sam was behind the wheel and driving down the hill, far too fast for the narrow lanes, but Melissa wasn't complaining. They reached the Jesus Pobre road and turned left, for Jàvea. 'Where are we going?' she asked, still keeping Fred awake by constantly tickling him or ruffling his hair. Fred was making the most dreadful groaning noises, but at least he was making noises.

'To the vet in Arenal. He looks after ma dogs. Ah reckon he's pretty good.'

'He doesn't like Fred.'

'Really? Ah'm sure he'll like him today.'

'But you...'

'Ah told yuh Ah'd be dropping by. Listen, save it till we fix the boy.'

'What's it to you whether he lives or dies?'

'He's a dawg, right? Dawgs are what Ah like, a whole lot more'n humans.'

'When I find out who did this...'

'Well, Ah got some ideas about that. But it'll keep till we fix the boy.'

In Sam's company, Melissa suddenly became the most welcome client at the vet's, and Fred was immediately carried into the surgery and laid on the table. Sam explained what had happened, and the vet peered into Sam's mouth, muttering. 'Is he going to be all right?' Melissa asked, hardly able to keep still.

'I must pump 'ees stomach,' the vet said. 'Zen we see. You wait outside.'

Sam escorted her into the waiting room, where there was the usual odd assortment of people and animals. 'Oh, Sam...' Melissa was feeling limp and had difficulty controlling the urge to drop her head on to the big shoulder beside her and have a good blub, even if he was a loathsome creature.

'He's gonna be all right,' Sam promised. 'A great big toughie like Fred? Sure he's gonna be all right. Listen, yuh guys play ball with me, and I'll see nothing like this happens again.'

'I told you, we don't have your bloody card...' Then she stopped short. That extra card with her own. So much had happened since she had first noticed it, she had not had the time to examine it; she had, in fact, forgotten all about it until this moment.

'Yuh were saying, honey?'

253

'Oh...' The surgery door was opening.

'*Señora?*' The girl assistant was beckoning.

Sam held Melissa's arm as they entered the surgery, which was full of unpleasantly excretory smells; another assistant, male, was mopping up the floor. Fred still lay on the table, eyes half open, tongue lolling. He gave no sign of being aware that Melissa was in the room. 'Oh, my God! He's not dead?'

'No, no, *señora*. But I 'ad to geeve 'eem a sedative, you understand. Now, I 'ave pumped out 'ees stomach, and I zeenk zere ees no bad matter steell in zere.'

'What was it, Miguel?' Sam inquired.

Miguel was happier speaking Spanish. 'Tell me,' Melissa begged.

'Strychnine.'

'Strychnine? God...'

'We got it in time. He's gonna be all right. But Miguel feels he should stay here for twenty-four hours, just so's he can make sure there are no complications.'

'Yes,' Melissa said. 'Oh, yes. You're sure—'

'I am sure, *señora*,' Miguel assured her.

'When can I see him again?'

'Tomorrow morning you fetch heem.'

'Oh, yes. Thank you.' Melissa began to cry again. 'Oh, Fred!'

Sam put his arm round her shoulders, and helped her from the surgery. 'He's gonna be all right,' he said again. 'Yuh gotta believe that.' He escorted her out to the Cadillac. 'Say, d'yuh mind if we pick up a paper?'

'I wouldn't mind picking up a sandwich, as well.'

'Will do.' He parked the car and installed her in front of a bar/restaurant overlooking the beach, ordered them both coffee and *bocadillos*, and left her looking at the calm Mediterranean while he went across to the news-stand and returned with the local paper before she had the time to work out what might be going to happen next, and what she was going to do about it. He might be a cold-blooded murderer who had indecently assaulted her – but he had undoubtedly saved Fred's life.

'Anything of interest?' she asked.

'Here, read for yurself.'

'I'm afraid I don't read Spanish.'

'This is an English-language newspaper. Seems like all kinds of exciting things were happening down in Benidorm last night.'

Melissa gagged as a piece of bread slipped down the wrong way. When she had recovered, and drunk some coffee, she took the paper. RIOT AT BENIDORM NITE SPOT. PURPLE CLUB WRECKED. TWO PEOPLE TAKEN TO HOSPITAL WITH BROKEN BONES. There was a lot more, and then the item which made her day:

The police are anxious to interview three people who were at the club last night, but who disappeared in the middle of the fracas. These were an elderly man, a middle-aged man and a

255

woman. They were accompanied by a large, very fierce, yellow dog. Anyone knowing of the where-abouts of these people is asked to contact the Benidorm police.

'Well, really,' Melissa said without thinking. 'Middle-aged?'

'Ah wouldn't describe Fred as yeller, either. But Ah guess it was dark.'

'What makes you think we had anything to do with it? You know Fred's not fierce. Or us, for that matter.'

Sam grinned. 'Nothing at all. Save that Ah agree, to describe yuh as middle-aged shows the reporter musta been blind.' He chuckled at her confusion. 'Don't trash me, huh? Say, that husband of yours is quite a guy.'

'What makes you say that?'

'Well, two guys taken to hospital with broken bones...'

'I'm afraid that wasn't Dave. Not that he's a pacifist, you understand. It's just that it takes a hell of a lot to get him sufficiently worked up actually to hit someone.'

'Is that a fact? Yuh know, Ah'm not sure Spain is really big enough for yuh guys. Now, let's talk.'

There were people all around them, and even a taxi rank across the way. 'We have nothing to talk about, right this minute, Mr Guichard. Salvador and his family are coming to lunch on Sunday, and I told him he can bring you. We can talk then.'

'Yuh really think you can mess me about?'

'I do not like being messed about myself. You had me at a disadvantage the other night, and you took me by surprise. It won't happen again. Believe me, I am eternally grateful to you for helping me with Fred, but I'm not going to forget that you are a self-confessed murderer as well as a lecherous bastard. I'll see you on Sunday.' And before he could recover from the surprise attack, she had left the table and crossed the street to the first taxi. 'Montgo,' she said, sinking back on the cushions, heart pounding at her own temerity.

The transistor was blaring, and the workmen gave her a wave as she went up to the house. David was waiting on the *naya*, fully dressed, and alone. 'Oh, Liss,' he said. 'Is he—?'

'He's going to be all right. Thanks to Sam.'

'He's quite a fellow.' He took her in his arms, held her close. 'I'm so terribly sorry.'

She turned up her face. 'We have a lot to talk about. We don't seem to have had much time to communicate recently.'

'Well, sit down and I'll fetch you a brandy.'

'Thanks, but no thanks.'

'You don't mind if I have one?'

'Now why on earth should I?'

He went inside and poured himself one. 'I have the impression you've been feeling I've been knocking back a bit too much recently.'

'Haven't you?'

He sat beside her. 'Yes.'

Waves of relief seeped through her mind. 'What did you do with Carrie?'

'Not a lot. She seemed quite keen on getting back to Hans, and I had Fred on my mind. That dog means as much to me as he does to you, you know.'

'Oh, Dave, that makes me so happy. Now just take a deep breath and listen.' She told him about Monday night.

He listened in silence, then remarked, 'Would you believe that I thought I was coming to Spain to enjoy a peaceful old age? You're quite sure—?'

'I am not making it up.'

'What are we going to do? We don't even know what he's really after.'

'I think we do.' She opened her handbag, took out her credit cards. 'I have four of these, right?'

'If you say so.'

'So here's number five.'

He took the card and turned it over, slowly. 'That's odd. There are only three sets of numbers, and each set is three instead of four. Seven-eight-three dash four-two-one dash eight-seven-six. This is a combination.'

'Right.'

'To what?'

'It must be to something pretty valuable, at least in Sam's opinion.'

'Well, let's give it to him and get him off our back.'

'Just like that? He's had at least two people killed to get hold of that card.'

'And we could be next on his list.'

'Just let him try.' She told him her plan.

'Holy smoke! And you reckon...'

'We'll have Salvador and his gun-toting daddy, Hans and his arm-breaking hobby, Dolores and her gun ... come to think of it, I'll ask Hans to bring his gun as well. And I'm going to invite the Bartons. These are all friends of ours. Sam is going to find himself surrounded and outgunned. And out-witnessed.'

'You think he'll give himself away?'

'Yes. When I flash this card at him.'

'You're quite a girl.' But immediately his mind turned to what to him was as important as anything. 'What were you thinking of serving?'

'Well ... I thought you might be interested in handling that.'

'Oh, yes?' He sighed and stood up. 'Time for another brandy, I think.'

'You remember those delicious curry lunches you used to have at the Pantry on Sunday mornings? Eat as much as you liked for ten pounds? You were always packed to the door.'

'With layabouts who couldn't afford a decent meal.' He returned with his glass to sit beside her. 'I may also remind you that at the Pantry I had a staff of sixteen.'

'I'd help, of course.'

He brooded, then grinned. 'It'll be the best curry lunch anyone in this neck of the woods has ever seen.'

She kissed him. 'And the most exciting.'

Casa Sagittarius just wasn't the same without Fred. Melissa could hardly wait for the next morning, when she could bring him home. ''E mus' be *muy tranquilo durante* ... ah, t'ree days,' Miguel told her.

'*Si, si*, definitely,' Melissa assured him. 'I hope you have learned enough never to eat raw meat again,' she told Fred severely as they drove home. 'Or anything offered you by a stranger.'

David had obviously done some thinking. 'I think I'm going to follow fashion and buy us a gun,' he told Melissa at lunch.

'Ah. Well ... perhaps it might be an idea. You also have to order the food for the lunch.'

He nodded. 'I'll do that this afternoon. When I get the gun.'

'I love it when you take command,' she told him.

As Fred was happy to spend the afternoon sleeping, Melissa walked down to the Grippenheimers', and predictably found Carrie swimming and Hans sitting by the pool, both in the altogether. They seemed perfectly contented with each other. 'Melissa!' Carrie cried, scrambling out of the water, golden blonde from the top of her head to the tips of her toes. 'How's Fred?'

'Resting. But he's coming along quite well.'

'When you find out who did it,' Grippen-heimer said, 'you bring him to me.'

'Do you know, I might just do that,' Melissa said. If we haven't shot him first, she thought. The idea grew on her every time she looked at Fred.

'Coming in?' Carrie dived back into the water.

'I can only stay a moment, thanks all the same. I just wondered if you'd seen yester-day's *Costa Blanca News*?'

'Oh...' Carrie had surfaced again on the far side of the pool, laughing. 'They said you were middle-aged.'

'An insult,' Grippenheimer growled.

Melissa began to worry about the future of the editor. 'I don't mind, really. It's just that, well ... there haven't been any repercussions, have there?'

'They'll never connect it with us,' Carrie said confidently.

'Not with those descriptions,' Grippen-heimer added.

'I hope you're right,' Melissa said. 'Well ... see you on Sunday.'

David had not yet returned, but to Melissa's pleasure, the Bartons dropped by just after four, in the midst of walking Corky. By now the fence was complete, and the property was secure, at least from sheep. Alvarez's men were still in evidence, but they had moved into the apartment, from whence the sound of their transistor radio blared forth to the accompaniment of much banging and crashing. Thus when the bell rang, as the remote control hadn't been connected yet, Melissa had to go down and open the gate for her visitors. 'My dear Melissa,' Lucy cried, embracing her, and looking past her at Fred, who had dutifully got up to accompany his mistress, slowly. 'We only just heard!'

'He's just about all right again now,' Melissa told them.

They both patted Fred, who was, as ever, intrigued by Corky.

'Who do you think could have done such a thing?' Lucy asked.

'I have no idea. But I can tell you this: if anyone tries it again, David is going to blow them apart.'

'You mean you're armed?' Barton was concerned.

'As of now, yes,' Melissa said, hoping she was right. But she could tell the Bartons weren't entirely sure this would be a sound policy, so she added. 'Come up and have a cup of tea. Or a beer. Or a brandy.' She was getting into Spanish habits.

'Love to, but we must press on,' Barton said.

'Well, listen ... We'd like you to come to

lunch on Sunday.'

'That's very kind of you,' Lucy began, a trifle hesitantly.

'Curry. David's doing it,' Melissa said.

'Oh. Well, in that case...' She glanced at her husband.

'We'd love to come,' Barton said.

Melissa couldn't make up her mind whether her own cooking had been insulted or not. She closed the gate when they left, and had a dip – wearing a suit, as the workmen kept looking out of the guest apartment doorway – and was sprawled on a daybed taking the evening sun and enjoying the quiet, the workmen having just departed, when David arrived home at half past five, smelling of brandy; but she couldn't possibly criticize, in view of her performance last week. 'You must have had a good afternoon,' she suggested.

'You could say that. I've bought the spices and ordered the meat for Sunday. We'll pick it up tomorrow, together with the prawns.'

'Right. We'll make tomorrow a big shop, so I can get all the bits. I'm going to make a raita. And we'll need bags of rice. Well, that sounds quite successful.'

'Then I found someone at the *ayuntamiento* who speaks a reasonable amount of English, and she took down my particulars...'

'Must have been fun.'

'And then said that it would take probably a month for a gun licence to be issued.'

263

'Oh, big deal. How are we supposed to defend Fred in the meantime?'

'Actually, my middle-aged darling, for the past couple of years we have managed quite well without arms at all.' Melissa threw a cushion at him. 'However,' David went on, 'she *then* said that if the rabbits were being a nuisance, as we had applied for the licence, and being bona fide residents – there are an awful lot of people who aren't, you know – with all of our fiscal numbers and what-have-yous, there was no reason why we should not go ahead and purchase the gun.'

'You're not serious?'

'Very much so. In Spain, it seems, having applied for something is the same thing as having got it, however many light years you may be away from receiving your licence, except in the case of such things as telephones, which depend on other people. But where you depend on yourself...'

'Dave!' she shouted. 'Show me!' Fred managed his first bark in two days.

'It had to be a shotgun of course. They won't licence a handgun without a big investigation. But if we are being plagued by rabbits, as I told her we are...' David led them both out to the car and opened the boot, where there lay the most splendid gun case. 'Voila!' He opened it and took out the shiny piece of metal and highly polished wood.

'That's a shotgun?' Melissa inquired.

'In Spain, apparently yes. In England I think it would be called a riot gun, and would be illegal for non-policemen. The barrel is a couple of inches too short. You'll see it is single-barrel, pump-action, seven cartridges in the magazine ... did you know you can get two kinds of cartridges?'

'Can you?' Melissa came from a gunless family; her father and brother had not even shot birds.

'Oh, indeed. You can get the ordinary twelve-bore scatter shot, such as we have here...' He opened one of the boxes of cartridges.

Melissa peered at them. 'They look positively lethal.'

'Well, they're meant to be. But only if you're standing fairly close. But you can also get solid shot. What they call deer shot in the States. Like these.'

Another box was opened, and Melissa gazed at the steel projectiles. 'What do we shoot with those?'

'Well, deer. You have to have a special licence to do that, of course, but when I told the gunsmith that I had applied for one, he was perfectly happy to give me the slugs.'

'There are no deer on Montgo.'

'True, but that's not a problem. Do you know this gun has an effective range of seven hundred yards? Of course, the buckshot would have scattered out of sight by then, but the deer shot would go through the side

265

of a car at that range.'

'Good lord!' She looked into the boot. 'How many do you have?'

'Ten boxes, five of scatter, five of solid. There are twenty-five in each box.'

'Twenty-five?' she shouted. 'Two hundred and fifty rounds of ammunition? What are you planning to do, start a war?'

'Better to have too many than to have too few,' he argued. 'Anyway, we need to practise. You need to, at any rate.'

'Me?'

'Suppose I'm not here, and someone tries to poison Fred again?'

'I'll blow the ass off them,' Melissa said. 'What about the shovel?'

'Eh?'

'To bury the body with.'

'Ha ha. Now, I thought we'd do some practising. You take the gun, I'll bring the cartridges.'

'It's not loaded, is it?' she asked, as she very carefully lifted the gun case from the floor of the boot; it was very heavy.

'No, it's not. And if you'll look closely, you'll see it has a safety catch in any event, which is presently on. I'll show you how to work it. Now then, I am going to climb up the hill with this cardboard box, and we'll shoot at it.'

'Up the hill?' Melissa considered. 'How far is it from the back door to the edge of our property?'

'Two hundred yards, maybe. I know it's only a fraction of the range of the gun, but it pays to start slowly.'

'And this thing will penetrate a car at seven hundred yards, you said. Suppose there's someone up the hill, within seven hundred yards? You didn't buy the shovel!'

'I wish you'd get it into your head that this is not a joke. Anyway, who on earth will be up this hill, at six o'clock on a Thursday afternoon?'

'Carlos and his sheep?'

He grinned. 'Then we'd have lamb for dinner.'

'And be back in court again on Monday.'

'Look...' He held her hands. 'There is no possibility of Carlos and his sheep being up the hill, Liss. We'd have heard the bloody sheep bleating.'

'There could still be someone. Young lovers...'

'Oh, come now. In Spain they're all still fast asleep. Don't chicken out on me now. We agreed to get the gun, right? And there's no point in having a gun if you don't know how to use it. Right?'

Melissa had to accept that, watched while he climbed the hill and placed the box. Fred also watched, with interest; he hadn't taken a close look at the guns being used by the Moors and the Christians on Monday, and was therefore unaware of what was likely to happen. But suddenly Melissa was. 'Fred!'

she said, as David came back.

'What about him?'

'He's terrified of loud noises. Especially gunfire. He nearly went berserk at the *fiesta*.'

'Then you'd better put him in the house.'

'He'll still hear it, noodle-gut.'

'Well, he'll have to put up with it. Really, Liss, we can't buy a gun and then not shoot it for fear of upsetting the dog.'

'I suppose not. Come along, Fred.' She took him into the master bedroom. 'You stay here and have a nap,' she explained. 'Daddy and I are going to make a loud noise for five minutes, but there's nothing to worry about.'

Fred gave her a dirty look, and curled up on one of the new rugs; he supposed he was being left behind while they went off galli-vanting and eating T-bone steaks. Melissa closed the door on him and rejoined David. 'Now here's how you load it,' he explained. 'What I propose to do is keep it loaded with two deer shot and five scatter, so that if any intruder isn't scared off by the scatter shot and keeps on coming, we then use the heavy stuff. Right?'

'If you say so,' Melissa agreed, becoming more uneasy with every minute.

'But today, as we're practising, I'm going to use only deer shot. Now you see, you press the cartridge in here. With each one you put in, the preceding one slips further into the magazine. It doesn't matter when you're using all one kind of shot, but when you're mixing them up, remember that the first one in is the last one out. So normally we'd put the deer shot in first. You with me?'

'Absolutely.' Which was a lie; she was feeling quite dazed by the whole thing.

'So there she is, fully loaded. Now, whenever you pump her, a cartridge is forced into the breech and the empty one is ejected. With practice, I should be able to fire all seven in about ten seconds. Virtually an automatic weapon, eh?'

'Sounds horrendous. What about me?'

'Well ... you cock it.'

Melissa took the gun, very carefully, and attempted to pump it. 'It's not moving.'

'Well, you have to exert a little bit of strength.'

Clenching her teeth and going red in the face, Melissa slowly managed to complete the action. 'God damn,' she said. 'You and your seven in ten seconds. I'll only make seven in seven hours.'

'We're going to have to work on that. Anyway, here's what you do.' David took the gun back. 'You'll see there's a back sight and a front sight. You release the safety catch, like so, you wedge the butt very carefully into your shoulder – it'll have quite a kick – and then you look along the barrel, lining up the two sights with your target.'

'What's the target?'

'That box, silly.'

'That's a pretty big target. Must be all of

two feet square. Shouldn't you paint a circle on it, or something?'

'Listen, if you can hit that box, you will either hit whoever you're aiming at or you'll scare him to death. I'll just show you how it's done.'

He levelled the gun, took careful aim, and squeezed the trigger. The bang was surprisingly loud, so that Melissa jumped, and the box quivered, while the bullet, smacking into the earth behind it, made a most impressive thump and sent up a cluster of dust. 'Well,' she remarked, 'you certainly terrified that box to death.'

'Let's see you do it, then.'

'Oh, listen, Fred's howling.'

'Is that Fred? I thought it was someone down the hill yodelling.'

'You beast! I must go to him.'

'Look, fire the gun first. He simply has to get used to noises if he's going to live in Spain.'

'Oh ... very well.' He cocked it for her, and she sighted along the barrel as instructed, took careful aim at the centre of the box, drew a deep breath, and squeezed the trigger. This time the box definitely moved.

'Oh, good shooting,' David said, starting up the hill. 'Good...' He stared ahead as he climbed. 'Shit on it!'

'What have I done?'

He held up the box; there was a large hole exactly in the centre of the side that had been

270

presented. 'Talk about flukes.'

'This is the story of Deadeye Dick, the only man with a corkscrew...'

'Don't be obscene,' David admonished, replacing the box and coming back down the hill. He was quite put out. Fred continued to yodel.

'I don't suppose you'd believe me if I said I'd aimed to put it there?' Melissa asked.

'Oh. I'm sure you *aimed* to put it there, my darling girl. But actually doing it...'

Melissa's dander was up. 'Then let's have another go,' she said. 'Hold on, Fred,' she shouted. 'I'm coming in a minute.'

'All right.' David cocked the gun and held it out.

'No, you go first.'

This time he aimed with great concentration, chewing his lip, while Melissa massaged her shoulder; it was quite sore. David fired, and again the box quivered. 'Damn,' he growled.

'I would say that was really quite close enough,' Melissa commented.

He cocked the gun and handed it to her. 'Let's see you hit it again,' he suggested. Melissa wedged the butt into her aching shoulder, lined up the sights, and squeezed the trigger. Once again the box jumped into the air. 'I don't believe this.' David went up the hill. The second hole was just beneath the first.

'Too low,' Melissa grumbled.

271

'You have got to be the most remarkable natural shot in the world,' he said. 'I've a good mind to enter you for Bisley.'

'What as?' she laughed, as she hurried inside to see to Fred.

Fred was as far under the bed as he could get, which was about halfway, and part of the reason he was yodelling was that he was stuck. Melissa grabbed his haunches and pulled, and he pushed with his front paws, and at length he emerged, puffing with embarrassment. She gave him a biscuit, which seemed to do much to restore his shattered nerves, heard the sound of an engine coming up the hill, looked out of the window, and saw a Guardia Civile Land Rover negotiating the gate, which the workmen had left open. 'Oh, my God!' She ran along the corridor and into the lounge, where David was lovingly unloading and cleaning his new toy. 'The police!'

'Where?'

'There!' She pointed at the back door. 'They must have heard the shots, or someone complained. What are we going to do?'

'Hide the gun and deny everything.' He leapt to his feet, pushed the gun and the boxes of cartridges into the broom cupboard.

'Oh, David!' Melissa went to the back door, and opened it just as the usual heavily armed policeman was about to knock.

'*Buenos tardes, señora,*' he said.

'Oh, ah ... *buenos tardes, señor.*' And as she was starting to pick up Spanish custom, added, '*Bien?*'

'*Si, muy bien. Usted?*'

'*Ah, si, si, muy bien.*' At least he understood her linguistic efforts, despite her atrocious accent. He then launched into an address in Spanish. 'I'm sorry,' Melissa said. '*Habla Ingles?*'

The man sighed, and began again, more slowly. 'We 'ave come about zee *coche.*'

'Oh, have you?' Nothing to do with the shooting. She was so relieved she could have hugged him. 'Have you found it?'

'*Si, señora,* we 'ave found eet.'

'Oh, tremendous! David!' she shouted. 'These kind gentlemen have found our car. Again.'

'Have they really?' David hurried along the corridor, having apparently just washed his hands; Melissa assumed he had been taking protective action against being tested for powder burns. 'You mean they're not here about the—'

'No,' she said firmly. 'This gentleman speaks English.'

'You are zee *Señor* Lytton?'

'That's me.' David looked past the policemen. 'Where is it? The car, I mean.'

'You must come weez me.'

'Oh? Last time you brought it here.'

'Zees ees not posseeble now.'

273

'Why not?'

The policeman made an expressive gesture. 'Zee car, eet ees no good. Zee car, eet ees ... kaput!'

Ten

'Kaput? No good?' Melissa shouted.

'You come,' the policeman invited.

'Yes, we come,' David agreed. 'But we had better come in our own car. It is the dog, you understand.'

'Zee *perro*?'

'Where we go, he goes,' Melissa explained. The policeman scratched his head. The mentality of the English was an endless source of wonder; it was useless to argue with them, they had no sense of logic. Fred was pushed into the back seat of the hired Fiesta, and they drove down the hill behind the Land Rover, turning west on the Jesus Pobre road, through La Jara, under the motorway, and out into the country roads beyond. 'This is the way to Salvador's village,' Melissa remarked.

'I have a notion that all the roads around here lead to Salvador's village,' David commented.

But they didn't go to Salvador's village.

274

They turned off on to a side lane some kilometres short, bounced along a very uneven track, and came to a stop on the edge of a continuation of the dry river. And there, in the midst of the rubble, was the unmistakeable shape of a Peugeot 506 Estate. It was just as well that the shape was recognizable; otherwise it was just a burned-out and blackened wreck. The Land Rover braked, while David and Melissa, pulling in beside it, stared in horror. 'Ees zat your *coche*?' asked the Guardia.

'It looks like it. I'd have to get closer to make a positive ID.'

'Zen you come.' The Guardia got out of the Land Rover and began scrambling down the rocks. Melissa followed. The remaining Guardia made some comment about being left alone with a *perro malo*, but they were in separate cars and Fred, apart from putting his head out of the window to puff, was showing no great desire to socialize.

Melissa, clambering over boulders and kicking beer cans and plastic bottles out of the way, felt physically sick. Over the past couple of years she had become very fond of this car. 'That's it. It's our car,' David said, having inspected the blackened number plates.

'You see...' The Guardia gestured through what remained of the doors. 'Zey tore up zee interior. You see...' He went round the front of the car to show them the burnt-out

275

engine; the bonnet had been raised on its arm, so there was no possibility it had been blown open by the heat. 'Zese people, zey are *muy malo.*'

'Yes,' David agreed.

'My God!' Melissa commented, as she arrived, panting.

'My feelings exactly. Well, officer, if you have no further use for us...'

'What weell you do?' the Guardia asked. 'About zee car?'

'See about getting a new one,' David told him.

They drove back into Denia, to the local office of their insurance company. 'Well,' Melissa said. 'What *do* we do? It'll take months for the insurance money to come through.'

'That's why we're going to file the claim now. As long as we make sure it's coming, we can go ahead with a new one.'

'Here? Unless you buy a Seat, it'll cost the earth.'

'Not now we're all in the common market, darling. Do you want another Peugeot?'

'Yes. It's the most comfortable car I've ever driven. And just made for Fred.' Fred, who found the back seat of a Fiesta somewhat cramping, puffed his agreement.

It was dark by the time they got back from Denia, having had their claim accepted, but having been warned that they could not

276

expect settlement for some time. 'Just as I thought would be the case,' David said. 'Well, what with our lunch party, we can't do anything about a new one until next week. Look, just forget about it. Maybe it was just an unlucky car.'

'It wasn't unlucky until we brought it to Spain,' Melissa pointed out. But she was actually more concerned with Sunday. As it was Spain, she had every hope that it would be a warm and sunny day. She wanted to eat on the *naya*, looking at the view and the pool, in which her guests would certainly wish to cool off. Her trouble was that she had only one *naya* table, and although she had shipped out her dining table from the London flat, she wasn't very keen on carting that into the open; it was an antique oak refectory which had been in her family for three generations.

She was equally concerned about the crockery and cutlery. Here again she had shipped out all of her good stuff, not intended for outdoor eating. David persuaded her that she should use the best, but he agreed on the need for another, larger table, so next morning they returned to *Garcia Meubles* in Gata, were welcomed like long-lost cousins, and *Señor* Garcia guaranteed that the additional table would be delivered the following morning. As it was only nine o'clock on Friday morning, that seemed quite hopeful.

When they stopped by the port to have a seafront aperitif before lunch and bought themselves a newspaper, Melissa was alarmed to read that the weather was expected to deteriorate in the next few days. 'Doesn't seem possible,' she remarked, looking at a cloudless blue sky. 'I was so hoping to be able to entertain outside. I mean, eleven people is going to be a bit of a crush inside the house.'

'And that's supposing there's no rough stuff.'

'There's not going to be any rough stuff,' she insisted. 'The object of the exercise is to overawe Sam, not take him on. I'm not sure even Hans could do that. But if it's raining...'

Worry about the weather became irrelevant when they got home, and found that a telegram had been delivered. It had been accepted by Alvarez's men. 'Eeet ees een Eenglish.' The foreman sounded quite put out, and Melissa saw that the envelope was opened.

'And you don't speak English? What bad luck.' It was addressed to her. She took out the sheet of paper, unfolded it ... 'Oh, shit on it!'

'Bad news?' David asked.

'Depends how you categorize bad news.' She read aloud. 'Brief visit Stop kindly meet charter flight from Gatwick arriving Alicante Airport three o'clock Saturday morning Stop accompanied by Audrey best love Gerald.'

'Would you like to read that again?' David requested.

'No. Of all the times for them to arrive. And why didn't he telephone? He has my mobile number.'

'Because, darling, if he had telephoned, you'd have been able to say, "Not on your nelly." Did you actually say three o'clock in the morning?'

'They must be getting one of those cheapo-cheapo midnight flights.'

'Sounds like Gerald, all right. Well, you can just call him and say it's not on.'

There was no reply from Gerald's mobile, or from Audrey's. So Melissa tried the house, and got the answerphone. Then she tried Gerald's office. 'I'm sorry, Mrs Lytton,' the woman said. 'But Mr Clarke is on holiday. Actually –' she sounded puzzled – 'he's coming to see you. Didn't you know?'

'I do now. Thank you, Janet. They've cut themselves off,' she grumbled, throwing herself across the bed. 'I'll have to go and meet them.'

'In the middle of the night? No way.' David stood above her. 'You do realize that the guest apartment isn't finished?'

'There's the small spare bedroom off the hall. They'll have to use that.'

'Brilliant. We'll put Fred in with them.'

'Audrey doesn't like Fred. She doesn't like any dogs.'

'I know,' David said.

279

★ ★ ★

He spent the afternoon preparing various meats and prawns for marinating, and the house became filled with delicious smells, which kept Fred very happy, as various items found their way into his mouth. The sight and sound of David happily at work always relaxed Melissa, and when she got down to thinking about it, she found the idea of her so politically correct brother and even more politically correct sister-in-law jumping with both feet into their very odd Spanish life-style, quite apart from being in at the show-down with Sam, intriguing. To complete her day, Garcia's van arrived with the new table and chairs that same afternoon, and installed them in the *naya*. 'You sure you want them here?' the foreman inquired.

'Why shouldn't we have them there?'

'When eet rains, the table weel get wet.'

'Is it going to rain?'

He gave her an old-fashioned look, and led his men back to his truck. Melissa went to the kitchen. 'They say it's going to rain.'

'Rubbish. There's not a cloud in the sky. Now let's be serious. What's your plan?'

'Well, we have to leave here at two o'clock tomorrow morning. No, we'd better make that half past one.'

'Or telephone a message to the airport telling them to take a cab.'

'For a hundred kilometres? You know how tight-fisted Gerald is. It'd ruin his holiday.'

'Yes,' David said happily. 'Well, what about leaving a message telling him to take the bus? There is one, you know.'

'I've checked that out. It takes four hours from Alicante to Jàvea; it doesn't use the motorway, you see, and stops in every village along the national route. Can you imagine? Flying half the night, and then driving till past dawn?'

'It was his decision, darling, to arrive at three o'clock in the morning.'

'And I intend to meet him. OK, he and I have very different approaches to life, but he is my brother. You don't have to come, you know. I told you that.'

'And I have said I am coming. So,' he added with great emphasis, 'is Fred.' Fred, not having the least idea what they were talking about, scratched half-heartedly at his left ear.

They had an early supper, with the intention of getting a few hours sleep, but inevitably, when Melissa looked at her watch, it was half past eleven and she was still wide awake. Then she did fall asleep, to awaken it seemed a moment later to the bleeping of the alarm. David was showing no signs of moving, so she abandoned him to have a shower and get dressed. By then he was sitting on the edge of the bed, blinking blearily. 'Leaving in five minutes,' she reminded him.

'The one thing for which I have always

been grateful,' he remarked as he staggered towards the bathroom, 'is that I have no brothers. And no sisters, either.'

She found Fred hardly more responsive. 'Do we really have to take him?' she asked, as he rolled on his back with all his legs in the air, eyes tight shut.

'Of course,' David said. 'What would Audrey do without him?'

The one advantage of going down to Alicante at half past one in the morning was that the *autopista* was deserted. Late workers and convivial diners were safely home, and not even the geriatric teenagers would consider abandoning the nightspots for at least another couple of hours. Only an occasional transcontinental truck rumbled through the darkness, but when they reached Alicante Airport they were surprised at the number of people about. Equally they were not surprised to see from the board that there was a half-hour delay on the flight. 'The best thing about Spain is that the bars never close,' David said, heading for the airport one.

The second best thing, Melissa thought, was that Spanish bars serve coffee as well as alcohol. She had it sugarless, black, suspecting she might have to drive home. Then it was the usual huddle outside the barriers and the doors, the usual peering through the glass to see if she could spot Gerald and Audrey; David preferred to remain at the bar and have a second brandy. 'Gerald!' she shouted, as she saw her brother's balding head. That apart, he looked very like her, although, at six years her senior, he had permitted the growth of a distinct paunch. Needless to say, being Gerald, although it was nearly four o'clock on a warm morning, he wore a three-piece wool suit, tie neatly knotted, and even had a buttonhole – in the starkest contrast to the sports-shirted men around him, some of whom were already in shorts. Audrey, short and plump, was equally overdressed, and she even wore a hat!

'Liss, darling, how good of you to come to meet us,' Gerald said, giving her a perfunctory embrace, as if he hadn't virtually ordered her to do so.

'What a flight,' Audrey complained. 'My God...!'

'You weren't hijacked, were you?' David ambled across from the bar, glass in hand.

'The delays,' Audrey complained. 'And then the service! David, you're not drinking alcohol! At three o'clock in the morning?'

'It's a national custom in Spain.' He put both arms round her and kissed her, despite her efforts to get away.

Melissa sighed. The cordial state of war that existed between her husband and her sister-in-law was obviously going to move from cold to hot, over the next few days. 'Where's your baggage?' she asked.

'Here.' Gerald pointed to the trolley.

She bent over to look at the five suitcases. 'How long were you planning to stay?'

'A week.'

'And golf clubs?' David asked. 'You don't mean to play golf?'

'Of course I do. Everyone in Spain plays golf. Except you, of course. Haw haw haw. But surely you know someone who does?'

David looked at Melissa. Who snapped her fingers. 'Donald Barton. He'll certainly play. We'll ask him tomorrow. I mean today. Later on.'

'Who's Donald Barton?' Gerald asked, as they wheeled the trolley across the road to the car park.

'One of our neighbours.'

'There's something vaguely familiar about the name.'

'Well, it's not a very uncommon name, is it? Now, let's see ... I'm not sure how we're going to fit everything in.'

'Where's your estate car?' Gerald asked.

'We no longer have it.'

'No longer have it?'

'As they say in Spain,' David said. 'Eet ees no good.'

'Or as they say in Germany,' Melissa added, 'it is kaput.'

'You've wrecked your car?' Audrey was aghast, and instinctively looked at David.

'We did not wreck our car,' Melissa said evenly. 'It was stolen.'

'We know *that*,' Gerald said. 'But you got

284

it back.'

'Then it was stolen again, and the thieves set fire to it. We'll show it to you, if you like.'

'Good lord!' Gerald commented, reaching for his golf clubs as if uncertain how soon he was going to be assaulted.

'I think our best bet is to get in the back, Audrey, and let the men load the luggage around us,' Melissa decided.

Audrey opened the door, and recoiled. 'What's that?'

'Fred. You remember Fred?' Fred, waking up, leered at his mistress's sister-in-law.

'It's not sitting next to me,' Audrey announced. 'It'll shed hairs all over me.'

'Yes,' Melissa conceded. *'He* probably will.' She got in first, and wedged herself against the sleepy retriever. Audrey crawled after her. Meanwhile David and Gerald were trying to cram five suitcases and a bag of golf clubs into the not very large boot. They actually made it, barring one case and the clubs.

'Which would you rather have on your laps?' David asked the women.

'The golf clubs,' Melissa said. The bag was laid across them; unfortunately, it also reached across Fred's legs as well, and he sat up. 'Something for you to chew on, darling,' Melissa told him.

'If he dares,' Gerald growled. He was inserted into the front with the suitcase on his knees, and David got behind the wheel.

'Are you sure you wouldn't like me to drive?' Melissa asked. There was no doubt as to who was going to have the most comfortable journey home. In fact, she reflected sadly as Fred gave a huge sigh and rested his head on her shoulder, the *only* comfortable drive home.

'I'm fine, thank you,' David replied.

'Is it far?' Audrey inquired.

'Just over a hundred kilometres.'

'A hundred?' she squealed.

'Less than an hour,' David promised her, braking to take his ticket at the *peaje*, and then gunning the Fiesta on to the *autopista*.

'If we ever get there,' Gerald commented.

In fact they got home safely, by which time extreme exhaustion had set in. Gerald and Audrey were very happy to be put straight to bed, despite the smallness of the room they were offered, and David and Melissa felt they could do nothing better than the same. Fred was already fast asleep and had to be dragged from the car.

Melissa awoke a couple of hours later to the sound of the blaring transistor; she'd forgotten that Alvarez's men worked on Saturdays. She pulled on a one-piece swimsuit, and half fell down the steps and into the pool, where the water rapidly revived her. Fred came down to sit on the coronation and watch her with bleary eyes, and as she swam on her back she looked up at the *naya* and

Audrey, wearing a dressing gown over her nightdress. 'Do you think you could turn down the radio?' she asked. 'Gerald and I are trying to sleep.'

'Can't be done. It's not my radio.'

'What?' She looked in the direction of the noise and found herself gazing at a workman, who had been enjoying watching Melissa but now turned his gaze on her. 'Oh, my God!' She hastily retreated.

David emerged shortly afterwards, and began doing things in the kitchen, and she went up to help. They finally got moving about ten, Gerald as ever resplendent in a blazer and tie. 'You'll stew,' David warned.

'Mustn't go native, old man,' Gerald insisted, looking disapprovingly at David's scruffy shorts, and even more critically at his sister's exposed legs; Audrey was wearing trousers – they could not possibly be called anything else, as they closely resembled what Melissa dimly remembered used to be known as Oxford bags. They did absolutely nothing for her already large behind. But perhaps they were intended as a protection against Fred, with whom she again had to share the back seat.

Both the visitors had to exclaim about the charm of the position of the house, the stupendous views over the valley and the distant mountains. Then David and Melissa drove them into the *pueblo* and then the *puerto*, both to show them the area and the beach and to pick up the final bits and pieces for Sunday. 'We're having a lunch party,' Melissa explained.

'For us?' Audrey cried. 'How nice.'

'We were having it anyway. There'll be ... good heavens, thirteen of us, now.'

'Thirteen!' She was impressed.

'You'll meet a good cross-section of the community,' Melissa said.

'And how,' David agreed.

On the way home they stopped by the Bartons', introduced the Clarkes, and talked about golf. 'Why, certainly,' Donald said. 'I belong to the local golf club. We'll have a round this afternoon.' It was arranged that he would pick Gerald up after lunch, and that the others would go over and meet them at the club at the end of the round.

'Then we could have a rijkstaffel, at that Indonesian place,' Lucy said brightly.

'What a lovely couple,' Audrey commented as they drove back up the hill.

Melissa looked at her in astonishment; it was totally unlike Audrey to like any new acquaintances until at least five meetings.

'Did you say you knew him?' David asked Gerald.

'Must've been mistaken,' Gerald grunted.

After Gerald had departed, relaxation was the order of the afternoon, save for David, who was busy marinating pork and arranging all the spices he had bought; he always mixed his own curries, which was why they invariably tasted so authentic. Melissa kept her eye on the weather while she prepared the side dishes. The morning had been beautifully clear, but soon after lunch, clouds began gathering on Montgo, making rather a mess of Audrey's sunbathing plans. Instead she spent the afternoon complaining, either about life in London or things she had not so far liked about Spain.

'Thank God we're eating out tonight,' David remarked in the privacy of their bedroom.

'Relax, darling,' Melissa told him. 'They've already been here twelve hours. Only another hundred and fifty-six to go. Less, in fact.'

'Shit! Don't tell me they're flying back at three in the morning as well?'

At half past six they said goodbye to a disgruntled Fred and swept up the impressive drive to the Barton palace to pick up Lucy, giving Audrey a chance to see how the other half lived, before going on to the golf club. Barton and Gerald had curtailed their round, Gerald having been thoroughly trounced, and had come straight in from the thirteenth green, already eight over par while Barton was one under, abandoning the remaining holes to allow plenty of time in the bar watering the nineteenth.

But despite the golfing disaster, Gerald was

in the sort of good humour he always reserved for the wealthy, especially if they could be regarded as potential clients – Melissa gathered the two men had spent much of the afternoon discussing investments, and that Barton had half promised to put some of his money with some clients of Gerald's who guaranteed good returns. The result was that the meal at the Indonesian restaurant was a great success. It would have been, anyway, as both the food and the service were up to even David's exacting standards, but he also insisted on ordering champagne, followed by French brandies, and by the time they finally broke up, about eleven thirty, it was obvious to Melissa that she was driving home. Lucy had come to the same conclusion about the Mercedes. 'See you tomorrow,' she giggled, endeavouring to fit the key into the lock while Barton relieved himself against a neighbouring bush.

'Really!' Audrey commented, falling into the back seat of the Fiesta beside Gerald. 'And I thought he was such a nice man. This country is so vulgar!'

'We prefer to think of it as uninhibited,' David argued. 'Are you sure you're capable, darling?'

'Quite sure,' Melissa said, starting the engine and driving slowly down the slope to the main road, leaving the Bartons still trying to unlock the Mercedes. 'I hope they get home.'

It was a dramatic night, for a wind had sprung up, and the clouds were scudding across the sky, causing the moon to appear for fleeting seconds before plunging the sky into darkness again. While in front of them, although still at a considerable distance, Montgo rose starkly against a distant backdrop of lightning flashes. Melissa chewed her lip and concentrated; none of the country roads around Jàvea were lit, and there was a surprising amount of traffic – but then, she reflected, it was Saturday night. Yet it would be just her luck to have a prang, when she was the most sober member of the party, while David drove all over the place pissed as a newt without ever touching another car. She'd never live it down. 'Why are you driving so slowly?' David asked.

'Because the car in front of me is driving slowly.'

'Why don't you overtake it?'

'I don't think that would be a good idea. This is a narrow road and he's weaving a bit.'

'For God's sake! Look, pull over and let me drive.'

'No way. Oops!' They had reached one of the bridges over the Jalón River, which was, as usual, dry. And the car in front of them had come to a full stop, in the middle of the road and just on the far side of the bridge, leaving them on the crown, Melissa having hastily stamped on the brake.

'Steady on, Sis.' Gerald had apparently

been asleep in the back, and had nearly joined them in the front. 'That could've broken my neck.'

'Blow at the idiot,' David commanded.

'At midnight? I'm sure there's a law against that, in Jàvea.'

'I'll have a word with him,' he decided, opened his door, and got out.

'Oh, shit!' Melissa remarked. 'Now there's likely to be a punch-up.'

'What did you say?' Gerald inquired.

'We'd better lend moral support.' Melissa got out as well, and after a moment's hesitation, Gerald followed her.

So did Audrey. 'What a heavenly evening,' she commented.

The clouds were still scudding across the moon, and it was certainly dramatic. 'What's that noise?' Audrey asked.

'Sounds like...' Melissa turned to look back along the road, saw the headlights behind them. 'Donald and Lucy, thank God!'

David was bending over the driver's window of the stalled car, having an animated discussion with the man behind the wheel. 'His exhaust needs attention,' Gerald grumbled.

The Mercedes pulled in behind the Fiesta, at the foot of the bridge. Barton switched off the engine and got out; Melissa gathered the reason they had been so far behind was because of a discussion as to who should drive, apparently won by Barton. 'What seems to be the trouble?' he inquired.

'Someone's broken down in front of us,' Melissa explained. 'If your Spanish is up to it, perhaps you could take over. David is liable to start punching at any moment.'

Barton came forward, somewhat uncertainly. 'The noise is growing louder,' Audrey remarked.

Melissa realized she was right. She turned her head to listen. All three of the car engines were stopped. And although the noise was still distant, it was definitely coming closer, rapidly. 'It must be the train,' she explained.

'You have a train?'

'Oh, yes. It runs from Denia down to Alicante and back, once every day. We hear it from the house.'

'At midnight?' Audrey asked.

'Ah ... no, that's not right.' Melissa looked down at the dry river, and then up along it, to where she could see the lights of Gata, some two miles away. At that moment, the clouds drifted from in front of the moon, and she gazed at a huge, roaring, tumbling wall of water, carrying on its crest every describable manner of debris. 'Get in the car!' she shouted, hurling herself at the door.

But Lucy had also got out, realized what was happening, and that there was no time to start a car engine. 'Quick!' she screamed, and grabbed both Melissa and Audrey by the arms to drag them backwards off the bridge.

'David!' Melissa shouted.

293

'Donald!' Lucy screamed.

'Gerald!' Audrey shouted.

The three women landed in a huddle beside the Mercedes, as the flash flood reached the bridge. The roar was tremendous, accompanied by the most terrifying additional noises, to which was added a ripping, tearing sound such as Melissa had never heard before and would never want to hear again. Then the water was over the bank, slurping round them with sufficient force to roll them in a heap against the car itself. They sat up, shaking their heads and panting, and gazed at what had been the bridge but was now just a frothing mass of water and debris; the masonry had been torn apart as if it had been cardboard, and the flood was careering on into the darkness.

'David!' Melissa got up by clutching the Mercedes. 'David!' she yelled.

'Liss!' He was on the other side of the river.

'Oh, thank God!'

'Are you all right?'

'Yes. Are Gerald and Donald with you?'

'Yes, I'm here,' Barton said. 'Lucy?'

'OK.'

'Where's the car?' Gerald shouted.

All their heads turned to look downriver, but the moon was again hidden in cloud and they could see nothing. The men had now been joined by the two Spaniards from inside the stalled car, and these were shouting as loudly as anyone. When the moon reappeared, it lit a silver path across the still racing water, glistening on wet boulders. Of the Fiesta there was no sign. Lucy took command. 'Listen!' she bawled. 'Can you get that thing started?'

'I should think so, by pushing it,' her husband replied.

'Then you get them to drop you home. I'll take the girls the long way round.'

'You mean there's another way?' Audrey demanded, in a tone which indicated, why didn't we take that way originally?

'A long way,' Lucy said. 'Through Gata. We still have to cross the river.'

'Oh, no,' Audrey declared. 'No, no, no.'

'Do you intend to spend the rest of the night here? In wet clothes?' Melissa inquired. Audrey burst into tears.

'Listen...' Lucy put her arm round her shoulders. 'The bridge we are going to take is the big one into Gata. There'll be no risk there.' She helped her to the car.

'See you in the funnies,' Melissa called, and got in herself.

'It's a jolly good thing you all got out,' Lucy said, as she made an eight-point turn on the none-too-wide road. 'Otherwise you'd have gone with the car.'

'Fred!' Melissa gasped. 'Suppose he'd been with us?'

'We nearly die, and all you can think of is a dog!' Audrey wailed.

★ ★ ★

They had changed into dressing gowns, borrowed in Lucy's case, and with the addition of a nightdress in Audrey's, and were drinking hot chocolate and brandies and still being greeted by a delighted Fred when the three bedraggled men turned up. 'Boy, that looks good,' David said, pouring.

'I think I'm for bed,' Barton said. 'I'm sorry about the car.'

'You win some, you lose some,' Melissa said. 'Or in our case, two or three.'

'We'll sort it out on Monday,' David said. 'Although I suspect we are going to get a bit of a reputation around here when it comes to losing cars.'

'I think I'd better report it for you,' Barton said. 'Or the police will be looking for dead bodies.'

'I can't possibly let you do that,' David protested. 'It's midnight!'

'No problem. I'll telephone them. Come on, Lucy.'

'About tomorrow...' Lucy said.

'It's here,' Melissa reminded her, looking at the clock.

'Well, then, today. If you want to call it off...'

'Not on your nelly,' Melissa said. 'Anyway, we wouldn't have any way of letting people know, would we?'

Alvarez's men did not work on Sundays, and as Audrey emerged next morning, she found all three of her hosts in the pool, reduced to their various fur possessions. 'Good lord!' she exclaimed. 'Don't you know it's unhygienic to have a dog in the pool?'

'How can it be more unhygenic than for humans?' David asked. 'Fred neither sweats nor wears suntan lotion.'

'But suppose he, well, does something?'

'Fred would never dream of doing anything in a pool. There's nothing to lift his leg against, don't you see? However,' he added magnanimously, 'if it really bothers you, I'll get him out. Come along, Fred.'

He headed for the steps, Fred swimming beside him, and Audrey gave a shriek. 'Don't you dare come out of the water until you've got something on.'

'Well, you come down and hand me my towel,' he invited, reaching the shallow end and standing up.

'Stop teasing,' Melissa told him. 'I'll get it.' She was close to the ladder at the deep end, and now climbed up, whereupon Audrey gave another shriek and disappeared into the house.

'Brilliant,' David said. 'I can hardly wait for lunch.'

'Now listen,' Melissa said. 'They are our guests, and we don't want to upset them.'

'Wouldn't dream of it,' David said. 'Would we, Fred?'

Fred winked at him.

★ ★ ★

297

'Do you have flash floods often?' Gerald asked at breakfast.

'Weekly,' David told them. 'Never lost a car before, though. Must be slipping. Of course, if I'd been driving, we'd have overtaken that Spanish chap long before we reached the bridge, and we probably wouldn't even know that anything had happened.'

'He's pulling your leg,' Melissa said. 'Last night was a freak.'

'When are the papers delivered?' Audrey asked. 'I want to read about it.'

'Delivered?'

'Don't you have a paper?' Gerald was scandalized.

'Of course we do. When we go out and buy one. But, as the nearest newsagent is about five kilometres away, I think we'll skip it today.'

'No newspaper?' Gerald's voice had risen an octave. 'How will we get the football results?'

'You have them, in the paper you brought with you,' Melissa reminded him.

'Dear girl, that was Friday's evening paper. What I want is Sunday's paper with Saturday's results.'

'Oh, you won't get that until tomorrow. English newspapers are always a day late.'

'But ... how do you keep an eye on the market?'

'We leave that to our stockbroker,' David said.

'Dangerous, old man. Dangerous. Now let me give you some advice...'

'Tomorrow,' David said. 'Right now it's all hands to the pump.'

He busied himself in the kitchen, while Melissa and Gerald and Audrey arranged the tables on the *naya*. The morning was again cloudless, and pleasant, although by looking through binoculars they could see that the Jalón River was still a torrent. 'I do think we should have reported about the car,' Audrey said.

'Donald said he'd do that. The hire-car company won't be open until tomorrow, anyway.'

'Well, we should do *something*! We could have been swept away and killed. We should complain. To somebody.'

'This is Spain,' Melissa reminded her. 'Not England. One looks after oneself. Nobody interferes, unless you actually harm or deeply offend them. Thank God!' She was more worried about the possibility of rain: would it really reach Jàvea? Her worst fears were confirmed when, about eleven o'clock, the clouds started to build on Montgo. 'Damn,' she said. 'Damn, damn, *damn*!'

'It may not actually rain,' David said, having emerged from the kitchen for a breath of air and a glass of champagne. 'It didn't yesterday.'

'It did in the mountains,' she reminded

299

him.

'Well, do you want to move everything back inside?'

'Oh ... blow it. Let's take a chance.' Where the tables were set, the *naya* was roofed.

'So tell me,' he asked, as the Clarkes were out of earshot. 'What's our plan? We haven't actually had the time to discuss it yet.'

'You've been too tied up with the food,' Melissa pointed out. 'My plan is simply to confront Sam, in front of a lot of people, show him the card, and tell him to do his worst, because he's not getting hold of it.'

David scratched his head. 'Dicey. I mean, if he really is a gangster, he'll probably carry a gun.'

'I've thought of that. But he's hardly likely to shoot twelve people, is he? And we'll have guns, as well. We have Dolores, and although I didn't actually tell Hans to bring his, I don't really think he needs it. And we have our shotgun, which we will place, fully loaded, in an accessible place.'

'Shoot-out at the Casa Saggitarius,' he commented. 'I had no idea I had married a combination of Bonnie and Ma Barker. I thought your family didn't do guns.'

'They don't. But I don't think any of them have ever had their crotch felt up by a thug, either. That made me very angry.'

'Remind me to approach you with caution in future. How do you suppose Gerald and Audrey are going to react to all this? You said we shouldn't upset them.'

'We're not going to upset them. Someone else may.'

'There's a happy thought,' he said, stroking Fred's head.

'Fred! We'll have to lock him up.'

'Oh, no we don't. Fred may well turn out to be our secret weapon. Remember that Dutchman.' Fred grunted.

The storm arrived at a quarter to twelve. The cloud on Montgo grew, but none of them were prepared for the sudden flash of lightning followed instantaneously by the ear-splitting crack of thunder. 'Jesus Christ!' Gerald leapt out of the chair in which he had been sitting.

'Gerald!' Audrey screamed. Melissa didn't know whether she was admonishing him for blasphemy or calling for help.

'Shit!' David emerged from the kitchen. 'The electrics have gone. Try the trip, Liss.'

Melissa put the trip switch up, but it immediately clicked down again. 'We'll have to wait a while. Where's Fred?'

'He was here a moment ago, looking for cook's titbits.'

'Fred!' She ran along the corridor. 'Oh, Fred!' Fred was in their bed with his head under her pillow. She sat beside him and gave him a hug and a kiss. 'It was just thunder. It can't hurt you. It can't...' There was another terrific boom from, it seemed, immediately above her head. Fred, who had emerged, immediately submerged again. 'Well, I suppose you had better stay there for the duration,' she decided.

'Does this mean lunch is off?' Audrey inquired when Melissa returned.

'Why should it be?'

'No electrics.'

'We cook on gas, fortunately. Of course, if it goes on too long, the champagne and sangria may warm up.' She went on to the *naya* to watch the rain teeming down past her nose, while another flash of lightning dazzled her, even as the thunder threatened to burst her eardrums. The only good thing was that there was no wind, so that no water was coming in to the *naya* to ruin the table settings, but she could see the pool filling above the decorative tiles even as she watched, while huge areas of the valley were turning from green to white with floodwater.

David stood beside her. 'When it rains in this part of the world, it really rains,' he commented.

'You can say that about almost everything,' she pointed out. 'Do you think anyone will come?'

'Well, if they don't, it's curry for breakfast, lunch and dinner for the next three weeks. Who's that, then?'

A BMW came round the corner. 'Umbrellas!' Melissa dashed out of the back door with a brolly to hold over Carrie as she got out of the car. Carrie was wearing quite the shortest shorts Melissa had ever seen in her life; they were even shorter than on Wednesday morning. Grippenheimer was wearing a red sports shirt decorated with small black swastikas. They were in the house before all of these facts had properly sunk into Melissa's brain. 'Champagne?' David was pouring, and hugging Carrie at the same time. 'It seems ages since last we met.'

'In bed,' Carrie reminded him. 'You had nothing on.'

'These are our neighbours,' Melissa explained to Audrey, who looked about to throw a wobbly.

'We have adventured together,' Grippenheimer said, seizing Audrey's hand to kiss it.

'Apparently,' Gerald observed. 'Are you German?'

'I,' Grippenheimer said, standing to attention, 'am a German admiral.'

'Oh, I say, I *am* pleased to meet you.' Gerald endeavoured to shake hands, and was prevented by Fred, who had recovered from his earlier alarm and was trying to do the same, with his mouth.

'My friend,' Grippenheimer said. 'He bites people.'

'Does he?' Audrey gave Fred a dirty look, but a fresh crack of thunder sent him scurrying back to the bedroom, and this time he remained there, even though another car arrived, a Mercedes, this time. Melissa returned to the back door, and ferried the Bartons into safety.

'Some weather!' Barton commented. 'This entire mountain is turning into a waterfall.'

Melissa escorted them into the lounge. 'The police haven't been able to find your car,' Lucy said. 'They think it was swept out to sea.'

'Makes you think,' Barton said. 'Supposing you'd been in it?'

'Champagne,' David recommended. 'I think you know everyone.'

A smooth roar. This noise was more solid than all the others put together, and Melissa knew it had to be Sam's Cadillac. 'Hi!' she shouted from the back door. 'Any news of Salvador?'

'I am 'ere, Meleessa.' Salvador got out of the front, and his mother and father emerged from the back.

'Thought it safer to come in one car,' Sam explained, giving her a hug; he was actually wearing a jacket over a sports shirt and had even shaved. 'Them mountain roads are really something. Like driving down a *barranca*.'

'I can believe it.' She ushered them into the house. 'We got caught up in a flash flood last night.'

'But zat ees very bad,' Julio said. 'You were not 'armed?'

304

'No, no. Only lost another car. Come on in. Now,' she said, 'I don't think you know any of these people?' Sam and Barton gazed at each other, and Barton involuntarily took a step back. 'You *do* know each other,' Melissa said.

'Never saw him before in my life,' Barton declared.

'It's ma size, Ah guess,' Sam said. 'People allus think they've seen me before.' But he did not offer to shake hands.

Melissa looked at Lucy, who had turned quite white. She had a sudden realization that she was losing control of the situation, without quite understanding how. She rushed into the introductions. '*Señor* and *Señora* Morales, and their son Salvador,' she explained at large. 'Salvador rescued us, twice, when our car was stolen, and *Señor* Morales is the *alcalde* – that's the mayor, Gerald – of a town in the hills.'

'Is that a fact?' Gerald shook hands. 'Pleased to meet you, Your Worship.'

'What ees zees worsheep?' Julio asked.

Gerald looked at Melissa. 'A drink,' she said brightly. 'Will you have champagne, or sangria?'

'Brandy,' Salvador suggested. 'We weell 'ave brandy.'

'Brandy it shall be. But what about your mother?'

'She weell 'ave brandy, also,' Salvador said.

'Right,' Melissa said again, and went off to

305

get it.

'Nice lil' place yuh have here,' Sam said to David.

'Nice of you to say so.'

'You're American,' Audrey accused.

'Ah guess Ah am.'

'I suppose the weather in the mountains is rather bad, right now,' Gerald remarked to Encarna, chattily.

Encarna smiled. 'She no speak zee Eengleesh,' Julio said. 'You no speak zee Spaneesh? Zen you must speek weez me, eenstead.'

Lucy joined Melissa at the bar. 'Liss, darling, I'm terribly sorry, but I don't think we're going to be able to stay for lunch.'

'Eh?'

'I'm suddenly not feeling very well. I get these turns, so—'

'Grub up,' David announced.

'Ah ... we're still one short,' Melissa protested.

'Well, you know, when it's ready, it's ready. The rice is just done.'

'But ... It's the Countess de la Jara,' Melissa explained at large. 'She's probably been held up by the weather.'

'A countess?' Gerald exclaimed. 'You're having a countess to lunch?'

'Doesn't everyone?'

'Oh. I say.'

'I was just explaining to Liss that we simply have to go,' Lucy told Barton, urgently.

'Oh, I think we should stay until the countess arrives,' he objected. 'I'd like to see her again.'

'Well, then, let's eat,' David suggested.

'That's a great idea,' Sam said. 'Mind if Ah use the lil' boys' room first?'

'It's just along the corridor,' David said, before Melissa could get a word in.

'I come weez you,' Salvador said.

'What ees 'appening, Beeg Sam?' he whispered as they went down the corridor together.

'Ah told yuh, she's up to some game.'

'But zeeze Bartons...'

'They're gonna get their comeuppance, any minute now,' Sam assured him. 'Ah fixed him. Ah didn't mean it to happen here, but that's the way the cookie crumbles.'

'You theenk Melissa knows who 'e ees?'

'Could be. She could be in cahoots with him. In which case...'

'And thees woman, Countess de La Hara ... I do not theenk zere is such a person.'

'Well. whoever she is, she'd better not stick her butt into ma business.' He finished what he was doing and waited for Salvador. 'Now remember, no rough stuff until the other guests clear off.'

'But zose people are Meleessa's brozzer and seester-in-law. Zey are staying 'ere.'

'Then they may well go up with her. Hurry up, or they'll come looking for us.'

Salvador zipped up his trousers, went out and opened the bedroom door. 'Zis is zeir room. Zee

307

card could be 'ere.'

'Maybe. They'll tell us.'

'What ees to 'appen to 'er? Meleessa.'

'That depends on how co-operative she is.'

'When I zeenk of zose legs...'

'Tell yuh what,' Sam said. 'When Ah'm done with her, yuh can have her, legs an' all.'

However disparate the elements of the party, they all admired the magnificent spread. David had put his best foot forward, and laid out the three curries, with their attendant chapattis and poppadums and Melissa's raita, and of course huge bowls of rice as well as side dishes containing sliced tomatoes, grated coconuts, raisins and sliced bananas, on the dining table, and the guests were required to help themselves before taking their places at the *naya* tables, which had been placed together.

The rain had slackened to a drizzle and although the entire valley was blanketed behind the water mist, the *naya* was perfectly dry. 'But look at your pool,' Audrey squealed. 'It's coming over the coronation.'

'Well, there's damn all I can do about it,' David pointed out.

'Well, I would, if I were you,' Barton suggested. 'Otherwise you are going to flood your downstairs apartment. There's a drain with a plug in it ... I'll do it.' He went down the steps.

'Take the brolly,' Melissa shouted, but he

was already splashing through the water to reach the skimmer, and thrusting his hand inside. 'He is such a dear,' Melissa told everyone.

Barton returned, while water flowed out of the back of the pool into the garden beyond the wall. It didn't make any immediate difference, but at least the level wasn't still rising. The party became very jolly indeed, as sangria and champagne and brandy went the rounds, together with refills of different curries. 'I like your teets,' Salvador confided to Carrie, who he had contrived to have sitting beside him, and who as usual was wearing only a thin shirt.

'Do you?' She giggled. 'Hans says they're shaped like pears.'

'Avocado pears,' David suggested.

'They would have gone well with the meal,' Melissa remarked, casting an anxious glance at Hans, but he was at the far end of the table and did not appear to have overheard.

'I actually thought Spaniards were bottoms men,' Carrie confided.

'Spaniards are both ends men,' Julio declared proudly.

Encarna was sitting with her eyes closed, gently rocking to and fro. 'Eet ees zee brandy,' Salvador told Melissa. 'Two brandies, and she ees peesed like ... 'ow do you say, Meleessa?'

'Like a newt.'

'And she's had two, has she?' Gerald asked.

'No, no, she 'as 'ad four.'

'Oh, lord,' Melissa said. 'Should we put her to bed?'

'Only eef she falls over.'

'Are Spanish luncheons always like this?' Audrey whispered to Melissa.

'Always,' Melissa assured her.

The main course was cleared away, and the fruit and cheese produced, with port and more brandy. Encarna woke up. 'Now,' Julio announced. 'I weell tell you all about zee Fascistas, and zee machine gun.'

'Machine gun?' Audrey looked nervously left and right.

'This fellow was a Communist during the war,' Grippenheimer told her.

'I am a Communeest now,' Julio said proudly.

'We used to have runts like you for breakfast,' Grippenheimer said contemptuously.

Julio gave a bellow of laughter. 'Zat is why your teez are all broken, eh?'

'Are they going to fight?' Audrey asked Salvador.

'Zey are too old,' Salvador commented. How little you know, Melissa thought.

'And are you a Communist, Salvador?' Lucy asked.

'Me? What for I am going to be Communeest?'

'Well, if your father is...'

'Communeesseem ees for when zee times

310

are bad,' Salvador explained. 'Now, zee time ees good. *Mi padre*, 'e ees a Communeest because 'e 'as always been a Communeest. What ees eet you say about zee spotted deeck?'

Lucy looked at Melissa. 'I think he means the leopard,' Melissa said.

'Zat ees correct, Meleessa. But you don't want to ask *mi padre* to share nozzeeng, unless 'e likes you. 'E ees a *practeecal* Communeest.'

'What about you, Mr...?' Audrey asked Sam.

'Guichard, ma'am. No, Ah don't reckon Ah'm a Communist. We don't hold with that kind of thinking in Chawleston.'

'I am going for a swim,' Carrie announced, standing up and stripping off her shirt.

'Talk about conversation stoppers,' David muttered.

It stayed stopped as she removed her remaining two garments before going down the stairs. It was still drizzling, and she shivered attractively before jumping into the water. 'Hi!' she shouted. 'It's quite warm. Who's coming in?'

'Gerald, it's time for your siesta,' Audrey recommended.

'I'm not the least tired, darling.' He turned his chair to look down at the pool.

'Well, we can't just abandon her,' David said, getting up.

'You just sit down and have another glass of

311

port,' Melissa commanded.

'I weell go,' Salvador said, and stood up. Then looked at Melissa. 'You no come een, Meleessa?'

'I don't think so, thanks very much.'

'Say, you all got more guests,' Sam said. They accumulated at the end of the *naya* to watch a car coming up the drive.

'Who else did you invite?' Melissa asked David. 'That's not Dolores.'

'Haven't a clue. Well, we have enough left over to feed them.'

Fred started to bark. 'Do you think we should tell Carrie to come out?' Lucy asked.

'Wouldn't do any good,' Grippenheimer said.

Melissa went to the back door, and opened it, to find herself looking at two fairly large men, wearing raincoats, and slouch hats. She didn't like the look of them at all, but reflected that if they were going to try to hold the place up, as she had heard had happened at more than one Costa Blanca lunch party, they were in for a nasty surprise when they encountered Sam and Grippenheimer, to name but a few. However, the first man merely touched his hat, and inquired, 'Mrs Lytton?' He was definitely English.

'That's me.'

'I'm sorry to interrupt your party, but we're actually looking for a Mr and Mrs Donald Barton. We stopped by their house, but the maid told us they were at a party up here.'

312

'Yes, they are,' Melissa said, her brain doing handsprings. The Bartons had a maid who came in even on Sundays?

'May we speak with them, please?'

'I suppose so. You'd better come in out of the wet.'

The first man lowered his head to step inside, and regarded Fred, who was regarding him. 'Is that dog safe?'

'He only bites people I tell him to,' Melissa said sweetly. 'Just wait here, will you.' She saw no reason why two total strangers should be vouchsafed the sight of Carrie disporting herself in the pool. She went on to the *naya*, bent over Barton. 'There are some people here to see you.'

'To see me? Here?'

'Your maid told them you were up here.'

'What sort of people?' Lucy had been listening in, and Melissa observed that her face had again gone quite pale.

'Two men. I'd say they were English. They're wearing raincoats and things.'

Barton glanced at Lucy; never had Melissa seen two people look quite so frightened. Then he looked at Sam. 'You filthy bastard,' he remarked.

'Now, is that any language to use in front of a lady?' Sam asked. And smiled at Audrey. 'Two ladies.'

'You mean ... You two know each other?' Melissa asked.

'Sure,' Sam said. 'We used to work for the

same outfit.'

'Oh, my God!' Melissa said, and sat down.

'Melissa,' Barton said. 'We're your friends, right?'

'Of course.'

'Then will you help us? We don't really want to meet these people. Will you keep them talking while we sneak out the front and get our car?'

Melissa wished she could consult David. But David had gone down to the poolside with Salvador. And whatever murky facts lay in their past, Lucy and Donald had helped them time and again. 'All right,' she agreed.

Lucy kissed her cheek. 'You're a brick. And it was a lovely lunch. We'll be seeing you.' She picked up her handbag and ran down the *naya* steps.

'Yuh reckon yuh'll make it?' Sam asked, drinking port.

'And I'll be seeing *you*,' Barton said, hurrying behind his wife.

Melissa returned to the hallway. 'I'm sorry,' she said. 'But they're both in the pool. They'll be with you in a minute.'

'We can interview ... see them in the pool,' the first man said.

'Not in my pool, you can't,' Melissa told him. The man looked at her, and past her. 'Apart from Fred,' Melissa said helpfully, 'there are several large men out there, who are all friends of the Bartons.'

'You're asking for a lot of trouble,' the man said.

'There's a lot of it about,' Melissa agreed.

A car door slammed, and both men swung round. The Mercedes' engine roared into life. 'It's them,' shouted the second man, running into the yard, in front of the car.

'No!' Melissa screamed.

Barton braked, and the Mercedes slewed sideways and came to rest against the BMW. The second man also ran forward. Fred gave a woof and threatened to follow, but Melissa grabbed his collar, instinctively, even if he almost pulled her off her feet. Her shout had alerted the others, and people came hurrying through the kitchen. Barton was gunning his engine, but the second man was standing in front of the car, risking his life, while the first man had reached the nearside door and was dragging it open, causing Lucy, who had not yet fastened her seatbelt or locked the door, to fall out, virtually into his arms. 'Ah said they wouldn't make it,' Sam commented.

Melissa did not reply, just watched. Barton had stopped the car, and was himself getting out, guarded by the second man. 'James and Alice Pemberton, alias Donald and Lucy Barton,' said the first man. 'I am Detective Inspector Milton, and this is Sergeant Tindall. We are members of the Special Branch. Scotland Yard. I am arresting you for the murder of Arthur Bigley on the night of 17 June 1998.'

'Aaagh!' Audrey screamed, and appeared to faint, but was caught by Sam before she could hit the floor.

Detective Inspector Milton gave her a dirty look, and then continued. 'You do not have to say anything in reply to the charge, but if you do say anything, it will be taken down and may be given in evidence.'

Eleven

Melissa found herself virtually pushed out of the doorway by the crowd behind her; even Carrie was there, wrapped in towels but dripping water all over the floor. Lucy was standing absolutely po-faced, while Barton wore a slightly embarrassed grin. 'Have you anything to say, sir?' the inspector asked.

'I would like to speak with my solicitor,' Barton replied.

'I am sure that can be arranged, sir. Meanwhile you will have to come with us. We have a warrant, signed by a Spanish judge.'

Barton looked at the crowd in the doorway, and shrugged. 'That's all, folks,' he remarked. 'David, I wonder if you would be so kind as to drive my car to the house? The keys are in the ignition. Oh, and Melissa, I'd be so grateful if you could look after Corky for us.

Just for a few days.' He felt in his pocket, handed her the house key. 'We'll be in touch.' He looked at Sam. 'I have things to tell too.'

Melissa watched them get into the car. Her head was spinning. If Barton was the other man ... so maybe he was a murderer. But so was Sam. And Sam was the immediate threat. And those were two English police-men, not Spaniards, with whom Sam seemed to have a working relationship. She stepped forward. 'Wait!'

The sergeant had started the engine, but he did not engage gear as his superior looked out of the window. Sam's huge hand closed on Melissa's elbow; he had passed Audrey on to her spellbound husband. 'Let 'em go, Lissy. Yuh don't want to get involved with folks like that.'

The inspector nodded, and the car drove off. Melissa shrugged herself free. 'You *are* a bastard. Shopping your friend...'

'We ain't friends, Lissy. We never was. Associates, maybe. Friends, no.'

'I wish someone would tell me what's going on,' David requested. 'You are saying the Bartons have committed a murder?'

'Plural, Dave. But one's enough to be going on with. Pity they don't execute people in your country any more. But they'll be away for a while.'

'And you were his associate?' Gerald asked. 'Good God! David...!'

317

Audrey had recovered. 'I want to go home,' she announced. 'Take me home, Gerald.'

'You are home, as long as you're in Spain,' David pointed out.

'Ah think this party is over,' Sam announced, as if he were the host. 'Mr Grippenheimer, Mrs Grippenheimer, it's been a great pleasure meetin' yuh, but Ah think these folks would like to be left alone. So...'

'Of course,' Hans said. 'We are in the way. We will take a storm cheque, dear lady.' He patted a bewildered Fred. 'Take care, Fierce Dog.'

'Wait,' Melissa said. 'Please, don't go.'

'I think he's right,' Carrie said. 'It's been great fun, but ... a little unexpected.'

'Hans, please!' Melissa begged, and drew a deep breath. 'Think of Benidorm.' She rolled her eyes from him to Sam.

Hans gazed at her for a moment, then gave a brief bow. 'I shall never forget that shared experience, dear lady. *Hasta la vista.*'

'Oh ... shit!' Melissa said.

'Liss, really,' her brother remonstrated.

'Anyway,' Melissa said. 'You're staying a while longer, aren't you, Salvador. Julio?'

'Sure,' Sam said. 'They're staying until Ah leave. Ah'm their transport.'

'Thank God for that. Well, then...'

'Ah think we should all go inside,' Sam said.

'Just whose house is this, anyway? David...'

David was recovering from his shock and

318

the amount of brandy and wine he had put away. 'I think he has a point,' he said. Melissa glared at him, but the others were filing back into the house; the Grippenheimers had already left. 'In here.' David showed them into the lounge, and took his position in front of the fireplace, suggestive of Hercule Poirot about to explain the unravelment of a murder case. 'Do sit down,' he invited.

Audrey half collapsed on to the settee, and Gerald sat beside her. Encarna sat on his other side, while Julio, Salvador and Sam stood behind them. Melissa remained by the *naya* door, with Fred. 'Now,' David said, 'I think you all need an explanation.'

'How did you get to *know* those people?' Gerald demanded. 'I told you their name was familiar. I read it in the papers.'

'They happen to be our neighbours. Now it turns out that they have a past. But they've been pretty good neighbours, so...'

'Brother, are you full of shit!' Sam said.

'*What* did you say?' Audrey asked, turning round.

'Good neighbours,' Sam said contemptuously. 'They've been after that card since yuh got here. Whose people d'yuh think stole your car in the first place? And the second place. Who d'yuh think set fire to it? Who d'yuh think has been trying to break in here? Who d'yuh think poisoned the lil' fella?'

'They did that?' Melissa shouted.

'Nobody else.' Melissa stared at David.

319

What fools they'd been. What trusting fools! 'Anyway,' Sam went on. 'They're gonna get their comeuppance. Now, I came here to talk.'

'That's what we meant you to do,' David told him. 'Before witnesses. You don't know this, Julio, but this so generous man who has done so much for your village is a gangster and a murderer.'

'What?' Audrey screamed.

'I say, old man, steady on,' Gerald protested. 'Just because he had an acquaintance with that fellow Barton...'

'He and Barton both worked for some big wheel in the underworld, who is now defunct. But he left something behind, a card containing a combination to a safe where there would appear to be something of enormous value. To get that card, they are prepared to kill, and they have killed.'

'Yuh know, Ah couldn't have put the situation better maself,' Sam said. 'So, yuh let me have the card now, sonny, and we'll leave yuh guys to have a quiet evening.'

'You heard that, Julio,' David said. 'That's a confession.'

''E wants zee card,' Julio explained.

'That's right. But he's not going to get the card.'

'Why ees zees?'

'Because you are going to place him under arrest.'

'Me? Why I am going to do zat?'

'You are an *alcalde*. A mayor. You have the authority.'

'But why I am doing zees?'

David's voice took on a note of desperation. 'I've just explained that he is a criminal. A murderer. A crook. And God knows what else.'

'You no like zees?'

'For God's sake, he breaks the law. You are the law in your village, and he lives there.'

''E ees *mi amigo*,' Julio pointed out. ''E ees *mi* village *amigo*. I do not arrest *mi amigo*.'

'Salvador,' David said. 'Be a good chap and explain it to your father.'

'Zere ees no explaining, Daveed. My Papa ees right. Sam ees our frien'. I work for 'eem.'

'You do *what*?'

'Who d'yuh think whacked those guys?' Sam asked. 'Salvador's ma right-hand man.'

Audrey, just waking up, subsided again. Melissa, up till now an increasingly horrified spectator, realized it was time for action, and turned to run along the corridor for the shotgun, Fred, getting into the act without understanding what was going on, bouncing beside her and barking. 'Get her!' Sam snapped.

'Oh no you don't.' David started forward, and checked as Sam levelled a large automatic pistol he had taken from the back of his belt, hitherto concealed beneath his jacket.

'Yuh gonna be stoopid?'

Audrey gave a shriek. 'Now look here,' Gerald said.

'Yuh get up and stand over there,' Sam commanded. Gerald looked at him, then at David, then at Encarna, who was snoring, then got up and stood beside David. 'Now we'll wait on the lil' lady,' Sam suggested.

Melissa raced down the corridor, and Fred got between her legs. She tripped over him and landed on her hands and knees. 'Oh, *Fred*!'

'Woof!' Fred said.

Salvador had caught them up. Now he held Melissa's arm and dragged her to her feet. 'Why you be'ave zo, Meleessa?'

'You bastard!'

'And now zee cursing and zee swearing. I deed not know zees about you.'

'And I did not know you were a killer.' She tried to free herself. 'Let me go.'

Salvador tightened his grip. 'You must leesten. All Beeg Sam wants ees zee card. You geeve 'eem zat, and 'e go away and no trouble you no more.'

'I'll see you in hell, first. Will you let go of me? You're hurting me.'

'Eef you do not geeve 'eem zee card, eet well be very bad. I am saying zees because I like you, very much.'

'Well, I don't like you one little bit. Get him, Fred. Kill, kill!'

Fred looked at her in utter consternation. For the past several days he had been told that this man was his friend, had indeed saved his life.

'Fred ees my frien',' Salvador said. 'You come now.'

'Fred, you are a goofball,' Melissa said, as she was dragged along the corridor.

'Well, hell!' Sam said. 'Where was she going, Salvador?'

'I zeenk zee bedroom, Beeg Sam.'

'So that's where the card is. OK, honey, you and me'll just wander along there and you'll hand it over, and nobody will get hurt.' He gave the pistol to Julio. 'Just keep these guys under control.' He grinned at David and Gerald. 'Yuh don't want to get fooled, either by his one arm or by his age. This guy has killed more people than you've had hot breakfasts.'

'He's right,' David said. 'Just don't do anything.' As if Gerald would be likely to do anything in any event.

'Now that's the first sensible thing any of yuh guys has said today.'

'We're going to die,' Audrey moaned. 'We're all going to die.'

'And that could be the second. Come along, honey. Let's get it done.'

But Melissa was now furious at the way things had turned out, they way they had been hoodwinked by both the Bartons and Salvador, the failure of Dolores to turn up,

323

and most of all the way Hans had just abandoned them in their hour of need. She was in the mood to go down with all guns blazing, even literally, and no matter who it involved, except perhaps Fred, but she was pretty sure Sam would not harm Fred. 'We're not getting anything done,' she said. 'You are not getting that card.'

'Now, listen up, honey, all Ah want to do is get out of here with ma friends. Ah'm getting tired of playing games with yuh all. So if yuh don't give me that card pretty damn quick, Ah'm gonna give you to Salvador for a spell. He really fancies yuh. Especially he fancies yur legs, and what you got between. An' it's all gonna happen right here, in front of yur hubbie and yur brother and yur sister-in-law, not to mention all of us. So what's it gonna be?'

'If you think I'm going to stand here and watch my wife raped...' David began.

'Show him, Julio.'

Julio hardly seemed to aim. He merely squeezed the trigger, and the vase on the mantelpiece between David and Gerald shattered into a hundred splinters. So did the mirror behind it.

'Good God!' Gerald said, dodging flying glass.

Audrey screamed and burst into tears, then threw both arms round Encarna, who had woken up at the sound of the shot, but did not seem to be particularly alarmed.

324

'David, please,' Melissa begged. 'Just relax.' She discovered that Fred was no longer beside her, predictably.

'Liss ... wouldn't it be sensible just to give him the card?'

'Now yur talking,' Sam said.

'I am not surrendering to this thug.'

'Liss...' It was Gerald's turn.

'OK,' Sam said. 'That's 'nough. Salvador, entertain us.'

Salvador approached. 'If you touch me...' Melissa warned.

'But I must touch you,' Salvador argued. 'You must not fight me, Meleessa. Zat way you get 'urt. I do not weesh to 'urt you. Well, only a leetle, until you geeve us the card.'

Melissa stared at him. He was going to do it. She was about to be raped. At the very least. She drew a deep breath ... 'Coche,' Encarna remarked.

All heads turned to watch the headlights coming up the drive. It was now almost dark, but they could see that it was a white Seat.

'Who the fuck is that?' Sam inquired.

Dolores, Melissa thought. Oh, Dolores. But ... 'I think it will be the Countess de la Jara,' David said. 'She was supposed to come to lunch.'

'Then she ain't got no sense of timing. Get rid of her. And if there's any funny stuff, someone gets hurt. Bad.'

David drew a deep breath of his own, looked at Melissa, and went into the kitchen.

She had no idea what to do, what she wanted him to do. The situation was completely out of hand, and Dolores's presence could only blow it apart. On the other hand, she was the only hope they had.

David opened the door. 'David,' Dolores said. 'I am sorry I am so late. It has been terrible. There was a leak in the roof, and the water got in. My apartment has been flooded. I have had to get the fire brigade to help me dry it out.'

'What rotten luck,' David said. 'Ah...' There was the sound of shuffling feet, and Melissa realized that she had pushed her way past him into the house.

'And you know,' Dolores said, 'I have had no lunch. Well, I always intended to have lunch here. But now I am starving.'

'Unfortunately,' David said, 'lunch ended a couple of hours ago, so...'

'But I am sure there is plenty left over. And your guests are still here.' She emerged from the kitchen doorway, surveyed the people in the lounge. Julio had had the sense to place a cushion over the pistol, but they still all looked fairly tense. Not that Dolores seemed to notice. Nor did she immediately appear to notice the shattered mirror. 'Melissa, my dear child,' she said, giving Salvador a glare that had him hastily stepping back. 'I am so sorry I am late. But I am here now. And I remembered to bring that little toy you asked for.'

'Oh,' Melissa said. 'Ah. Well...'

'So won't you introduce me to your friends?'

'Well...' Melissa looked at Sam, who was beaming in a disarming fashion. 'This is my brother, Gerald.'

'Countess.' Gerald, awaiting instruction in a situation he had never encountered before, bowed over her hand.

'And my sister-in-law, Audrey.'

'Countess,' Audrey gasped. 'Countess...'

'She's had too much to drink,' Melissa explained, hurriedly. 'And Encarna Morales, and her husband, Julio.' Dolores snorted. 'And their son, Salvador.'

Dolores looked even more contemptuous. 'And this is Sam Guichard.'

'Pleased to meet yuh, ma'am,' Sam said, clearly prepared to wait on events.

'You're an American,' Dolores accused.

'Never was a truer word spoken, ma'am.'

Dolores was frowning, but she had more important things on her mind, for the moment. 'So where are Donald and Lucy Barton?' she asked Melissa. 'You told me they were coming.'

'Did I?' Melissa couldn't remember doing that.

'They were here,' Sam said. 'But they left early. Said they had some place to go. Yuh saying yuh know them?'

'Guichard,' Dolores remarked, pennies apparently having been dropping. 'An American, named Guichard.'

'Say, we know each other?'

'You!' Dolores said. 'You stole my house!'

'You the sister of that guy? Called himself a count. Well, what do yuh know. He was a crumb. And that sure was one crummy castle. Cost me a fortune to put it right.'

'You are a fucking bastard!' Dolores announced, turning her back on him and opening her shoulder bag. From where she was standing, only David and Melissa could see her draw her magnum, but Melissa remembered the night of the running of the bulls.

'Take cover!' she shouted.

'*Santa Maria!*' Dolores shrieked, and turned, opening fire as she did so. Sam got the message and dived to his left. Salvador dived to his right. Melissa dived to the floor.

Dolores's first shot hit the bookcase on the right of the hall; several paperbacks disintegrated. Her second bullet struck the wall just beyond the bookcase, bringing down a shower of plaster. Her third struck the side of the door. Her fourth struck the other side of the doorway. And her fifth shattered a picture Melissa had carelessly hung close to the entrance. Obviously she was better with ashtrays.

The evening was filled with noise, the echoes of the firing being overtaken by a high-pitched baying scream from Audrey, who, although not in the line of fire, had thrown herself to the floor behind her chair. Gerald had also disappeared behind a chair.

'Julio! Shoot the bitch!' Sam shouted.

Julio threw away his cushion and raised the pistol. But Dolores still had one bullet available, and she had got the range. Her next shot struck Julio's hand and the gun at the same time, and both disintegrated, Julio staring in consternation at his mangled fingers, which were dripping blood on to the settee. It was Encarna's turn to scream.

David had retreated into the kitchen. But now he emerged again. 'I say, Dolores!' he protested.

'David!' Melissa shouted, scrambling to her feet, as Dolores turned towards him, still holding the gun.

'That's all right,' David said. 'A magnum only holds six bullets, and she's fired them all. Now, Dolores, put down the gun, like a good girl.' He obviously felt he had regained control of the situation.

'Say, he's right,' Sam said, recovering his nerve.

'What ees eet wees zees woman?' Salvador inquired, also getting up. 'She ees crazy, no?'

'No, no, she is crazy, yes,' Melissa told him.

'Well, I am going to bust her ass into a hundred pieces,' Sam announced, moving forward.

'Oh, shit!' David's voice took on a note of alarm, and Melissa, also starting towards the countess, realized why.

With the greatest calm, Dolores had again opened her bag, dropped the empty magnum into it, and replaced it with a machine pistol. Equally methodically, she now proceeded to slap a magazine into place, and then dropped two more into the pocket of her jacket. Then she humped the bag on to her shoulder, and turned back to the room.

'Jesus Christ!' Sam bawled, and made for the *naya* door, Salvador at his shoulder. Julio and Encarna both began babbling in Spanish. Melissa assumed Julio was wishing he had his boyhood machine gun, even if he had no means of squeezing any trigger. Dolores ignored him, stepped past Melissa into the doorway, and levelled the pistol, but as she fired, Melissa dived to the floor again, threw both arms round the countess's ankles, and brought her down with a thump and a grunt; the burst of fire went wild.

'What in the name of God are you doing?' Melissa shouted. While she certainly wanted Sam taken care of, she reckoned that had been accomplished, and she equally did not want her house littered with blood and dead bodies. 'What *is* that thing?'

'This,' Dolores said proudly, sitting up, 'is a PM-63. It is Polish. It can fire six hundred and fifty rounds per minute. Unfortunately, there are only forty rounds in the magazine. But I have spares. And you see, it has the great advantage of being trigger-controlled rather than selective, which means I can fire

330

one, two, or a dozen shots at a time, as I wish.'

'But you just can't shoot it at people like that,' Melissa told her. 'I mean, people don't do that sort of thing.'

'I am not people,' Dolores pointed out. 'They're trying to escape.'

The pool gate had crashed shut as Sam and Salvador, abandoning the senior Morales, had decided to get out while they could. Dolores freed herself from Melissa, brushed David aside, and ran for the back door. She reached it as Sam wrenched open the Cadillac's door, got behind the wheel, and gunned the engine desperately, trying to make the seven-point turn necessary to swing the huge car round to face the right way for the gate. Dolores levelled the gun. Melissa reached for her again, but it was too late. With the greatest calm, Dolores took aim and used a single shot to put out one of Sam's tyres. The Cadillac lurched, and Dolores shot out a second tyre. The Cadillac swung the other way, and Dolores loosed a burst into the engine. There were a series of short explosions, and the Cadillac came to rest against the exterior wall of Melissa's bedroom, smoke drifting upwards into the rain.

'Dolores!' Melissa screamed. Doors banged as Sam's car was evacuated by the two men. Dolores evaded Melissa's grasp, and stepped outside into the rain, loosing a short burst as she did so, and then reloading from the spare magazines in her pocket. Then she followed the fleeing men into the darkness.

'Liss!' David came pounding down the hall. 'Are you all right?'

'She's gone bonkers!' Melissa shouted. 'Well, she always was bonkers, but now she's OTT. Someone's going to get killed.'

'Woof!' Fred agreed, emerging from the bedroom; Dolores had loosed another burst just outside the window, and he had decided that even under the bed did not provide shelter enough.

'A countess!' Audrey wailed from behind her chair. 'Behaving like that.'

'I'm sure she has a perfectly adequate reason for her behaviour,' Gerald suggested.

'Oh, get stuffed!' Melissa told her brother, and listened to another fusillade while Fred seemed to be trying to get inside her jumper. 'Dave! They may be thugs, but we can't just let her shoot them.'

'Absolutely,' David agreed. 'How do you propose to stop her?'

'What about our shotgun? If we told her that if she doesn't stop shooting we are going to shoot *her*...'

'I don't think that will have the slightest effect on Dolores. She'll know we don't mean it. No, there's only one thing for it: I will have to go out there and take her gun away from her.'

'Are you out of your mind? She'll shoot

you.'

'No, she won't. She likes me. It's Sam she's after.'

'David...'

But he'd already stepped past her and out into the rain. From the driveway beyond the master bedroom she heard another burst of firing.

Gerald moved cautiously down the corridor. 'Gone off, has she? Look here, that chap is bleeding all over the place.'

'She went off about twenty years ago,' Melissa said. 'And Julio brought it on himself. Come on.'

'Come on where?'

'We have to help David.'

'What, out there? It's raining.'

'And he'd get shot!' Audrey wailed. 'Get shot, don't you hear?'

'Oh ... give her a sedative,' Melissa snapped, and ran to the bedroom to fetch the gun. Tongue between her teeth, she pumped a cartridge into the breach, then opened the bedroom door and went outside herself. Fred went with her; however much he disliked the gun she was carrying, he obviously wished to be beside his mistress at the end. 'Dolores!' she bawled. 'It's me. If you shoot either me or my husband, I'm going to blow you away.'

'Woof!' Fred supported her.

'Or if you hurt my dog,' Melissa shouted. There was no reply, not even from David, to her surprise. But perhaps they couldn't hear her above the steady pounding of the rain, which had already soaked her to the skin. She approached the Cadillac, which was blocking the drive.

'Psst,' someone said from the bushes.

Melissa turned sharply, presenting the gun.

'Zat woman ees a Fasceest swine,' Salvador remarked.

'You could be right. And you and your lot are Communist swine. I ought to blow you apart.'

'But I am your frien', Meleessa. I am Fred's frien'.'

'Not any more. Where is Sam?'

''Ow I am knowing zat, Meleessa? 'E gone down zee 'eell. Or up zee 'eell. 'E eese afraid.'

'And you're not?'

'My papa shot people like 'er, een zee war,' Salvador said proudly.

'All wheels turn,' Melissa reminded him. She couldn't make up her mind what to do about him. If he *had* been intending to rape her, he deserved to be shot, and she knew that he was a murdering thug. But he was those things because Sam had made him do them. He had also saved Fred's life, and he was actually quite a cute little man. In any event, she had never shot anyone in her life, and she had no intention of starting now, unless it was somebody trying to harm David or Fred. 'Listen, your papa is never going to shoot anyone again, and right now he could be bleeding to death. Get in there and help him. And just remember that if you try anything, I have the shotgun.'

'Zat Fasceesta weell come back een zee 'ouse.'

'Over my dead body. Oops. That wasn't very appropriate, was it? My brother and sister-in-law will help you until I get back. Oh, Lord!' She was distracted by another burst of firing from down the drive. 'Do it!' she shouted at Salvador, and ran round the corner of the house, tripping over Fred as she did so and landing in a flower bush. 'Fred!' she shouted. 'Get out of the way! David! Are you all right?'

'I see her,' David replied, from next to the gate. 'Keep your head down. Dolores, for God's sake, stop acting the fool.'

'They are in the *barranca*,' Dolores announced. She was standing in the gateway itself. 'American swine!' She loosed another burst.

'David!' Melissa said urgently, crawling through the flower beds on her hands and knees, but retaining hold of the shotgun.

'Sssh,' he advised.

She realized he was doing his mathematical calculations again, as to just when Dolores might need to change magazines.

'Look, lady,' Sam called from the darkness below them. 'If yuh keep up this shit Ah'm gonna bust your ass.'

Once again the chatter of the machine pistol filled the night. Melissa became aware that a cold wet nose was running up and down her neck, accompanied by very heavy breathing. 'Sssh, Fred,' she begged.

'Hello!' came another voice from out of the darkness beyond the gate. 'David? Melissa? I heard shooting.'

'Hans!' Melissa shouted. 'Thank God you've come back!'

'I was always coming back, dear lady. I only waited to make sure you really needed me.'

'Well, be careful. There's a trigger-happy...'

There was a burst of firing, followed by a shout from Grippenheimer. 'My God, she's shot him!' Melissa cried, inadvertently rising to her feet. In reply there came a single shot, smashing into the house just above her head. 'Bloody hell!' she screamed, hurling herself to the ground again.

'Woof!' Fred barked, following her example.

'Aaagh!' Dolores shrieked from down the hill; apparently, however much she enjoyed shooting at people, she did not enjoy being shot at in turn.

'Shit!' David bawled. 'Are you all right, Liss?'

'Yes,' she gasped. 'What...?'

'Hans, was that you?' David asked.

'Who did I hit?' Grippenheimer asked, curiously.

'Me, nearly,' Melissa said. 'Look, for God's

sake, put away that gun.'

'My dear lady...' He was obviously approaching. 'If you are in trouble, I must help you.'

David decided to ignore him for the moment. 'Dolores?' he called. There was no reply. 'Oh, my God!' he said. 'I think you got *her*!'

That wasn't possible, as the bullet had hit the house. Melissa saw David's shadow as he stood up, only a few feet away. She stood up also, and went down the drive. Now she could see Grippenheimer, coming up to the gate, gun in hand. Of Dolores there was no sign. 'I think she's fallen down the *barranca*,' she said.

'Who?' Grippenheimer inquired.

'The Countess de la Jara.'

'But she is a lunatic.'

'That doesn't give you the right to shoot her.'

'Not even if she's been shooting other people?' David asked.

'Aaaagh!' Dolores screamed again; she was indeed in the *barranca*. 'Put me down, you Communist pig!'

'Jus' take it easy, lil' lady,' Sam said. He emerged on to the drive, carrying a kicking Dolores in his arms as if she were a delinquent baby. Her machine pistol was stuck in his belt.

'Dolores!' Melissa cried. 'Are you hit?'

'No, she ain't,' Sam said. 'Not yet.'

'Put me down, you hairy bastard!' Dolores bawled, kicking desperately but ineffectually.

'Hans! Hans! What is happening?' Carrie emerged through the rain mist. 'You have been shooting at someone?' This possibility did not seem to alarm her.

'He shot at me!' Dolores wailed. 'I will make a *denuncia*!'

'There's going to be a queue,' Melissa told her.

'I think,' David said, 'that we should all go inside and have another drink. Sam, you've had your fun. Now hand over that gun.'

'You reckon? Ah came here to get something, and Ah allus get what Ah want. Catch.'

Acting with tremendous speed and power, he threw Dolores into David's arms with such force that they both fell over, then drew the machine pistol and threw his arms round Melissa, the pistol held to her head. 'Drop the gun,' he told her.

It was already slipping from her grasp. Much as she hated herself, she knew she was scared stiff, perhaps for the first time in her life. Never had she heard such concentrated menace in anyone's voice.

'Good girl,' Sam said. 'Now yuh guys listen up. Just nobody move.'

Nobody did, save for David and Dolorees, who were sitting in a flower bed trying to extricate themselves from each other.

'Now,' Sam said. 'Lissy an' me are gonna take a lil' walk into the house. There she's gonna give me what Ah want, and then me and ma friends are gonna take off and leave yuh people in peace. But just remember. If anyone tries to interfere, Ah'm going to blow this lil' lady apart, and Ah sure would hate to have to do that.' His grip on Melissa's arm tightened, as he turned her towards the back door.

But Melissa had regained her nerve, as she realized that he wasn't going to do anything to her until after she had handed over the card ... and sitting immediately behind her was Fred, who at last seemed to be coming to terms with the continuous gunfire with which he was surrounded. 'Fred,' she said. 'This bad man is hurting me. Do something.'

Fred appeared to consider this, once again confused. It was Sam who precipitated matters. 'Move along, lil' fellah,' he commanded. 'Ah ain't got the time to play games.'

'Get him,' Melissa said. 'Kill, kill!'

This made Fred more confused than ever, but Sam was on a short fuse. 'Git out the way, dawg!' he snapped, and as Fred still couldn't make up his mind what to do, pushed at him with his foot. It wasn't a kick, but in the gloom Fred couldn't be sure of that. He saw the large foot coming towards him, sidestepped, and sank his teeth into Sam's ankle. 'Jesus Christ!' Sam screamed. And again, as Melissa sank *her* teeth into his forearm, causing him to release the pistol.

339

'Boy,' he said, 'am Ah gonna bust your ass! As for you, dawg...'

But by this time Hans had come right up to them. 'You, sir,' he said, 'are insulting a lady I much admire, and my friend Fierce Dog.'

'Listen, yuh stupid German—' Sam began.

'Oh, my God!' Melissa said. 'Hans...'

Her intention was to save his life, but she was too late. As Sam stepped towards Hans, there was another of those terrifying clicks she remembered so well from Tuesday night. Sam gave a little grunt, and sank to his knees, while Fred looked at Melissa, seeking instructions. 'Good boy,' she said. 'Are you all right, Hans?'

'I have cut my knuckles,' Hans said.

'We'll put something on it,' she said, wondering if he had broken Sam's jaw; Sam was certainly making some peculiar noises.

They were surrounded, Hans now holding his pistol to Sam's head. 'You want to have those bites seen to,' he recommended. 'You may well have rabies.'

'*What* did you say?' Melissa demanded.

'I was thinking of the Fierce Dog, dear lady.'

'Hans,' Carrie said severely, 'I have told you that you simply cannot go around hitting people. It is not polite.'

'I think it would be a good idea if we all went inside and had a drink,' David suggested.

No one argued except Dolores, and she

didn't seem to be against the drink, only Sam. 'We should shoot him,' she declared. 'No one will know.'

'Except all of us,' David pointed out.

'Well, give me back my gun.'

'Not on your nelly,' Melissa said. 'I am keeping this as a souvenir.'

'That is stealing.'

'So report me to the police. Up you get, Sam, you can make it. Just remember that hitting people very hard is Hans's sole recreation, apart from breaking their arms, of course – and also that Fred, once he has tasted flesh, is insatiable.' She led the way up the steps from the pool and through the *naya*, paused to survey the lounge, and Gerald, Audrey, Julio, Encarna and Salvador, all of whom seemed to have consumed several brandies during their brief absence, and all of whom now started to their feet in consternation at the sight of the sopping, mud-stained group, Audrey falling over her chair in her excitement. They had at least bound up Julio's hand, with, Melissa saw to her annoyance, one of her linen napkins.

'Beeg Sam?' Salvador asked. 'What ees 'appening?'

'Ah, shaddup!' Sam recommended, still rubbing his chin.

'He's not feeling too bright,' David said. 'Our dog bit him.'

Although Fred was not at that moment present, Encarna started screaming again.

'And Hans hit him,' Melissa added. 'Can't you shut her up?' she begged Salvador.

Salvador gave his mother another glass of brandy before attending to Sam, who had also collapsed into a chair.

'That woman should be locked up,' Carrie declared, dripping all over the carpet, but then, they were all doing that. 'Shooting at my Hans...' Melissa gathered she was referring to Dolores.

'I did not shoot at your Hans,' Dolores replied with dignity. 'Or he would be dead.'

'Aaaagh!' Audrey screamed. Fred, having had to lift his leg after all the excitement, had been the last into the house, and being as wet as anyone, had now decided to stand in the middle of the room and shake – mainly over her.

'Quiet!' David said, in a voice which he had last used when expelling a delinquent Arab sheikh from the Pantry.

Everyone turned towards him. He was holding the shotgun.

'It's time to call a halt to this nonsense,' he said. 'Dolores, you know as well as anyone that Sam bought your castle from your brother in good faith, and that your brother had every right to sell it. You have been behaving like a stupid, hysterical woman. Just listen.'

They did, to the sound of another car engine coming up the drive.

'Oh, hell!' Melissa remarked. 'That has to

be the police.' She went to the back door, opened it, gazed at a vaguely familiar face. But no uniform. However, the blazer was also familiar; the bloodstains had been removed.

'Forgive the intrusion, *señora*, but is Dolores de Soto here? Her car is parked on the road.'

'Duarte! I thought you were in hospital.'

'I must not laugh,' Duarte explained. 'Otherwise, I am on the mend, eh? But I am looking for my cousin.'

'Dolores is your cousin? Well –' she led him into the lounge – 'you're welcome to her.'

'Duarte!' Dolores exclaimed. 'I have been manhandled, ill-treated...'

'And you have been shooting at people,' Duarte said, apparently recognizing the carry-all.

'Yuh can say that again,' Sam agreed. 'Yuh responsible for this dame?'

'She is my cousin,' Duarte repeated. 'Dolores, you have been a naughty girl.'

He reminded Melissa of Carrie remonstrating with her cat, but he obtained a more positive reaction from Dolores than Carrie from Antoinette: the countess burst into tears.

'Now I am going to take you home,' Duarte announced. 'Gather up your things.'

'You mean you want to take the guns?' David asked.

'They should be confiscated,' Hans recommended, having pocketed his own weapon.

'We weell take zem,' Julio offered.

'I don't think that would be a very good idea, either,' Melissa said.

'I will be responsible for the guns,' Duarte said.

Melissa looked at David; she didn't really want to become involved with the police – again.

David came to a decision. 'If you promise to make her behave, we'll give her back her hardware and let you take her home. But she's your responsibility.'

Dolores sniffed.

'I understand,' Duarte said. 'I apologize for her behaviour. I will see that it does not happen again.'

'Right,' David said. 'And as a sign of peace, I want you to give Sam a big hug and a kiss.'

Dolores and Sam looked at each other.

'Could be an idea, ma'am,' Sam said. 'What the hell, we're both wet.'

Dolores bent over him for a quick peck, then picked up the refilled carry-all and walked to the door. 'You must all come to dinner,' she said. 'I will send you an invitation.' She stepped into the rain, followed by Duarte.

'Well, now. Ah guess we should be leaving too,' Sam said. 'Julio needs looking at, and Ah guess Ah'd better get this bite seen to. Both these bites,' he added, regarding his forearm. 'And this bruise. Say, old fellah, where'd yuh learn to hit like that?'

'I was heavyweight champion of the navy of the Third Reich,' Hans announced.

'Wasn't that a while back?'

'He keeps in practice,' Melissa assured him.

'Well,' Sam said, attempting to get up. 'Ah guess...'

'Just one minute,' David said. 'You came here looking for trouble.'

'And Ah sure found it. Ah know when Ah've been licked.'

'And you reckon you can just walk away?'

'You aimin' to call the cops? Yuh'd be opening a can of worms. Yuh ain't got no proof of anything, save that yur dog bit me. And yur wife bit me as well. An' that Julio got shot.'

'That I am not going to call the police,' David said, 'is because you saved Fred's life, as Salvador may have done. But you came here looking for something, right?'

'Well, sure. But maybe we can take that up some other time.'

'There's no time like the present. Liss, fetch the card.' Melissa looked at him in consternation, but this was the David of the Pantry, lord of all he surveyed. She went to the bedroom, where she had left her handbag, and returned with the card. 'Is this what you were looking for?' David asked.

'Jesus, yuh mean it was right there all this time? Well, now, yuh just hand it over, an'

345

we'll call it quits.'

'I have a better idea. Keep your gun on him, Hans. Liss, there's a pair of scissors in the kitchen. Let's have them.'

Melissa gasped as she realized what he intended, but she went into the kitchen, and returned with the scissors.

'Just what yuh aiming to do with those?' Sam asked, looking uneasily from her to Grippenheimer's pistol.

'Remove temptation,' David said, laying down the shotgun and taking the scissors. He cut the card into two, then cut the two halves into four, then cut the four quarters into eights, then, tongue between his teeth, carefully cut the eights into sixteen. Everyone in the room watched him in horrified silence, even if most of them had no idea what he was actually doing. Then he carefully gathered the tiny pieces of plastic into his hand, and emptied them into Melissa's waiting hands. 'You know what to do.'

'Back in a flash.' She went down the corridor, emptied her hand into the toilet bowl, and flushed. Then she returned to the lounge.

'Yuh have got to be crazy!' Sam said. 'Yuh know what yuh have just put down the john?'

'So now you can go home and dream,' David suggested. 'Off you go. And if any one of you turns up here again, Fred is going to tear his leg right off. Aren't you, Fred?'

Fred puffed happily.

'I want to go home,' Audrey said. 'Gerald, I want to get out of this madhouse. Isn't there a *parador* we can go to?'

'We'll see about that in the morning, dear,' Gerald promised.

'We could stay to dinner,' Carrie suggested.

'Dinner!' Melissa took a deep breath. 'Right! Dinner.' She closed her eyes against the thought of the chaos waiting in the kitchen.

'I will prepare it,' Carrie said grandly. 'You have done enough.' She pointed at Audrey. 'You can help me.'

'I want to go home.'

'I'll help you,' Gerald volunteered. Carrie was still wearing her very short shorts and no bra under her very thin and very wet shirt.

'Oh, all right. I'll go,' Audrey snapped, getting up.

They all disappeared into the kitchen. Hans was drinking his fourth brandy and muttering to himself, apparently unable to believe he hadn't hit anybody with his pistol.

'There's lots of leftover curry,' Melissa shouted. 'It'll be interesting to see what they do with it,' she added. 'You know something that's been puzzling me, Dave? How did Dolores know we were having the Bartons to lunch? I never told her.'

'Maybe she met Lucy some place.'

'Lucy didn't like her. Or at least ... they were so two-faced. You don't suppose she might actually have been, well, working with them? Or for them?'

'Someone like the countess, working for a thug like Barton? Hardly likely.'

'I suppose you're right. But you do realize that we have just thrown away a fortune?'

'Save that we don't know which bank has it. Anyway, who needs a fortune? We have enough to go on with.'

'There's a point. Well, I suppose we have to fetch Corky. Fred will like that.'

'Corky can wait a moment. Liss, you were just magnificent. I'm sorry your party went phut.'

'Forget it. I think it went like a bomb, literally. People will be talking about this party for years to come.'

'I've made a bit of a hash of things, haven't I?' he asked, as she sat beside him on the bloodstained settee, while Fred sat on the other side to lick his face; Fred could tell when someone needed sympathy.

'In what way?'

'Well, getting drunk...'

'David, you were magnificent.'

'Was I, really?'

'Given time, yes. But as you say...'

'I'll give it up.'

'Oh, for God's sake, don't let's go to extremes. But...'

'I'll ration myself. That's a promise. And I'll see if I can open a restaurant down here. I need something to do.'

'Great. I'll be your maître d'. Well, some of the time.'

'What are you planning to do with the rest?'

'Well –' carefully she stroked Fred – 'I was due last week.'

'And nothing happened? I'm not surprised, with everything else that's been happening.'

'Nothing yet. Anyway, I don't feel the least PMT.'

'One swallow doesn't make a summer,' he pointed out.

'But,' she said, putting her arm round him and determinedly ignoring the racket from the kitchen. 'It does encourage one to try some more, doesn't it? Especially if Gerald and Audrey are going home tomorrow.'

He grinned, and kissed her. 'And we can get rid of the rest of the mob.'

They both looked at Hans, who was now fast asleep.

'Grub up!' Carrie called from the kitchen. 'I hope you guys are as hungry as we are.'

'Woof!' said Fred.